Chasing Love

Also by Lisa Herrington

The Renaissance Lake Series
The Fix
Fall Again
Million Reasons
Mistletoe in Maisonville
The Pursuit
Sunny Paradise
Chasing Love
Coffee and Twinkle Lights

Standalone Books
One Starry Night

Chasing Love

Lisa Herrington

Writerly House Publishing

CHASING LOVE

Published by Writerly House Publishing
www.WriterlyHouse.com
www.LisaHerrington.com

This is a work of fiction. Characters, names, places, and events are products of the author's imagination. Any similarity to events or places, or real persons, living or dead, is purely coincidental.

Copyright © 2023 Lisa Herrington
First Published September 2023

All rights reserved. No part of this book may be reproduced or transmitted in any form or by any means, electronic, mechanical, photocopying, recording, or otherwise, without written permission.

ISBN: 978-0-9990626-6-1

10 9 8 7 6 5 4 3 2 1

For James

Chapter One

Jail was the last place Marlow Ripley thought she'd end up on her wedding day. As she sat on the floor of the empty Maisonville jail cell in her seventeen-thousand-dollar wedding gown, she tried not to think about how she ended up here.

There were over five-hundred guests waiting to see her walk down the aisle and well over a hundred thousand people watching to see video of her wedding and reception online.

As she glanced over the black ink smeared down the front of her dress, Marlow shook her head. *"Ruined,"* she said. Her whole life *was ruined*. Everyone must have heard the news that she'd taken off. As a social media influencer, she understood the chaos that would follow once word got out that she'd been arrested, too.

Thankfully, no one was there to video her throwing up on the police officer who'd pulled her over. If she'd just been a little faster or if he had been a little more understanding, she'd be out of the state by now.

Running away made her feel so free and independent for the first time in years that she'd ignored how fast she was driving. Why couldn't Officer Bowman bend the rules just that one time?

Marlow buried her head in her hands as she thought about riding in the back of that police car. When the uptight officer ordered her out of the car, he barely looked at her.

"I'm going as fast as I can," she cried, and he told her to stop. Officer Bowman surprised her when he crouched down and used wet-wipes to clean her gown and shoes. It was considerate and unexpected since he'd ignored her pleas from the back of his car. As he gently blotted her hemline and shoes, she could see the concern in his eyes before he pulled that austere demeanor back into place.

"Let's go," he ordered and pointed for her to walk into the police station, but the tight spanx underneath her dress had twisted when she slid out of the back of his police cruiser. Wearing handcuffs, she couldn't fix it, and as she tried to walk, the flesh-colored fabric cinched tighter, gripping her legs like a vise.

Marlow cried out as she tumbled forward, but before she hit the ground, Officer Bowman scooped her up and carried her inside the building. It was thoughtful and, again, uncharacteristic of the uptight policeman who wouldn't give her a break.

It was clear the moment he realized what he was doing was unprofessional. "Officer Shannon, can you help her, please," he called out to a female officer. Marlow smirked because he was the one who didn't know how to treat a woman.

Officer Bea Shannon was older and immediately took over. Marlow made an ugly face at Zachary, and he smirked back at her. The animosity between them was palpable to everyone in the booking room.

He'd never met a more privileged woman, and she'd never

disliked a man, other than the one she just left at the altar, more.

Of course, Marlow had thrown up on the man. But what did he expect? She'd just run out on a seventy-five-thousand-dollar wedding in one of New Orleans' most famous churches, The St. Louis Cathedral.

Her getaway car, the silver Jaguar she'd gotten as an early wedding and birthday present last month, was adorned with streamers, a just married sign, and bells tied to the bumper. Sure, she was driving fast, but was that an arrestable offense?

Thankfully, the older woman was more patient with Marlow. Officer Shannon smiled sweetly at the disheveled bride as she discovered the problem with her dress. "Hold still, honey," the silver-haired woman said as she knelt and firmly pulled the elastic undergarment back into place.

After fingerprinting Marlow, she tried to help clean the ink off her fingers. That was when the would-be-bride shook her head and swiped them across the expensive lace instead.

"That was for my mother," Marlow said. Bea Shannon could see the sadness in the young woman's blue eyes and looked sympathetic before she locked Marlow inside a cell.

Marlow could hear the officers in the outer room. It sounded like a herd of them stormed inside. This was supposed to be the happiest day of her life. It had taken fourteen months to plan the wedding since her famous senator mother, Michelle Ripley, had to approve every single detail. "Oh, Marlow, the invitations can't be white, and cream looks gauche. Only linen paper will do," her mother complained. Then she demanded calligraphers send examples of their work because each invitation had to be hand-addressed by a professional.

The wedding, just like her life underneath Senator Ripley's thumb, was exhausting. But as soon as Marlow's social media fans found out about her engagement, everything blew up even more. They followed along every step of the way and swooned over all the wedding minutia.

Each week brought some new wedding decisions and thousands more followers. Finally, the wedding-palooza, as she'd not so affectionately called the event, had an end.

She was to marry Royce Chatham III that morning, and after the reception, Marlow was going to be a married woman and not just the daughter of Senator Ripley. Sure, she had doubts, but she also had hope that once they were past her mother's wedding obsession, their lives would settle. They could find a way to be happy.

There was a professional videographer live streaming her hour-long makeup session and two-hour hair creation. The dress reveal was minutes before she showed her almost husband. Thankfully, she'd asked for the moment to be private, and that was when it all went to hell in a hand basket.

She didn't even know what a hand basket was, but her grandmother used to use that expression all the time, and it seemed to fit the situation. The dress reveal was supposed to be their private little moment together, the only thing Marlow had asked for without her mother's input.

When she walked in to surprise him, Marlow was the one taken aback. Her only reaction was to throw a crystal vase full of white roses at his head. She was a good shot, and although he ducked, she nailed him in the forehead. He'd have to wear that scar for days, if not longer—the rat.

Marlow didn't want to think about what had happened at the church anymore. Swiping at her eyes again, she smudged her mascara even more. Her head hung low, and she looked at her once spectacular satin high-heeled shoes, stained and scuffed beyond repair. It must have happened on the wet street near the church, where she ran to her car before anyone saw her.

Hurt and angry, Marlow knew she'd dodged a bullet by not getting married today. Her mother was probably losing it. Slowly, she pulled off each shoe, screamed in frustration, and threw them as hard as she could until they clanged into the metal bars before hitting the floor.

Zachary Bowman stepped into the room to look at Marlow. "You okay in there, Miss Ripley? You still feel like you might get sick?"

Marlow locked onto Officer Bowman's stare. "Hoping I'll embarrass myself more?" He wasn't fooling her. He was mocking her with all that sympathy. No one was that nice.

It was a shame because he was handsome, and that uniform made him look sexy. Too bad he was male. Marlow was swearing off men forever— specifically, men who arrested her.

She rolled her eyes at him, but he moved in closer and bent down so they were face to face except for the bars between them. "Look, I know you aren't having the best day. But I wanted to let you know that we've notified Senator Ripley and told her you're okay."

"Not having the best day? Right." Marlow shook her head. Who did he think he was fooling? "You actually talked to my mother?"

Officer Bowman continued watching her without answering.

Marlow smirked. "I didn't think so. It was one of her minions, right?"

Officer Bowman nodded.

"Whatever. How long are you going to keep me here, Officer Bowman? And where is my car?"

"Your release isn't up to me. Your car was impounded."

"Impounded?" Marlow stood up and glared at him. "Aren't there any real criminals you could go after, Officer Bowman?"

He leaned in. "You're in the little town of Maisonville, Miss Ripley. You're about the biggest criminal we've seen around here in quite a while."

"Lucky me."

"You were driving 120 miles per hour on a winding, country two-lane road. I'd say you are lucky." He smiled smugly. She never liked boring by-the-book types, and he was the king of the irritating do-gooder club.

Before Marlow gave him another piece of her mind, Officer Shannon entered the room. She looked nervous when she told them that Senator Ripley was there and wanted a private word with Marlow.

"What? Already?" Marlow said, turning away so they wouldn't see her eyes fill with tears, and that was when Senator Michelle Ripley stepped into the room.

"Thank you for finding her, officers. May I have a moment with my daughter?"

Zachary felt like he shouldn't leave Marlow alone with the senator even though she was her mother. But Senator Ripley had already gotten it approved by the chief of police, Tim Gallegos. Zachary would obey the chief, especially during his first week in Maisonville. Still, he couldn't help but feel uneasy.

He and Officer Shannon reluctantly left them alone. As Zachary stepped into the outer room, Chief Gallegos nodded his way, proud that Zachary was the one to apprehend the runaway bride. Zachary's late father was good friends with Tim Gallegos, and he wanted to make him proud.

When the chief got the call that Marlow Ripley was found in their town, he rushed back to headquarters to greet the senator and her entourage personally.

The press would be there soon, and Zachary really hated reporters. Sure, there were some hard-working journalists, but his ex was a news anchor in his old hometown, and if there weren't any juicy stories to report, she would make one up.

Everyone in St. Marksville found out about his break up with her when he did, and he wasn't ready to be on the evening news again, even if it was about someone else's failed relationship.

Chief Gallegos could see his newest officer frown as the news van approached the police station. He stood next to Zachary and explained that he would handle the press and then release Marlow to her mother. "See you on Monday, Bowman," Gallegos said before heading out the front door to make a statement.

Zachary had Sunday off, and without another word to anyone, he slipped out the back door. But as much as he hated drama, he couldn't stop thinking about Marlow Ripley. She looked like a Barbie Doll with that big blond hair and blue eyes. His first week on the job had been exactly what he'd wanted- quiet and routine. When the all-points bulletin went out across the radio that Senator Ripley's only daughter had gone missing on her wedding day, he'd laughed, figuring that she'd gotten cold feet or something. That wasn't a crime, and he wouldn't have stopped her. But when she flew by him in that sports car, he had no other choice. She could have lost control of that car and hurt herself or someone else.

It was hard for him not to laugh as he thought about how angry she was at him for pulling her over. Marlow Ripley had waved her arms, *"Can't you see I'm in the middle of a crisis?"* And he was sure that hadn't been the first time she'd ever had to say that to someone.

Zachary shook his head as he pulled into the parking lot of

the local diner where he'd arrested her just a few hours ago. She was something, wearing that fancy dress and yelling at him.

Wedding-Day Barbie might have been angry at him for arresting her, but she looked destroyed over facing her mother. Senator Michelle Ripley may have had a smile on her face when she walked into the jail, but she didn't seem to have an ounce of sympathy for her daughter as she dismissed him and Officer Shannon. There was more to that story, but a powerful politician like Senator Ripley would do everything possible to keep negative information about herself or her daughter out of the news.

It didn't make sense, but he felt terrible leaving Marlow there as if he had any other choice in the matter. He didn't know her. He would never really know her. His job was done. He needed to get some dinner and forget about it.

But as Zachary walked into Miss Lynn's Diner and saw his childhood friend Olivia, he was pretty sure he wasn't done talking about the run-away bride, Marlow Ripley.

Chapter Two

The Main Street Grocery, better known by locals as Miss Lynn's Diner, was locally famous for its home-style food, a fusion of popular Southern, Creole, and Cajun dishes. The diner was locally renowned for the delicious food but also for Miss Lynn. Everyone adored the remarkable woman for her loving disposition and her homemade pies.

In the short time Zachary had been in town, he'd eaten at the diner almost daily. But this evening was different. While the small-town residents were hospitable, and the warm summer days had lulled Zachary into a false sense of comfort, Maisonville still had its share of craziness.

The car chase and arrest of Marlow Ripley reminded him not to let his guard down. He dragged himself into the diner as he tried to forget about her because a lot of things could be settled over a good meal.

Olivia Dufrene, who'd been a year older than him in school back in their hometown of St. Marksville, waved him over to sit at what they called the lunch counter even though it was dinner time.

She was a dark-haired, blue-eyed, bossy waitress and his closest friend in town. "You look like you need a day off," she said as she handed him a menu and a glass of iced tea with mint ——a summer favorite at the diner.

Miss Lynn sat next to Zachary as she motioned a finger around his tired expression. "Does this have anything to do with that hot-tempered bride that screeched into our parking lot earlier?"

He gave her and then Olivia that boy-next-door grin but didn't reply.

Miss Lynn leaned in closer to whisper where only the three could hear. "Word has it that she is Senator Michelle Ripley's daughter who went missing from her own wedding?"

Zachary didn't discuss specifics about his work. It had been a personal rule he never broke. "My first week on the job has been interesting."

Olivia gave him a pointed stare. "Leonie Ford still your real estate agent?"

On his first day in town, Zachary met Leonie Ford standing in front of him at the local food truck that specialized in coffee drinks. It didn't take her but a few minutes to recognize that he was new in town and then to offer her services. That day, Leonie frowned when he told her that he was friends with Olivia. There was something wrong between the two women, and no good would come with interfering. But now, faced with the evil stare that Olivia perfected in high school, Zachary had to do something.

"Livvie, I've been here eleven days. She showed me one house and a town home. What gives?"

Olivia smiled at him, and he felt the chill even more. "She passed her real estate exams three months ago and broke up with her fifth boyfriend this year. I think you need to be careful."

"Don't tell me you're now going to mother me, Olivia?"

Olivia smirked, but he saw her blue eyes soften.

"It's been a while since anyone looked out for me. Thanks," Zachary said, staring into Olivia's eyes a little too long when her boyfriend, Alexavier, walked into the diner. Alexavier Regalia stepped up next to Zachary and looked questioningly at his girl.

Alexavier was the Mayor of New Orleans, and he'd met Zachary Bowman last year when Olivia and her son Lucas had some trouble back in St. Marksville. There was mutual respect between the men, but Alexavier couldn't help but notice that Olivia had been distracted since her friend moved to town.

"Hey," Olivia said to Alexavier as she smiled at him. Her blue eyes shimmered as she locked on to him, and he instantly was ready to do whatever she needed.

"Everything okay, Olivia?" he asked as he leaned in to kiss her.

Olivia shrugged. "Apparently, Zachary, who's been in town all of two minutes, has gotten the attention of Leonie Ford, our resident maneater, and arrested Senator Ripley's only daughter."

Alexavier knew Leonie Ford and paused momentarily before turning to look at Zachary. "The senator's daughter was supposed to get married today. Her wedding was all over the news and social media."

"I'm not on social media," Zachary admitted.

"Well, it's not very social, but I don't know how you avoid it," Olivia added.

Alexavier Regalia was the most well-liked mayor in recent New Orleans history and was popular online. Someone started a Facebook page dedicated to him, like a Where's Waldo type thing, but dedicated to pictures of the handsome Italian man spotted around the city, usually with a coffee in his hand.

Alexavier winked at his girlfriend because he knew she wasn't enthusiastic about his fan page. She smiled smugly at him before he pulled Zachary away to discuss what happened with the Senator and her daughter privately.

Since Olivia's two worlds collided, which was how she referred to her present-life and past-life acquaintances meeting, she worked at finding peace with it all. Still, there were times when Olivia felt uncomfortable over it, and she worked hard to keep those negative feelings from affecting her relationships.

Miss Lynn could almost feel the waitress' irritation and walked around the counter to wrap an arm around her. She and Olivia instantly became familial once the dark-haired beauty began working at the diner years ago. "No need to worry, Olivia. I will get the details of what happened with the Ripley women down at the jail house from the chief. You know he can't refuse my pies."

Olivia grinned at Miss Lynn. She suspected Chief Gallegos was a fan of more than Miss Lynn's pies, but so far, it had been a lot of harmless flirting.

The sweet older woman leaned in and added, "I know Leonie Ford flirted with Alexavier a few months ago, but she was dealing with a breakup, and he is a handsome fellow. Plus, she didn't know you two were dating."

Olivia smiled as she stared at her boyfriend. "He is really handsome, isn't he?"

"And smitten with you, dear. So, let's give Leonie a break?"

Olivia nodded. Miss Lynn vehemently disliked "catty" or "girl-hating" behavior. She told Olivia and other staff members that women had to help each other. The way she saw it, the world was a difficult place, and women needed to build each other up and not tear each other down. It didn't matter if they were stay-at-home moms, working mothers, single girls, or divorcees. All women needed to do a better job sticking up for one another.

Olivia wasn't so sure she would ever be friendly with the young real estate agent, but she would try and be the bigger person. At least as long as Leonie Ford didn't speak to Alexavier again-or *look in his direction*. She smiled over her last thought as she headed out to refill drink glasses for their customers.

Miss Lynn waited for Alexavier to finish talking to Zachary and then for the police officer to order his food. When she delivered his plate of pork chops and dirty rice, she questioned him again throughout his meal. The young man would not give her even a hint of what happened and seemed immune to her gentle prodding. Most people in town couldn't wait to gossip with Lynn, and she didn't know what to make of Zachary's discretion.

Had she lost her touch?

After eating dinner, Zachary took a piece of pie for later and another for Mrs. Bowers, who owned the boarding house where he rented a room temporarily. As he pulled out of the diner parking lot, he didn't miss the three black Suburban SUVs with tinted windows that sped past him.

It was Senator Ripley's caravan. Obviously, someone had erased Marlow Ripley's earlier arrest from all public records. People with that kind of power and money rarely paid for their mistakes, and Zachary didn't like the double standard.

Marlow Ripley had been a hot mess on what was supposed to be her best day, and while he didn't like her mother bailing her out of the speeding ticket or arrest, he was still curious about why it all happened in the first place.

Shaking his head at the shenanigans that woman probably got herself into because she was trouble, with a capital T, Zachary pointed his squad car toward the boarding house. He would eat dessert with Mrs. Bowers and get some much-needed sleep.

He'd worked ten days without a break and was exhausted. Still, he enjoyed Mrs. Bower's company over dessert for an hour before bed.

It felt like the middle of the night when Zachary was jolted awake. He glanced at the clock on his nightstand to see it was four in the morning. Someone was straining to unlock his door.

There was no mistaking the shaking of the door handle, then the vibration of the door, and the entire wooden frame because this was an old home, and whoever was working to get inside his room was putting all they had into pushing it open.

He was on his feet with his gun in hand when he wrenched the door free.

"You!"

Standing there, in the dark hallway, was Marlow Ripley, still wearing that wedding gown, smeared mascara, and now all that blond hair was cascading past her shoulders and around her face, accentuating those large blue eyes.

He lowered his gun while she stared at his bare chest and down his body. Zachary slept in boxer shorts.

Marlow was bone tired, which was the only reason she wasn't controlling her reaction to a mostly naked Officer Bowman. She had no idea he looked like that under his uniform, and honestly, she hated how hot he looked right now. As she focused back up at his face, he grinned at her.

"Tell me you aren't staying here too," she said with less fire than she'd had before.

"Why are you trying to get into my bedroom, Miss Ripley."

Marlow cut her eyes at him. "As if I would ever try and get into your room, Mr. Bowman."

There was the girl he'd arrested earlier that day. Still grinning, he shrugged. "Well, it is my room, and here you stand with a key and what looks like determination in your eyes."

Marlow shook her head. "Mrs. Bowers said it was this room. None of the others have furniture."

Mrs. Bowers was having the hardwood floors refinished in all the bedrooms but two. It hadn't been a problem since Zachary was the only tenant, but he couldn't imagine the spoiled woman in front of him living where carpentry work needed to be done.

Not his problem.

He pointed toward the room next door to his and watched as she picked up the hem of her dress to walk over there. She was barefoot, and he remembered her pretty pink-painted toes when she threw her shoes across the jail cell earlier that evening.

Marlow struggled with the other lock, and he shook his head. *Would he ever get any sleep with her there?*

He walked over and held out his hand for her key. Reluctantly, she handed it to him, and with a little force, he opened the door. Next, he reached over and picked up the large suitcase she had in tow.

Marlow walked into the room and watched as he set her bag on the bench at the end of the queen-sized bed. The room was smaller than his, but every inch was decorated in a retro Laura Ashley floral print with the drapes matching the bedspread and pillows. The walls were painted a complimentary rose color, and although it was circa 1987, it looked like it suited the runaway bride.

Zachary clenched his jaw. He didn't know what suited her,

and he needed to stop thinking about her at all. "Goodnight, Miss Ripley," he said.

But before he got out of there, Marlow spoke. "Thank you," she whispered, and Zachary watched as she blankly stared at her bag.

"You're welcome," he replied, less annoyed than before but still not wanting to get involved.

Without another word, Zachary headed straight to his room, firmly closed his door, and locked it.

Clearly, mayhem followed that woman wherever she went. But she was not his problem. He was not going to get pulled into her turmoil. Zachary clenched his jaw as he pulled a pillow over his face, struggling to stop thinking about all that blond hair he would like to run his hands through. Then he told himself, *"This is not the beginning of something."*

Chapter Three

The next morning, Marlow was in the bathroom brushing her teeth when Zachary walked in on her. She wore a pale pink nightie made of silk and lace. He smiled before he thought better of it. Marlow raised her eyebrows at him, then quickly rinsed her mouth with water.

"Seriously? Do you mind? I'm having a private moment." She wiped her mouth on the hand towel and looked at him. "Do you always barge into bathrooms without knocking?"

"Only when the common bathroom isn't locked."

Marlow looked confused. "We have to share this bathroom?"

"Yup," he replied before pulling out his toothbrush and standing beside her at the sink.

Marlow opened her mouth like she was shocked and then shook her head disapprovingly before storming out of the bathroom and into her bedroom.

It was exactly the behavior he'd expected from her, but it still made him laugh. He had an appointment and needed to hurry to grab something to eat.

A few minutes later, Zachary was sitting at the kitchen island eating a bowl of cereal when Marlow walked into the room. She wore a pink sundress with a fitted bodice and a billowing long skirt that skimmed her hips. When she turned around, he instantly stopped eating. Two thin straps held together the back of her dress, and that was it. Her entire back was visible down to her tiny waist. He swallowed hard as he stared at every inch of her exposed skin. Her hair was long and wavy, sweeping down her lightly tanned body, and Zachary couldn't stop his physical reaction over her. This version of Marlow Ripley would stop traffic.

When she turned around, he looked back at his cereal bowl. But Marlow knew he'd been staring at her. "All I have with me are the clothes I packed for my honeymoon."

Zachary shrugged as if he didn't care.

"I was supposed to be in Bora Bora right now."

Still, he didn't say anything.

Marlow poured herself a mug of coffee and continued standing there as she drank it. *Was he judging her? It felt like he was judging her.* Marlow couldn't stand it. "You don't have to act so rude, Zachary Bowman."

He squinted his eyes as he glanced at her. "Just sitting here eating my cereal, ma'am."

"When someone speaks to you, the polite thing to do is respond," she said, setting her mug down on the countertop with a little force. "And don't call me ma'am."

Zachary couldn't help himself. "Sorry, Runaway Barbie." He said and then laughed at her, which made her even angrier.

Marlow stormed over to him to point her finger into his chest. "Don't you dare make fun of me."

Zachary stood up and stepped into her space. The air around them was charged. He stared into her blue eyes, and she couldn't find her words. There had been real anger in her voice, but now it felt like something else.

"Am I interrupting something?" Leonie Ford asked as she stepped into the room. She looked Zachary up and down as she smiled slyly at him.

He wore navy athletic shorts and a light grey t-shirt that barely eased around his muscular arms. Leonie could almost make out his toned abs through the material, and her expression showed how much she approved of his body.

She heard someone clear her throat and turned to see who had been yelling at her handsome new client. "Leonie Ford," she said and held her hand out for Marlow.

Marlow locked eyes with the taller woman and shook her head. "He's all yours, Ms. Ford." With that, Marlow picked up her coffee mug and quickly exited the room before she said more of what she thought about Zachary Bowman.

When Leonie walked in, she hadn't decided if she wanted to go out with Zachary yet, but she didn't like that another woman was already on his radar. He'd just gotten to town. She needed to decide now, or the girl who'd stormed out of the room might take him for herself. The blond seemed the type that got what she wanted, and Leonie preferred not to compete for attention.

"Friend of yours?" Leonie asked, poking the sensitive situation.

Zachary shook his head slightly but watched the other woman walk toward the staircase. Leonie didn't like that one bit. She slipped her arm around his to pull him toward the front door.

"I have two great places to show you today. I think one of them is going to be your style," she said, leaning in like it was a private conversation. She was a master at flirting, but Zachary Bowman didn't give much away.

It was time for Leonie to turn on the charm and capture his attention. She'd always had a fear of missing out, FOMO, especially when it came to the opposite sex.

As they headed toward her red jeep, Leonie squeezed his bicep a little harder and grinned up at him. "Let's grab lunch after we finish today. That way, we can discuss the houses." She gave him a confident look, and he shrugged, which was a yes in her book.

They sped off with the tan rag-top rolled back on Leonie's jeep as Marlow watched from an upstairs window. She'd heard Leonie laughing at something as they drove off, and it irked her more than it should.

So what if he had a girlfriend? A pretty girlfriend with shiny brown hair and legs to the ceiling. The way he'd looked at Marlow that morning in her pink nightie and then again in her sundress, she would have thought Zachary was single.

But who was she kidding? Men were wolves, and Officer Zachary Bowman was no different. Sure, he had that boy next door charm——thick eyebrows and a strong jawline. *If you liked that sort of thing.* She didn't. In fact, she planned never to date again. Perhaps she could get a dog and forget men altogether.

She walked back downstairs, intending to make a plan of action. Her mother had disowned her last night. Insisting she apologized to Royce Chatham and agreed to marry him again, ignoring the fact that she had anything to do with hurting Marlow.

But forgiving her ex-fiancé wasn't going to happen. She didn't care how much that wedding cost or how much it embarrassed her mother. Michelle Ripley deserved every ounce of humiliation she got, and Marlow told her so in that quiet jail cell.

Marlow had never admitted how she felt about her mother to anyone and had to sign a nondisclosure agreement while still in college. Michelle maintained tight control over her public image and considered her daughter an extension of that reputation.

Never mind that Marlow had spent her entire life trying to be good enough for her mother. When that didn't work as a teenager, she tried to get her attention another way. Their relationship needed a lot of work. It had only felt normal when her grandmother was there to help.

Nona went into assisted living when Marlow was barely twelve. She hadn't realized then that her mother was using the event to further her career. Visiting Nona every week was emotional for Marlow. She missed her so much, and going from living together to only weekly visits was the most challenging thing in her young life. She was too young at the time to understand how that personal event could catapult her mother, the politician.

From when Nona got sick until she went into the nursing home, there was always a camera around to film doctors or hospital visits. At first, a reporter declared that Nona's fans were worried about her health because she was a well-known artist. Michelle would fortuitously show up as the overly concerned daughter. But eventually, that story got old, and Michelle Ripley needed to make it look more authentic. She bought Marlow an iPhone that happened to have video capabilities. Then, she had someone give Marlow photography lessons on how to frame the perfect picture and videos of them.

Michelle couldn't have known the future of social media,

but she'd given her daughter all the tools she needed to excel. Michelle's popularity grew from constantly being in front of a camera, but she resented how Marlow was even more prevalent in that world.

But Marlow didn't want to be a famous influencer anymore. It had all just gotten so out of control, and she wasn't even sure how often she was paid or how much. Her mother's lawyers and accountants handled that part of the business, and she got an allowance.

Getting away from Royce and the wedding had been the priority yesterday, but escaping her mother's control was the gift she hadn't dreamed would ever come.

However, her mother was ruthless. Marlow watched Michelle mistreat people on their household staff and in business. It was usually over some small thing like forgetting to water the plants or not returning an email in a timely manner, which was far less than running out on a massive public event like her wedding.

The senator discarded people effortlessly once they weren't of any use to her. Marlow had no doubt it would be the same for her now.

She needed to get to the bank and remove her mother's access to her account.

Sitting at the kitchen island in the boarding house, Marlow tried to write out her to-do list.

*Remove Michelle from bank accounts.

*Find cell phone

Tapping her pen on the paper, she thought she'd thrown her phone into the passenger seat of her car. She added it to her list.

*Get the car back

She rested her forehead on the countertop because it was

Sunday, and the banks weren't open. She would need to go first thing in the morning to remove her mother's access to her account.

Rethinking that idea, Marlow knew it wouldn't be enough. She would need to move her money all together to another bank.

*Open a new bank account

In the meantime, she could withdraw as much cash as possible from an ATM and get her car. Marlow would drive as far as she could until no one knew her name.

Florida was always an option. She'd considered living at the beach full-time when her mother left her alone as a teenager for months. *Why not now?*

It was strange how wanting to have all the control in your life was different than getting it all at once. Feeling overwhelmed, she finished her coffee and put her cup in the sink.

That was when Mrs. Bowers walked in. She'd been lovely to Marlow when the chief of police dropped her off there in the middle of the night. The older woman didn't even ask her for a dime.

"Hi," Marlow said, thinking an elderly woman had to be her guardian angel.

"There you are, child." Mrs. Bowers patted Marlow's arm sweetly. "Have you had anything to eat?" she asked.

Noticing Marlow was dressed and had on her sandals, she added, "You can't run errands on an empty stomach. My, don't you look pretty in pink."

Marlow's face warmed as the sweet older woman complimented her. People always thought Marlow's life was perfect, and she didn't need reassurance. It had certainly been a long time since anyone gave her an appreciative remark, and she wasn't quite prepared for it. "Thank you. I had some coffee. I'm okay. But I don't have my phone, and I'm unsure where to find an ATM or the impound lot to get my car?"

Mrs. Bowers had a twinkle in her eye. "I believe there is an ATM inside the Piggly Wiggly, and if you walk a couple more blocks to Miss Lynn's diner, she could probably tell you where to find your car."

"Thanks," Marlow said, but before she turned to leave, Mrs. Bowers hugged her. Marlow's eyes watered. Yesterday was her wedding day, and her mother hadn't even hugged her then. She couldn't remember the last time anyone had done it.

Royce would kiss her on the cheek or forehead, but they'd made some ridiculous pact when they got engaged. There had been little to no affection between them, and there wouldn't be until they were married. It wasn't like she'd saved herself for him, but he told her it would make things special. *What a liar.*

Marlow blinked back her tears and told the endearing woman she would see her later. Then Mrs. Bowers hugged her again and walked out to the porch with her so she could point Marlow in the right direction.

Unfortunately, the ATM at the Piggly Wiggly was out of order, and as she walked two and three blocks further, there wasn't anything called Miss Lynn's Diner.

Marlow watched several people walking into The Main Street Grocery and hoped someone there could help her. When she opened the heavy glass door, she saw it was a diner, and the entire room of customers turned to stare at her.

News of who she was and what she'd done yesterday had to have traveled quickly throughout the town. Marlow wasn't shy anymore as the daughter of a famous politician, and thanks to social media, she'd spent most of her life in the spotlight. But this was a little awkward.

Suddenly, a woman with a kind face walked over and gently

put her arm around Marlow. As she guided her to the lunch counter, the white-haired woman cleared her throat, "Is this how we treat company?" she scolded the patrons and then shook her head. "This isn't the first time we've had someone famous visit the diner. Mayor Regalia comes here all the time."

Slowly, some men and women nodded, and many smiled, but they all turned around in their chairs. As Marlow sat on the retro-looking stool, the woman leaned in, "I'm Miss Lynn. What can I get you, my baby?"

"I was looking for Miss Lynn's diner. I guess this is it?"

The older woman winked at her. "The one and only. You looking for a job, honey?"

The place looked like it had been in a time warp, straight from the fifties, with booths covered in green leather and a lunch counter trimmed in chrome. The floors were large black and white checks but with a rustic flair. It was definitely circa nineteen-fifty New Orleans style with the green and white striped awnings out front and the gas streetlights surrounding the area. It was perfect, and Marlow smiled that she thought it was a grocery.

"No. No, ma'am. I'm looking for the impound lot to pick up my car. Mrs. Bowers said you would know where it is?"

Miss Lynn grinned that Mrs. Bowers didn't tell Marlow where to find the impound lot. The woman was a schemer with ulterior motives behind sending the almost-bride her way.

"Have you eaten yet? You look like you could use a little breakfast and maybe a coffee before you head out?" Like Mrs. Bowers, Miss Lynn was also known to interfere in people's lives. Of course, only in the name of helping them. And Marlow looked like she could use a little help.

Chapter Four

Looking around the diner again, Marlow Ripley wished she could sit for a while and leisurely enjoy more coffee. Unfortunately, she didn't feel like she had time to waste. *And what was up with everyone in this town trying to feed her?*

"I've already had breakfast. Thank you. If you could point me in the right direction, I'd appreciate it." Marlow smiled, aiming to sound grateful for the hospitality.

Miss Lynn gave her a short nod and then wrote the directions to the impound lot down for her. It was only a ten-minute walk, but Marlow was ready to get as far away from New Orleans and her mother as possible. She'd instantly felt welcomed in Maisonville, but it was just too close.

Thanking Miss Lynn, she quickly left the diner before someone else could distract her. This small town was a beautiful place with a lake on one side and a river on the other. Marlow remembered going on vacation with one of her nannies to Maisonville one summer when she was younger. Her mother was working on her campaign or building her personal brand and couldn't be bothered with something like vacations. It had been one of Marlow's fondest memories, swimming all day or boating. Happiness seemed to be the priority to Miss Lena and her family that summer. They were in or on the water every day and would eat the best meals, like bowls of homemade pasta or grilled burgers, before falling like a stone into sleep. Marlow had never slept better at any other time in her life.

Of course, when her mother realized how attached Marlow had become to her nanny and her nanny's family, she fired the woman. That was the first time Marlow had to move to Washington, DC, with the senator.

The days were long and miserable because Marlow was locked up in their house with a tutor. Michelle couldn't stay out all night at political dinners without paying a babysitter a fortune, and they both agreed that Marlow should always live at home in New Orleans.

Senator Ripley stayed away for extended periods, and Marlow grew to hate Washington, DC, and politics. She'd also learned a valuable lesson not to get too close to her caretakers so she could attend school with her friends. It had been the beginning of the end of her childhood, and those friendships faded, as did her carefree days.

The walk through the small town reminded her of that lovely time. She noted that the walk to the impound lot, which was near the police station, wasn't too bad. Summers were hot, but a breeze was coming from the water, and the large oak trees draped with moss shaded the sidewalk. The picturesque town could be the perfect backdrop for her photography, she thought before scolding herself for daydreaming. Sure, she'd loved visiting Maisonville as a child, but she could not stay.

As she walked past a family getting onto a pontoon boat, Marlow smiled that lovely memories were still being made during summer in Maisonville. Of course, not for Marlow, as she recalled the moment Officer Zachary Bowman pulled her over for speeding yesterday, the know-it-all. He'd called her Runaway Barbie, and that wasn't funny. She grumbled as she walked past the police station and stared straight into a giant chain link fence. It was the impound lot because she could see her car parked in the far corner.

The sign on the fence said the office was closed until Monday. It also gave towing costs along with the bold typed words 'Cash Only.' Marlow thought she might cry. Small towns tried to lure you in with all their hospitality and charm, but they had zero ATMs and closed impound lots, which made life difficult. Not to mention, it would cost a small fortune to get her car out of jail.

Of course, she'd never been to an impound lot before and, at the moment, couldn't remember needing cash, particularly on a Sunday, but still, she had to get out of there.

Since running away from the church yesterday, not much had gone right for her. She squeezed her eyes shut, wanting to forget about that moment. Taking a deep breath, Marlow reminded herself that everything hadn't gone wrong. She turned back toward downtown, relieved that she wasn't Mrs. Royce Chatham III of the New York Chatham's. The thought of being married to Royce made her stomach ache.

Marlow didn't care if she was broke, on foot, or homeless. At least she'd escaped what she now knew would have been a marital prison.

As Marlow walked another block, she caught sight of a little drugstore. How had she missed that place earlier? It was clear that Maisonville was trying to tempt her as all those beautiful Oak trees distracted her earlier. But right there, in front of the pharmacy, was a brand new ATM.

Marlow smiled at the clerk as she stepped inside. She didn't need her mother's credit cards. Her eyes glowed as she inserted her bank card into the machine, and the screen lit up. Finally, things were turning around for her.

Her mother would have a fit if she saw Marlow looking desperate. She always had strange ideas of what optically was inappropriate for Marlow. It didn't matter if it was something as simple as a human necessity like eating. Marlow had a picture in one of her yearbooks where she and her friends were sitting on the lawn of her all-girls school eating pizza, and it sent her mother into a frenzy. "How could you let them photograph you putting that trash food into your mouth?" Michelle had yelled. As if it meant Marlow was fat. Her mother was high-strung, and most of the things Marlow did made her act crazy.

But how Michelle felt didn't matter anymore. The truth was that Marlow was a little desperate to have money in her hand and her car. Both equaled freedom.

Marlow grinned. She was free. But as soon as she put her PIN into the machine, it swallowed the card completely. A message in bold type said the card was reported stolen and to contact the bank during regular hours.

Marlow stood there staring at the message. This couldn't be happening. She'd never carried cash. Her mother said it was too dangerous. She dug into her wallet to verify, and all she had was a ten-dollar bill.

How would she buy food or pay for the boarding house where she was staying? Forget about getting her car out of the impound lot.

Marlow stood there stunned at the situation, but there was nothing else she could do. She didn't have anyone she could call, or anywhere else she could go. Had she ever felt more helpless?

Overwhelmed over her circumstances, Marlow remembered the sweet woman from the diner. *Didn't Miss Lynn offer her a job?*

Marlow was more determined than before as she returned to Miss Lynn's place. The older woman hadn't offered her a job. She simply asked Marlow if she needed one. Of course, Marlow had no experience waiting tables or in any kind of food service. Would they even hire her? A stranger with a degree in marketing and zero real job experience except as a social media talking head. But for the first time in her life, she needed money.

The diner was packed with customers when Marlow walked back inside. Miss Lynn waved to her from across the room as she slid into a seat at the lunch counter. "Be with you in a minute," Miss Lynn said as she carried a tray of six large, iced drinks.

A beautiful dark-haired waitress handed in orders to the kitchen, and after watching them for a few minutes, Marlow understood their routine. She grabbed an apron, a water and tea pitcher, and hit the floor, filling glasses, and handing new customers menus after she seated them.

Miss Lynn didn't stop her, but the other waitress gave her a side glance here and there. Marlow had the hang of it for a while, and the diner hummed with happy customers.

"Hi, I'm Olivia. You good?" The dark-haired waitress introduced herself after she delivered a large tray of food to a table.

"Good," Marlow replied, feeling like that was her way of welcoming her.

As the rush slowed and everyone was watered and fed, Marlow cleared one of the oversized tables, balancing a giant round tray weighted down with used dishes, silverware, and trash. She hadn't felt that useful in a long time, and her pride got the better of her. She hoisted the tray above her head, sliding between two crowded tables by the front door.

It was all going fine until she heard a male voice yell, "Watch out!" *Was that Zachary Bowman?* She instantly thought.

Leonie Ford had turned to face Zachary as they walked inside the diner for a late lunch. She was talking animatedly with her hands and giving him her most enthusiastic attention. But Leonie wasn't watching where she was going. She backed into Marlow with some force. In one fell swoop, Marlow and the dishes crashed onto the floor.

"Sugar. Honey. Iced. Tea," Olivia said through gritted teeth as she hurried over to help clean the mess.

"I'm so sorry," Marlow said as she scooped broken glass. There was brown gravy and red sauce in her hair and all over her apron, expensive pink dress, and leather sandals. She didn't seem to care about herself, just that she had ruined so much dinnerware. *Miss Lynn would surely reconsider hiring her now.*

When Marlow turned around, Leonie was rubbing her shoulder and arm as if she was injured. But Zachary was bent down, picking up broken plates to help clear the mess, which seemed scattered everywhere.

"I'm fine, but I could use some ice for my arm," Leonie said, still attempting to gather some attention from Zachary. He didn't look up, but Marlow did, and that was when Leonie lowered her eyes at her. "Did you hear me? I need some ice, so this doesn't bruise."

Leonie wasn't usually so ugly, but she'd had a wonderful couple of hours with Zachary. He was a great guy. When they finished looking at houses, she was confident he would ask her out. But after being in the diner for less than thirty seconds, Blondie managed to get his attention immediately.

Miss Lynn brought over some ice for Leonie while Olivia, Marlow, and Zachary made short work of the disaster. Zachary carried the broken dishes back into the kitchen while Marlow mopped the floor. Olivia put an orange cone down to warn everyone that the area was wet before she seated a new group of customers on the far side of the dining room.

Marlow avoided Zachary as he walked out of the kitchen, and she walked toward the back room to clean the mop and pour out the soapy, dirty water. She shook her head, humiliated over breaking all those dishes and falling right on top of them.

After fleeing her wedding that was live-streamed to two hundred and fifty thousand people worldwide, she hadn't thought she could be embarrassed again. But she'd been wrong. She walked into the kitchen and handed all her tip money to the cook and asked him to give it to Miss Lynn for the dishes she broke. Then, without another word, she slipped out the back door and walked back to the boarding house.

Zachary stood near the front counter, hoping he could talk to Marlow for a minute. She seemed so down, and he knew firsthand that the first hit to a person's life was brutal, but another punch and then another could knock most people out. He didn't like to see people down. He didn't like seeing Marlow that way.

Olivia had seated Leonie in a booth but didn't wait around for her drink order. She wanted to be a good person for Miss Lynn, but it would take a little while to accept Leonie Ford. It was apparent to Olivia that Leonie was interested in more than Zachary's real estate needs. And if she had to guess, Leonie was trying harder now because of Marlow Ripley.

"Hey," Olivia said to Zachary as she walked by him to hand

the cook an order. The cook told her about Marlow and handed over the tip money just as Miss Lynn walked up.

"She just left the tip money and walked away?" Miss Lynn asked, confused that Marlow, who'd stepped in when they needed a hand, thought she would be angry over a tray of broken dishes. "She earned every penny of that money, and I have a sneaking suspicion she truly needed it too."

Olivia tried to ease Miss Lynn's worry. She had an idea and winked at Miss Lynn before she turned toward her childhood friend. "Zachary? Could you take this to Marlow and tell her we aren't upset about the dishes? Let her know we need more help around here if she's interested?"

The last waitress Miss Lynn hired, Tenille Sims, had tried to continue working after she got married. However, she also helped Mrs. Bowers with her boarding house and now also with the boarding house renovations. On top of that, Tenille and her husband had rental cottages on their property in New Orleans that she managed. Tenille couldn't be there as often as they needed her, especially at the moment with the busy summer vacationers. The town had an ordinance that allowed summer rentals only during June and July, which meant the diner was overly crowded seven days a week for eight straight weeks.

Zachary nodded and looked like he was about to bolt after Marlow when Olivia grabbed his arm. "Um, I think there's a woman sitting in a booth waiting on you. Want me to tell her you had to leave?"

Truthfully, Olivia wouldn't have a problem letting Leonie Ford know that Zachary was interested in someone else, but Miss Lynn had lectured her about building other women up. As she looked over at Leonie, who was excited to have lunch with Zachary, she did feel the teeniest bit sorry for her. But

Zachary and Leonie Ford were not going to date. Olivia was sure of it.

Zachary looked at Leonie sitting there and then at Olivia and Miss Lynn. He wouldn't purposely hurt anyone's feelings. Plus, Zachary needed Leonie to help him find a house. But he didn't want more than friendship with his real estate agent.

Holding his hand out for the tip money, he grinned at Miss Lynn and Olivia. "I'll just tell Leonie something came up and then take this to Marlow."

Miss Lynn patted him on the back and thanked him for being thoughtful. It was more of a push to get him moving, but no one would know that except for Olivia.

The two women pretended to be busy as they covertly watched Zachary give Leonie the bad news. It wouldn't be the first time someone broke up with her at the diner. And Leonie wasn't one to take rejection quietly.

Would she cause a scene with Zachary Bowman over lunch?

Chapter Five

Zachary looked sincere as he spoke to Leonie. Miss Lynn and Olivia couldn't hear what he was saying, but he no doubt let her down easily. The young real estate agent hugged him. Then, in a surprise twist, she encouraged him to go before sitting back down in her seat.

"See, she's a good apple," Miss Lynn said.

Olivia smiled at the sweet older woman who wanted to see the best in everyone. "I have to admit, that conversation wasn't near as explosive as I thought it would be," Olivia replied before she checked on her other customers.

Miss Lynn laughed at Olivia. She wasn't wrong about Leonie flirting with Zachary. It was clear that the young real estate agent was interested in the town's newest police officer. But she had a feeling about these things, and Marlow Ripley needed some of what Zachary Bowman had to even out her tumultuous life. She hoped the handsome police officer figured it out before it was too late.

Zachary walked out of the diner like he wasn't in a hurry,

but once he got to the sidewalk, he began jogging toward the boarding house.

It didn't seem very long since Marlow left, but when he didn't catch up to her, he got a little worried. He took the steps up to the porch two at a time and didn't see Mrs. Bowers outside sitting in her rocking chair until he opened the screen door. Tipping his head her way, Mrs. Bowers grinned. "She's inside," Mrs. Bowers whisper-yelled, hoping he was looking for Marlow.

Zachary nodded at her but didn't waste a second by talking. Taking the stairs inside the house as fast as he had the outside, he only slowed when he stepped onto the landing. Marlow had a towel in her hands as she walked toward the bathroom. She hadn't noticed him and still had the same depressed look.

"Hey," he said, startling her. Marlow looked up at Zachary and then toward the bathroom. He wondered if she was ready to run again. He cautiously stepped closer. "Miss Lynn asked me to give this back to you." He held out the tip money, but she didn't reach for it. Instead, her eyes filled with tears that she didn't bother swiping away.

He stepped closer, and that was when he swept her ketchup-stained hair out of her eyes. This time, she looked up. Zachary saw she needed a friend and instantly pulled her into his body.

As his strong arms wrapped around her, Marlow leaned into him, and that was when he felt her tears soak through his shirt. After a couple of minutes, she wiped her eyes and stood back to look at his clothes.

"You shouldn't have done that," she said quietly.

"You looked like you could use a hug."

"No. I mean, yes. But I'm afraid you have food stains all over your clothes now, too."

Zachary looked down at his clothing, which was the mirror image of her stained dress, and smiled. She'd worn an apron, but still, the food had soaked through to that fantastic dress. He leaned close to her ear and whispered, "No good deed goes unpunished."

Marlow laughed, but it was insincere. It would take a lot more to turn things around for her. He could feel how upset she was, and it had to do with more than the accident at the diner.

He wanted to tell her that it would all be okay, but he didn't know what had truly happened to her or why she didn't leave with her mother last night. Where was her father? Didn't she have anyone that she could call?

He was still holding her tip money. "This is yours. I'm guessing since you are still on foot that you need these funds."

She stared back at him, and he could tell she was weighing the idea of telling him the truth. "The impound lot is closed on Sundays. According to the sign, it will be at least four hundred dollars."

Zachary had a lot of questions like wasn't she rich or didn't they take credit cards? But from the defeated look on her face, this wasn't the time to push her.

The money in his hand didn't look like it would be enough, but it was a start. "Well then, you should take this cash. Olivia and Miss Lynn said they could use your help waitressing. I think you should do it."

Marlow accepted the money this time. "Thank you. I need to shower. Maybe I can pick up the dinner shift." She shrugged and, without another word, headed into the bathroom.

Zachary stood there after she shut the door. He probably

needed a shower, too. And he shouldn't be thinking of Marlow Ripley in there naked. It had been a long time since Zachary had been with a woman, and it had to be the reason he kept chasing after Marlow Ripley. That bombshell had a ton of problems, and hadn't he moved to Maisonville to secure a calm and happy life?

He went to his room to change clothes. The food stains transferred from Marlow to him had only dirtied his shirt. He tried to focus on something else, but he couldn't stop thinking about how well she fit into his arms.

What was he doing?

Marlow Ripley ran away from her wedding yesterday. While he didn't know the circumstances, she had no doubt been in love with the groom at some point.

Ending a relationship was hard, but especially an engagement. Zachary couldn't understand getting as far as the church ceremony and then leaving. That kind of heartbreak took time to get over. She needed space to put it all into perspective and then time to mourn the loss.

Whatever was going on with her mother hadn't just happened over the wedding. It was the type of resentment that took years to develop. Yep, Marlow Ripley had a lot to figure out. As Zachary headed out of the boarding house, Mrs. Bowers stood up. "Everything okay," she asked.

"Yes, ma'am. She's in the shower. I need to run an errand. Do you need anything?"

The sweet older woman shook her head. She was worried about Marlow, too. "I'll be back soon, Mrs. Bowers. You have my number if you decide you need anything," he said and then added, "Or if Marlow needs me."

That seemed to make Mrs. Bowers feel better, and he tipped his head before telling her goodbye. In under two weeks, he'd already grown fond of the caring older woman, and she looked after him almost like family. It seemed to be a habit with her since she also fussed over Marlow.

It took him by surprise the first day he was at the boarding house. Mrs. Bowers had served him breakfast. Then, after his first day with the Maisonville Police Department, she'd baked him fresh cookies. They were warm when he walked in, and he ate six of them, which made her happy.

He'd started calling her before he returned to the boarding house after work each evening to see if she needed him to pick up something. Several times, he brought home an extra dessert from the diner for her. They would sit on the porch or at the kitchen counter and eat the treats and talk. It was oddly comfortable living in the two-story home, and he would miss Mrs. Bowers when he moved into his own place.

He'd told Olivia the truth yesterday because no one had looked out for him in years. His mother died of cancer when he was in college, and his father, who had been the chief of police in their hometown, needed help over the past couple of years before he succumbed to pulmonary disease.

Taking care of others came naturally to Zachary. He figured he got it mostly from his loving mother and service-oriented father. It was why he and his ex-fiance, Chloe Patterson, stayed together as long as they did. He took care of her, and she expected it.

Their breakup hadn't surprised him as much as it should have, but Chloe was difficult. No matter how much he gave, she still wanted more. When he learned that his father was dying and needed more help, Chloe Patterson found a way to make everyone feel sorry for her.

Nope. Zachary refused to be foolish over a woman like that

again. He scrubbed his face with his hands as he reconsidered what he was about to do.

After losing his father, Chloe started coming around again. He had two aunts he hadn't heard from in years who also showed up in St. Marksville. None of them had any idea he'd already made plans to move, and he felt like he'd dodged some real trouble there.

Maisonville was his new home and possibly a refuge from the drama coming for him. Zachary just needed to keep his head straight to buy his new house and that boat he'd always wanted. He was happy to be in the small water town where no one knew his story.

Before reaching the drugstore, he turned his car around to return to the boarding house. *This was the smart thing to do,* Zachary told himself.

Dating had been off the table for a long time, and when he finally settled down, it was going to be with a woman who was selfless and loved with her whole heart. It was the way his mother loved everyone and what he wanted in his life. Otherwise, he would live alone, work as a public servant, and fish as often as possible— the good life.

Of course, it would help if a life-size Barbie Doll hadn't moved into the boarding house. But he'd been around plenty of beautiful women, and he could control himself. Runaway Barbie would be on her way soon. She wasn't someone that stuck around——just ask her groom.

His jaw tensed as he tried to retract that harsh, judgy voice in his head. He didn't know what had happened to that beautiful girl, and he had no right to criticize her. A block away from the boarding house, he made a U-turn in the street. He was acting ridiculously and needed to follow through with his initial plan.

After all, Zachary made a decent living as a police officer. He certainly wasn't wealthy like the Ripley Family, but he had received some money from his father's life insurance policy and then again after selling his family home. He had enough money in the bank to put down on a house, make payments on a boat, and remain comfortable for many years.

It was the reason he decided to help Marlow. There wasn't anything more to his actions except it was the right thing to do.

The longer her car sat in that lot, the more debt it would accrue, and if she were going to work as a waitress, it would take her quite some time to get it out. There was no need to let that car run up a huge bill. Perhaps a little bit of kindness would give that woman some hope.

Zachary withdrew the cash from the ATM at the drugstore so that she could get her car tomorrow. It would be easy enough to slip it underneath her door, and they wouldn't have to talk about it.

After getting the money, the smile on his face was ridiculous, and he knew it. But he liked to help people, and he couldn't wait until she realized she could get her car first thing tomorrow.

When he pulled up to the boarding house, it looked quiet. It had warmed up quite a bit, and Mrs. Bowers must have gone inside. As soon as he entered the boarding house, he heard Marlow talking to Mrs. Bowers. Their voices came from the kitchen, so he headed in that direction. Zachary paused to watch them bake a batch of cookies together. He hadn't seen Marlow smile like that before. She looked happy. Her eyes glowed as she pulled a tray out of the oven and slid another pan inside. Had he heard her right? She said she'd never baked cookies before.

"My mother doesn't cook or bake. When I was a kid, we

either picked up food or had it delivered. Baking is a dangerous skill. Now that I know how to make cookies from scratch, I might eat them all the time." She laughed as Mrs. Bowers handed her a cookie before eating one herself.

"These are delicious, dear. I think you make a fine baker."

Marlow's whole face practically glowed. "My mother would be so angry to find out I'm baking cookies. I swear her worst fear is me getting fat."

Mrs. Bowers shook her head. "My husband always told me that he liked my curves," she said, which made Marlow smile even bigger.

"My mother gave me diet pills when I hit puberty. She would lecture me about watching my weight all the time. It was about the only thing she ever said to me. She was and still is obsessed over it." Marlow set the other half of her cookie down, and Mrs. Bowers reached out to squeeze her hand.

Zachary decided it was time to interrupt. "Those cookies smell amazing," he said, and both women turned and smiled at him. Marlow scooped a warm chocolate chip cookie into a napkin and handed it over.

"Thanks. I also have something for you," Zachary said as he handed an envelope full of money to her. He couldn't wait to try and cheer her up again. "For your car," he said, but the look on her face wasn't what he'd expected.

"Who told you to give me money? This is none of your business." Marlow glared at him before turning and running upstairs to her room.

Chapter Six

"Oh my," Mrs. Bowers said. She reached her hand out to pat Zachary's arm.

He realized he must have looked hurt by Marlow's response and cooled his expression. "That wasn't exactly the reaction I thought she would have over getting her car back tomorrow."

"I know, dear."

Zachary took a deep breath. "Let me go upstairs and talk to her," he said to Mrs. Bowers, who looked worried about them both.

He slowly walked up the staircase for what felt like the twentieth time that day, trying to think of what to say to Marlow Ripley. As he neared her door, he could hear her walking around in her room. The old wooden floors creaked, and she was pacing back and forth.

The walking sounds instantly stopped when he knocked, but she didn't answer. He knocked again. "Come on, Marlow. I need to speak with you."

Marlow opened her bedroom door wide enough for him to

walk inside. As Zachary sat on the end of her bed, she stood with her arms crossed— a defensive stance to match her mood.

"I didn't mean to offend you, Marlow."

"I am not naive, Officer Bowman. Unexpected generosity always comes with a price."

Zachary stood up to match her. "What are you talking about? It was a simple gesture between friends. I don't expect anything from you."

She squinted her eyes as if it helped her see him better. "Nothing in life is free."

Who taught her that lesson? He was sure he didn't want to know. "I had a little extra money and wanted to help. That's all. A friend helping a friend." Zachary crossed his arms across his chest now because his hands were restless. He wanted to hug her again and show her he meant no harm, but that wasn't a good idea for either of them.

"I can take care of myself. I had a plan, you know. It wouldn't have taken me long to earn four hundred dollars."

"Marlow, that impound lot charges a fee each day the car remains there. It could easily be six or seven hundred dollars by the end of the week."

By the way she looked at him, he had to guess she didn't know.

She sat down and put her head in her hands. He sat down beside her but far enough to give her space.

"Are we friends?" she asked, looking up to watch his response.

"Why wouldn't we be?" he asked, staring back at her.

Marlow shrugged as she seemed to weigh his words more carefully. Then she admitted, "I'm not great at reading people. If you're trying to deceive me, you should know it's cruel."

That felt like a dagger to his heart. He would never be cruel to her. "Just friends, Marlow," he reassured her.

Nodding this time, she looked down as she told him, "I haven't had any real friends in a long time."

Zachary gently bumped his shoulder into hers. "Well, it looks like you're wracking them up in Maisonville. Miss Lynn is a big fan of yours and Mrs. Bowers. Even Olivia was concerned when you bolted out the back door of the diner. You add me to the mix, and you already have four new friends. And you've been here less than twenty-four hours."

Marlow stared blankly at him. It had felt like a week since her wedding fiasco, and it had only been a day. She needed to get herself together. *Make a plan. Execute the plan. Simple.*

"I'm not a very good friend, Zachary. My life has been spotlighted since my mother won her first election. I was trained to perform on command. My job since I graduated has been as an influencer on social media. I don't even know who I am without that life?"

That felt like a lot of honesty on her part, and he stared at her closely. There were a lot of layers to Marlow Ripley, and she kept them hidden.

"Well, it looks like you are a single woman starting a new job as a waitress with or without an incredible sports car."

"Wow. Don't make it sound so glamorous."

Instantly, his smile faded. As he sat there expressionless, Marlow froze. Zachary Bowman was impossible to figure out. He turned hot and cold faster than the faucets in that old home. When he stood up, she stood with him.

"Who says life is supposed to be glamorous, Marlow?"

She wanted to tell him she was kidding, but he wouldn't believe her. For a split second there, Marlow had thought they had a connection. She was wrong. The way he looked toward the door told her Zachary was done talking. There was no mistaking how he dismissed her because she'd experienced her mother doing the same in her everyday life.

"No one," she whispered as she looked down. If she left there today, Zachary wouldn't think twice. They weren't friends, and he didn't know her. And she wouldn't tell him her sad little rich girl story either.

It was her authenticity on social media that made her pseudo-famous, but she'd never let the whole truth of her life come out. She absolutely wouldn't do that now with him—— the cop who'd arrested her and changed her escape plan.

Nope. Zachary Bowman could keep thinking whatever he wanted about her. Marlow did not care. She had no one, and she liked it that way. *Less baggage to carry around,* she used to say, when people she thought were her friends stopped coming around.

Zachary looked a little more exasperated at her. "So, what do you want to do about your car?"

Marlow looked at the envelope in his hand. She did need that car, and if it didn't come with conditions, perhaps she could accept his generosity. "Thank you for lending me the money. I promise I'll pay you back."

"No need. Pay it forward." Zachary didn't look back as he walked away.

"Okay, thank you," she said and watched him go.

No matter how grand her life looked to others, the truth was that Marlow had been on her own for a long time. There just weren't many good people around since her grandmother passed away.

Zachary Bowman was a good person. She could tell he did the right thing when no one was looking. Even when times were difficult, that man followed every rule down to the letter.

It didn't matter that he'd said they were friends because he didn't like her.

Every time she caught him looking at her, it felt like he could see her soul. She wasn't perfect, but she'd tried to be good to others. But there was no way she'd ever reach the bar that man set for himself and others.

She slipped on her shoes and tried to put Officer Goody-Two-Shoes out of her mind.

As she returned to the diner, she tried to think about the things she needed to get done. She needed to go to the bank first and then get her car. She had plenty of money in her account to pay Mrs. Bowers and Zachary Bowman. By tomorrow night, she could have everything handled and log onto her social media accounts.

It might take a little time, but she could, and she would figure out a budget based on what advertisers paid her.

Assuming anyone wanted her anymore after she ran out on her wedding. How had she let her mother and advisers talk her into filming all the wedding planning? Those sponsors would probably want their money back now that the wedding of the year didn't happen.

How far could she get on her savings and waitressing money?

As she walked into the diner, Marlow tried to forget about the trouble she'd created for herself. If she'd learned anything, it was that the only way to handle a problem was to face it head-on. She had a list and determination.

"What's wrong?" Miss Lynn asked as she reached to lift Marlow's chin to look at her.

"I'm good. Just have a lot on my mind, Miss Lynn."

"Well, of course, you do. Is there anything we can do to

help you?" Miss Lynn looked over at Olivia, who headed their way immediately.

It was like the older woman and the beautiful Olivia read each other's minds.

"Is this about Zachary?" Olivia asked.

Well, almost like they read minds, Marlow thought. "Absolutely not. Officer Bowman and I are not friends. In fact, I doubt that we will talk to each other again."

"Really?" Miss Lynn asked.

Nodding, Marlow tried not to explain herself, but those two women kept watching her.

"Well, he did give me the money to get my car out of the impound lot, but I'm going to pay him back tomorrow after I go to the bank."

Miss Lynn smiled. "That was very thoughtful of him."

"I told you that he had a thing for Marlow," Olivia said with a smirk on her face.

It was hard to understand why those two looked so happy, but Marlow had to set them straight. "I'm sorry, Olivia, but he doesn't. Yes, Miss Lynn, it was thoughtful, but I think he did it to get rid of me. I mean, who gives a perfect stranger an envelope of cash? He insisted I take it and then told me, instead of paying him back, to pay it forward. Then he got mad and stormed off."

"He stormed off?" Olivia asked. "I don't think I've ever seen Zachary mad."

"Well, I can promise you that he was mad. He didn't even look back at me when I said thank you. He's positively one of the most frustrating men I've ever met."

Olivia nodded. She was surer than before that Zachary was interested in Marlow Ripley. First, he helped pick up the dishes she'd dropped and then was worried when Marlow left without her tip money. But the fact that his tough armor was breaking down over the blue-eyed girl was a significant sign. But Marlow didn't know him yet. "I'm sorry he hurt your feelings, Marlow," Olivia said. "Deep down, he really is a good guy."

A group of customers walked in as Marlow nodded at Olivia. "It's okay. I don't think his girlfriend likes me very much either." She shrugged, grabbed some menus, and walked over to seat the new customers.

Miss Lynn looked at Olivia, and they said, "Leonie Ford?" simultaneously.

"He couldn't?" Olivia said and then stomped toward the kitchen.

Miss Lynn didn't think it was true, but it wasn't the time to bring it up. They had a rush of people until eight, and Olivia left shortly afterward. Miss Lynn and Marlow worked well together, helping customers and cleaning up, too.

When a beautiful redhead walked in and hugged Miss Lynn, Marlow stopped and watched the exchange. Red was holding hands with a handsome man and animatedly talking as she rubbed her baby bump.

Miss Lynn turned around and motioned for Marlow to come over. She was smiling so big that Marlow thought they must be her family.

"Marlow, this is Sydney and Ryan Gentry. Sydney used to work here a while ago until Ryan hired her to help him renovate homes and then swept her off her feet."

Sydney hugged Marlow before stepping back and realizing she'd shocked the new waitress a little. "Sorry. I'm a hugger," Sydney said, and Marlow grinned.

The woman was the most stunning pregnant woman she'd ever seen. "It's okay. Nice to meet you both."

Then, another couple came in behind them. "This is my lucky night." Miss Lynn turned and hugged that couple, too.

"Marlow, this is Ryan's sister, Reagan Gentry, and her fiance, Dr. Young."

"You can call me Seth," Dr. Young said, and Reagan reached over to shake Marlow's hand.

"Can I get you guys a table?" Marlow asked, and Miss Lynn laughed that she hadn't seated anyone.

"We've just been so busy, and I haven't seen any of you in weeks," the sweet older woman said.

Marlow handed over menus and took drink orders before giving them a few minutes to figure out what they wanted to eat. She would have guessed it had been months or a year since Miss Lynn saw that group.

But she gave Marlow a quick smile as she told her they were all close friends and usually came in to eat once every week or two. It was clear that Miss Lynn loved them all, and Marlow wasn't used to seeing that much emotion or affection between people.

The rest of the night flew by, and after closing, Marlow walked back to the boarding house. She was surprised by the tears that filled her eyes when she thought of the happy couples and Miss Lynn's love for them.

It was beautiful, and even though she didn't have that, she was thankful to witness it in person.

Marlow dried her eyes. This place had a charm that she couldn't describe. But she didn't fit in here. Once Marlow got things straightened out at the bank and got her car back, she would stop by the diner and tell them goodbye. They were all lovely, happy people, and Marlow felt like a burden.

It was foolish to feel attached to a place she hardly knew, but leaving would still be hard. Everyone had helped her without a second thought, including Zachary Bowman. But it also broke her heart to see what she had missed her whole life.

As she walked into the boarding house, Mrs. Bowers waved to her from the kitchen island. She was eating a bowl of cereal, and if Marlow didn't know better, she would have thought the sweet woman was waiting up for her.

After telling Mrs. Bowers about her evening and the people she'd met, Marlow went upstairs to prepare for bed. She was exhausted and needed to be out the door by seven in the morning. She wanted to be the first customer at the bank and mentally went through her checklist again.

Dragging herself to the bathroom to brush her teeth, Marlow could have sworn Zachary's door closed. Had he been watching her? Avoiding her?

It didn't matter because she was leaving tomorrow, and he would wish he'd been nicer to her. She smirked. He probably wouldn't, but it made her feel better to think he might miss her a little.

Chapter Seven

"What do you mean she withdrew all the money in my account?" Marlow asked the private banker.

He was a heavy-set man stuffed into a brown suit. Marlow noticed his shirt collar was too tight, and his neck bulged even more when he was nervous.

"Her name is also on the account, Miss Ripley."

"But it's my account. Michelle was just a co-signer. I was told she needed to be on there. No one explained that she could empty the account at will." Marlow stood with her hands on her hips as she looked at the clock. She'd gotten to the bank branch in Maisonville before they opened and was the first customer. No matter where in New Orleans her mother went, she couldn't have beaten her to a branch.

"When?" she asked him with her eyes narrowed.

"What?" The banker asked.

"When did she withdraw the funds?"

He swallowed hard before he answered her. "Yesterday. She called the bank president and talked to him. I can see in the notes that he electronically had the money moved for her."

Of course, Michelle didn't even have to go into a bank branch. Marlow shook her head before she put her hands on his desk and leaned in so they were face to face.

"You can close my account. I won't ever do business with you again," Marlow said before storming out.

The threat sounded hollow even to her. She didn't have any money or know how to manage her social media business. But she would figure it out on her own and one day have plenty of money. She would show them all, but especially her mother.

Marlow headed toward the impound lot. It was on the other side of town, but she was angry and needed the exercise to calm down. She wore a lavender linen jumper and her platform tennis shoes but was too furious for the heat to be a problem. The shoes had been her favorite to wear because they made her appear three inches taller and were comfortable.

Three blocks down, emotions flooded Marlow. She'd had a plan, made a list, and now would have to start again. She couldn't leave Maisonville that afternoon or possibly for a long time. She stopped walking.

All that frustration grew inside her until she balled her hands into fists and stomped her feet. The bottled-up rage over her life erupted as she screamed toward the river in what could only be described as throwing a fit.

Marlow felt a little better after letting go, but when she turned around, Zachary Bowman was looking out his car window at her.

He'd left early that morning, no doubt attempting to avoid her. But let her lose control for one minute, and he would be the one to witness her at her worst.

The man didn't even have the decency to pretend he didn't see her losing it. Without acknowledging him, Marlow turned and walked to the impound lot.

At least she could still get her car today. Of course, she couldn't pay Mrs. Bowers or Zachary back. It was time to get practical, and earning money was of the utmost importance.

It didn't matter what the fallout was from her ditching her wedding. She needed her social media business and would have to search her car for that phone and do damage control.

Social media was always more about *what have you done for me lately* and less about *what have you done.* So, she would have some explaining to do over the wedding-palooza. Still, perhaps a genuine apology for leaving them hanging on Saturday would keep her from losing her entire audience. After all, the name she coined lent to the idea that it was an exaggerated event.

Surveying her surroundings, Marlow considered her photography business, too. People liked her art, and she could potentially sell prints again like she had in high school and college.

She got her artful eye from her grandmother and was proud to have inherited the gift from her. While she built things back up, she could waitress. Miss Lynn seemed open to having her work there for a while.

Waitressing hadn't been on Marlow's radar as the daughter of a self-made millionaire, as her mother loved to tell everyone. Of course, Michelle Ripley had first played the single mother card to earn votes, too. Once she rode that campaign to the end, she proudly would give speeches on how, in America, if you worked hard enough and long enough, you could be successful.

Michelle may have fooled everyone else, but her mother, Marlow's grandmother, was a successful artist. They'd always lived a privileged life.

Michelle expected Marlow to play the perfect daughter

because it was a lifestyle she was selling to her voters. *You, too, can be successful and have an ideal daughter like me.*

It was exhausting. If Marlow was honest, so was being an influencer, but she hadn't any other choice.

She couldn't wait for Michelle to find out she was waitressing in Maisonville. It would send the almighty senator into orbit. You would think Marlow was a stripper by the way Michelle would freak out.

It would be perfect. Plus, Marlow enjoyed the work, and it kept her mind off her troubles. But she didn't need any distractions, and Zachary Bowman was a considerable obstacle. Sure, it was a small town, and he was a police officer, but why did he have to live in the same boarding house?

Before she went down the rabbit hole of her recent bad luck, she thought about how he was in bed when she got home last night, even though it wasn't super late. And he was gone this morning before she was too, and she'd gotten up early. While she didn't know for sure, it felt like he was avoiding her.

Good. Marlow didn't want to see the good-goody officer either. The disapproval in his eyes every time he looked at her was enough. She had a lot to figure out, and having someone around who judged her at every turn reminded her of her mother.

He was nosy, too. And when Marlow thought about it, it was his fault that Marlow was stuck in Maisonville in the first place. Everyone in law enforcement in the state heard that she was on the run. He could have looked the other way. But oh, no, not Officer strait-laced Bowman.

Marlow worked herself up over Zachary when she walked through the metal gates of the impound lot. The truth was that there was no good reason for Zachary Bowman to have given her the money to get her car, except that he was genuinely a kind person.

As she began to soften, she considered that maybe he had no ulterior motives. But they absolutely were not friends. No. He was probably ready to get rid of her and knew she would leave once she got her car back.

He wasn't entirely wrong, but how dare he try to get her out of there. Just as she began to get fired-up again, she opened the office door, and sitting there talking to an older man wearing overalls was Zachary Bowman.

Zachary looked her up and down. "Everything alright, Miss Ripley?"

She wanted to throttle him for calling her Miss Ripley again. The only thing worse would be calling her ma'am, but she was sure he would say that again, too.

"Perfect," she said through gritted teeth, and he nodded slowly. He didn't have time to figure out what was wrong with her again. He'd already overstepped every boundary he'd set with her, and it was time to stop it.

He would make sure Marlow could get her car and then get back to work. Seeing her at the riverfront that morning, he could tell something had happened, and she was upset. But Zachary needed to stay out of it. Besides, in his free time today, he wanted to read up on housing prices in the area.

Marlow Ripley needed to stop pulling him into her pandemonium and get her own life together. She caused too much of a commotion for him.

Marlow turned away from him, and he had to admit she looked beautiful in light purple. Not to mention, when the cute blond genuinely smiled her blue eyes shined.

"Can I help you, little lady?" Barry, the garage manager, asked.

"Hi, I'm Marlow Ripley, and my car was towed to this lot on Saturday."

"That silver Jag. Whew, it's a beauty," he said.

"Yes, sir. I want to pick it up."

The man nodded and waved her over to the counter so she could sign the paperwork.

"The towing fees, plus the yard and tax, comes to $595, Miss Ripley."

Marlow's expression dropped as she reached into her wallet to pull out all the cash she had from Zachary and tips. It was going to be close.

When she set down her last dollar, her stomach felt hollow. She was still twenty dollars short.

Zachary stood and, without a word, put down a twenty-dollar bill. The older gentleman smiled at her and handed over the keys.

Marlow turned but didn't make eye contact with Zachary when she whispered, "Thank you."

Every time she wanted to dislike him, he showed up and helped her.

He leaned down and said, "You're welcome, ma'am."

And instantly, her blood boiled. Zachary held out his hand for her to walk out of the office in front of him, but on the inside, she wanted to let him have it. He was pushing her buttons on purpose.

Why was he equally annoying and sweet? He inserted himself when he hadn't been asked and stepped away once she was okay. She couldn't think about him or his behavior anymore. She was sleep-deprived and confused.

All night, she'd mentally prepared herself to get in that car and drive until she was too tired to keep going. But now, she didn't even have a dollar to her name.

Sure, she had her car back, but she couldn't afford to put a single gallon of gas into it.

It turned out to be the Mondayest Monday that ever Mondayed, and she didn't have a moment to cry about it.

She needed to get to the diner and work the busy lunch shift to pay Mrs. Bowers a little money and buy herself something to eat. Watching her weight had never been easier since she couldn't even afford fast food.

Without saying another word, she climbed into her sports car. There was an odd feeling sitting inside the Jaguar again. She checked the small console, and her cell phone was where she'd left it, lifeless. Had there ever been a time when the battery was dead, and it wasn't urgent to find a charger?

Marlow didn't feel like the same girl who'd spent almost every day posting something on social media and the last two years broadcasting live events, especially during her engagement, had taken over her life.

She certainly wasn't the same woman who'd received the Jaguar as an early wedding gift. Royce had surprised her with it four weeks before their wedding. He said he could tell she was getting overwhelmed with the wedding date coming at them so fast, and when he saw the car, it reminded him of her——sexy lines and fun.

A year of dating and another year and a half of wedding planning, and he hadn't known her at all. She wanted his time and affection, not a showy car.

He'd never liked her driving the old Bronco that used to belong to her grandmother. Nona had needed the larger vehicle to carry around her canvases and prints. Marlow had a connection with that light blue tank that her Nona had painted the same color as the sky. She'd driven it since she was sixteen and planned never to get rid of it.

The Jag was just a car to her. A vehicle from someone she hadn't known at all. Royce Chatham worked for her mother, and she'd met him at a political fundraiser for one of the senator's peers.

During their engagement, she'd questioned whether her mother had set the whole thing up. Marrying him meant that Marlow was expected to be in DC all the time. Royce was constantly huddled up with Michelle, discussing important business unless they wanted Marlow to post something on their behalf.

She should have been more in control, but her life, their lives, were always in a whirlwind of activity. Marlow needed quiet so she could put things into perspective.

She started the car, and the engine hummed as she slowly pulled out of the impound lot. It was a smooth ride, but the little town looked different as she saw it through the windows of this car.

Maisonville gave her much-needed space to breathe. She'd laid awake the last two nights, replaying the life decisions that led her here.

Knowing what she knew now, Royce couldn't have ever loved her. Marlow had been lonely for a long time when they met, and a little attention had felt like something special. She'd been so wrong.

In college, she'd had what she called situationships, a cross between a situation and a relationship. It was fun but not meaningful. She and Royce only had sex a handful of times, and it seemed like he needed to be drunk to be with her.

She'd questioned his sexuality because who doesn't like sex? She'd questioned her sex appeal, too. But Royce Chatham always had an excuse, and he'd mastered making her feel like she was overreacting.

Her mother would swoop in and say she could tell something was wrong between them. Marlow couldn't believe for the first time in her life that Michelle cared or was connected to her.

Looking back now, none of that felt real. Marlow didn't deserve the betrayal, but clearly, her mother and Royce had discussed the couple's sex life.

Chapter Eight

As Marlow pulled into the diner parking lot, she realized Zachary had followed her. What was his problem? As she got out of the car, ready to confront him, he nodded her way and then drove off.

She would never understand men. He wanted to watch over her but didn't want to talk to her. At least she wouldn't have to explain what happened at the bank to him. In hindsight, she should have removed her mother's access to her account years ago. Officer Bowman would have probably told her not managing her personal bank account was irresponsible. She already knew that, but she certainly didn't want to hear it from him.

Marlow doubted herself as she walked into the diner. She'd struggled with those feelings of not being good enough as a teenager. Her therapist agreed with Michelle that it was probably from her father abandoning her at a young age. Once she was away at college, she second-guessed everything she'd ever been told.

Sure, Mason Ripley hadn't been a part of her life since she

started kindergarten, but before that, she'd only had fond memories of her father. In those early days, he'd been caring and fun. They spent a lot of time together, which confused her when he was instantly gone from her life. Marlow eventually agreed with the therapist, but secretly, she felt like her grandmother dying was the first time she'd felt truly alone. Especially when her mother constantly complained about the hassle of being a single working mother.

Her mother sat in on those therapy sessions and planted the story of father abandonment until they stuck. The truth was that Michelle Ripley rarely showed up for Marlow.

Everyone seemed to adore her mother, and it looked like Marlow was the luckiest girl. No one understood that Marlow could never please her mother, but she tried to earn her approval like many others.

Dating Royce had surprisingly made her mother happy, and that made even less sense to her today. As Marlow put her things down in the backroom of the diner and found an apron, Miss Lynn walked in behind her. "How did things go at the bank, honey?"

When Marlow shook her head, the sweet white-haired woman hugged her. Nothing else needed to be said between them, which was odd for Marlow. Her mother never intuitively knew how to comfort her.

"Well, we are busy-busy-busy out there, and you can pick up as many hours as you would like. I think the mayor wants to take Olivia and Lucas to the beach for a long weekend or something, but she won't ask off if she thinks I can't handle it. You think it over and let me know how many hours so I can add you to the schedule."

Marlow nodded in agreement and then got straight to work. The great thing about working in the busy diner was that she didn't have time to think about her situation. No one in Maisonville seemed to care who her mother was or about her running away from her wedding anymore.

Most were just happy about the menu specials or what flavor of pies were available. Marlow had never known comfort from food, and to see so many people happy over it was funny to her.

Time seemed to pass faster than ever, and Marlow enjoyed turning off her anxious mind and clearing dishes, delivering food, and all the duties associated with her new job.

There was only a short lull before the dinner rush, and she found herself behind the lunch counter with Olivia for the first time all day. Olivia was stunning but a bit intimidating.

"Thanks," Marlow said as Olivia handed her an iced tea.

"You have to pace yourself around here. The summer crowd is relentless, and you need to hydrate."

Miss Lynn joined them. "Oh my, Marlow. You haven't had a break? My baby, you have to eat something. We can't have you wasting away."

Marlow smiled at the two women fussing over her. "This tea is what I needed. I don't usually eat during the day."

Miss Lynn looked at Olivia and then back at Marlow. "What do you mean you don't eat during the day? Honey, you need fuel for your body."

"My mother doesn't have the healthiest relationship with food, and we never had regular meals. As a teenager, she was worried I would get fat."

What she didn't tell them was that Michelle gave her diet pills when she turned thirteen and talked to her constantly about the food she ate.

"It was exhausting, so I learned to eat a small dinner. I don't even think about food during the day anymore."

Olivia had nothing to say about that, and Marlow could tell it wasn't usual for her. Lynn paused for a moment to consider what she'd heard, but it didn't take long for her to speak her mind.

"I understand wanting to keep your figure, but your health is important. You've been walking all over town and need more calories, dear."

She wrapped an arm around Marlow and, for the first time, realized she could feel the young woman's rib cage. Attempting not to seem alarmed, she turned and cut a piece of strawberry ice box pie. "Take this pie, for instance. I make it from scratch, and while there is sugar, it is mostly made of fresh strawberries. It's practically a health food. You need to try it."

Marlow's eyes got bigger. "Oh, I couldn't."

Miss Lynn pressed harder. "It is your job to push the pies to each customer, and how can you sell it if you don't know what you're selling? It would be best if you tasted each of my pies by the end of the week, Marlow. You hear?"

Olivia grinned as she glided out from behind the counter to help a few new customers. It sounded like Marlow's mother was a piece of work. Had she tried to give her daughter an eating disorder? She wanted to say everyone wasn't cut out to be a parent and that sometimes you learned more about what not to do from them. But Marlow looked like she'd been through too much already, and there was no reason to pile on the negativity.

Marlow watched as Olivia left her alone with Miss Lynn. That beautiful waitress couldn't possibly eat pies and look that great. But she was alone with the older woman who looked expectantly at her.

Marlow had no choice but to accept the dessert. She thanked Miss Lynn and then went out back to eat it. Maybe

Marlow did need a break. She sat in the covered area with comfy outdoor furniture. After grumbling over getting fat, Marlow took a bite of the strawberry pie that sold out each day before the dinner shift was done.

There was an explosion of strawberries in her mouth as she swallowed that first bite. Then, her mouth watered for more. She examined the piece of pie closer because she had never had anything that tasted that decadent and delicious that wasn't chocolate. It took her only a few minutes to eat the entire piece, and then she swiped the extra cream off her plate with a finger.

Miss Lynn stepped outside to check on Marlow and grinned when she saw the empty dessert plate. "Good?" she asked but already knew the answer.

"Amazing, Miss Lynn."

The older woman winked at her. "I'm headed home, but Olivia is fine for now. You relax for a few more minutes. I'll see you tomorrow, honey."

Marlow leaned back in her chair and was seriously smiling over food. That had never happened. Never. Michelle would freak out if she saw Marlow now. As they planned the wedding, her mother had disciplined her daily over dieting.

It reached its peak when Michelle forced her to keep a food diary so she could review it weekly to verify Marlow kept her calories in check.

Marlow's eyes watered, and she looked around to see if anyone was watching her. The quiet in this town might do her in. Alone with her thoughts was becoming a dangerous place as she considered all the demands her mother had of her. She was twenty-five and had learned it was easier to comply than to deal with the wrath of Michelle Ripley. Would she ever not care what her mother thought of her?

She was tired of worrying over her dysfunctional relationship with Michelle or wondering what she'd been doing with Royce Chatham for the last two years. Or rather what he was doing with her. He hadn't loved her, and the wedding had been a transaction.

The night Marlow had met him, they sat at the hotel bar and drank a bottle of wine together. He was sincere, interesting, and a little bit funny. Marlow hadn't been attracted to anyone since college, and spending time with an intelligent, attractive man was exciting.

Strangely, when her mother found out, she was all for it. It was the first time in Marlow's life that she and her mother seemed to agree on something.

Why didn't she pick up on how odd that was instead of feeling happy she had Michelle's approval for once?

Their relationship was a push and pull where Marlow spent more time in DC than she'd wanted. But Royce took her on vacations every few months, with the first being a week in the Hamptons to meet his family. Next, they went to Italy, and then the whirlwind courting was on super-drive as he suggested they go to France together.

He proposed in Paris, and it was the last time they'd slept together. Looking back, he was constantly distracted and never seemed that into her. But she enjoyed his company, and he talked to her mother like she was an equal and not like he was in awe of her. If Marlow thought about it, that was the reason she'd agreed to marry him. She respected him and how he handled Michelle Ripley like no one Marlow had ever seen.

How could that have all been fake?

It was time to return to work and lean into the diner's distraction. Marlow pulled her long hair up into a ponytail and headed back inside. Memory Lane wasn't a place she wanted to visit, and the dinner crowd would be filling up Miss Lynn's diner any minute.

Marlow and Olivia were closing together, and she looked forward to getting to know her better.

After washing her hands and tying her apron back into place, Marlow headed back behind the large counter to help a few customers.

The familiar diner hum didn't let up until eight, and she smiled as she looked out the front plate glass windows at the deep orange and yellow sunset.

It had been a very long day, and she looked forward to crawling into bed at the boarding house. It was beginning to feel more comfortable, and she did not doubt that she would pass out as soon as her head hit the pillow.

The smile she'd planted on her face finally felt genuine as she grabbed the water pitcher to fill everyone's glass.

When she heard the little bell on the front door sound off, she turned around to welcome the customer and hand him a menu. But time slowed down, and her breath hitched as she came face to face with the last person on earth she wanted to see.

Royce Chatham was in a dreadful mood as he stared a hole through Marlow Ripley.

Chapter Nine

The water pitcher hit the floor harder than was natural. The ice and cold water went everywhere, but Marlow was frozen in place as she locked eyes with the man, she swore she would never speak to again.

He didn't flinch when she dropped the pitcher or when everything around them got soaked from its contents. Royce just stood there and looked into her eyes. "Marlow, can we talk?"

Olivia was by Marlow's side in seconds and threw down towels as she tried to stand between the couple. "Can I help you to a seat, sir?" Olivia asked, aiming to distract them. The look they gave each other was so full of emotion, and it was unclear if it was lost love or full-on hatred, but the air felt palpable between them.

Royce finally looked at Olivia. "I'll have a seat at the counter if that's okay with you?" Cordial as ever, and Marlow wanted to scream at him. He was a big fat pretender. He was no gentleman.

Olivia handed him a menu and gently guided him to a seat as far away from Marlow as possible. The man watched his ex as she got on her hands and knees to clean up the water mess.

"You okay?" Olivia asked as she stood in front of Marlow, blocking Royce's view.

"Yeah."

"He's the guy? The one you blew off?"

"Yeah."

"Good for you."

"Yeah." Marlow half-grinned.

"I'll wait on him. You take the floor tables instead. I've got this."

Marlow's mood lifted from the thoughtful gesture. Olivia barely knew Marlow, yet she was willing to run interference for her. It was incredible, and her heart ached over the kindness.

Marlow put away the cleaning supplies and headed to a large table of five people, thankful she had time to consider what she wanted to say to Royce.

Olivia had never seen Marlow act so calmly. After everything she'd been through in the last few days, the girl kept getting back up and taking care of business. Marlow proved she was made of sturdy stuff, and Olivia liked her even more than before. She'd stand by Marlow and help in any way she could.

A smile was plastered on Olivia's face when she returned to the unwelcome customer. "What can I get you to drink?" she asked, never taking her eyes off him.

Royce let that charming facade fade for a minute as he realized Marlow switched stations with the attractive brunette. "I thought Marlow was working the counter seats?"

As she suspected, he'd been watching them from the parking lot for a while. Olivia leaned forward. "Oh, she was before you got here. But I'm sure you know she doesn't want to speak to you." Olivia's blue eyes shimmered as she smiled slyly at him. He didn't seem like a man who was used to straight talk. "Now, what can I get you to eat?"

Royce's face reddened as he looked down at the menu. He wasn't happy with the situation and needed a few minutes to figure out what to do next. Michelle Ripley would disapprove of him causing a scene. He needed to keep his cool. "I'll have the house salad with grilled chicken and extra dressing on the side, please, and an ice water with lemon."

Olivia bit her bottom lip. She wanted to ask him if he was watching his girlish figure, but she didn't. Lots of men ate a salad or drank water, but there was something about how this guy waxed his eyebrows and buffed his fingernails that she didn't like. Sure, he had manners, dressed well, and talked the talk, but his mannerisms weren't authentic. She'd spent plenty of time with her boyfriend, who had been in local politics for eight years. Alexavier Regalia was a beloved politician, but he was also genuine and trustworthy. This guy's tan was even fake.

After putting his order in with the kitchen, Olivia grabbed napkins and utensils to help set up an empty table where Marlow was clearing. "I don't like that guy."

"Me either," Marlow agreed as she flashed Olivia a grin. In fact, as she watched him across the diner, sitting on the barstool and looking down at his phone, she couldn't imagine what she ever saw in him.

"Want me to call Zachary? I could get him to come sit at the bar until Mister Pomp and Circumstance is done."

Marlow appreciated Olivia's concern, but she wasn't in danger from Royce. Even if he stayed until they closed, Royce would only force her to talk to him. She didn't care about him.

But strangely, the idea of facing Zachary, who'd avoided her, was worse. She certainly didn't want him meeting high-handed Royce Chatham and assessing her even more.

"Thanks, but no thank you. I don't need Zachary Bowman. I can handle Royce."

Olivia wasn't so sure, but against her better judgment, she followed Marlow's wishes and didn't call Zachary. She did rush Royce's food to him and then handed his bill over before asking if he needed anything else.

Royce took the receipt and again looked annoyed at Olivia, who was clearly rushing him. He didn't say another word to anyone. He just ate his dinner, left cash on the counter to pay his bill, and exited the diner in a huff.

Olivia looked out the back door, and sure enough, Royce Chatham had pulled his car around to the back and was parked next to the Jaguar. It was thirty minutes before closing when she told Marlow. "He's out back waiting for you. Alexavier is picking me up. Want us to give you a ride home?"

Marlow grinned. "It would probably be an hour before he realized we were closed, and I left already."

Olivia laughed at the idea, but Marlow interrupted the moment by admitting she would talk to him once they closed. "My mind is made up, and nothing he has to say will change it. I may as well get this over with," Marlow mumbled as if she were talking to herself and not Olivia.

Reaching out to hold Marlow's hand, Olivia wanted her to know she wasn't alone. "Alexavier and I can wait to make sure it goes okay."

"You have a kid to get home to, and this may take a while. Seriously, I'm tougher than I look."

Olivia nodded. Marlow continued proving she was

stronger than any of them had given her credit. But Olivia knew leaving Marlow alone with her ex in the back parking lot after closing was not a good idea.

Of course, she'd considered herself more streetwise than others, but her ex managed to trick her in the most sinister way. It was better to be safe than sorry.

Still, she nodded at Marlow in agreement because there was no reason to discuss it further. As soon as she told Alexavier, he would insist on waiting until that meeting in the dark was over.

When the last customers finished up, Olivia and Marlow had most of their closing chores done. Together, they were quick and able to leave at the same time as the kitchen guys. Olivia locked the front door behind everyone and watched the chef and prep cooks pile into a small pickup truck and leave together. Marlow slowly walked around the building alone, and Olivia tried to act natural when all she wanted to do was walk with her.

Her expression had Alexavier alarmed as she got into his SUV. It wasn't until she reassured him that she was okay that he relaxed. He understood why his girl was nervous for Marlow and turned off his headlights so they could pull across the street and silently watch over the senator's daughter.

Marlow threw her bag into the passenger seat of her car as Royce got out of his Mercedes. She leaned against her car door and shrugged him off when he tried to hug her. "Don't touch me, Royce."

He looked hurt, but she knew it wasn't real. "I miss you, Mar. Don't you miss me?" Royce reached for her wrist and gently stroked her with his thumb.

It made her want to throw up. "I hate you, so what do you think?"

"I'm sorry, Mar. I didn't mean for it to happen. It had been so long, and a man has needs."

Marlow pulled her arm out of his grasp, balled up her fist, and slugged him in the jaw as hard as she could. He held his face, and she held her hand, both were bleeding.

Suddenly, Alexavier's SUV pulled into the parking lot near them, and Olivia ran out of the car to stand between Marlow and Royce. Alexavier scrambled to get in front of both women. Olivia was going to be the death of him, he was sure of it. "It's probably best that you leave," Alexavier told Royce, but Marlow had already lost her temper.

She verbally let Royce have it. "You had needs? I had needs, too. I needed you to be a decent human," she yelled as she threw a handful of dirt and gravel scraped up from the parking lot at him.

Olivia and Alexavier ducked out of the way as Marlow did it again, yelling, "I needed to be able to trust you. You are a sorry excuse for a man, you know that? And right now, I need you to stay away from me. You got that?"

Olivia held out her arms to block Marlow from getting closer to Royce. She couldn't have the poor girl going to jail for assault. But Marlow reached down and picked up another handful of debris and managed to throw it right into Royce's face this time.

He turned to try and wipe his eyes as he yelled back at her. "I'm trying to apologize to you, Marlow! Can't you see that? I told your mom you were crazy, but she didn't believe me. You tell her that I tried to put this behind us and get back together. You tell her!"

Marlow picked up more rocks and threw them at him. Royce Chatham got back into his car and sped out of the parking lot as she pummeled his car with more rocks and dirt.

Olivia put her arms down, and Alexavier took a deep breath, thankful he didn't have to make the guy leave physically.

Marlow dusted off her good hand and held the bloody one to her chest. She had dust and dirt on her hair, face, and clothes. She looked like she'd been in a brawl, but she wore it like a warrior.

Olivia tenderly tucked a strand of Marlow's blond hair behind her ear. "Are you okay?"

When Marlow looked up, she was smiling. "I've never hit anyone before. But it felt so good."

Alexavier grinned at them and shook his head. It wasn't exactly the way he thought his night was going to go, but he had a big Italian family and tons of cousins that got into worse fights than this. He'd mostly been a peacemaker. "Do you need us to drive you home?" he asked.

Olivia looked concerned. "You might need to go have that hand looked at."

Marlow shook her head. "Thanks, guys. I'm good. I'm going home and get into the shower."

Olivia and Alexavier watched as Marlow proudly held her head high as she got into her car. Apparently, slugging her ex did make her feel better. She waved out her car window to them as she pulled onto the road toward Mrs. Bowers' Boarding House, and neither of them could speak over the shock of what had just happened. In the blink of an eye, things could change, and there was nothing anyone could do about it.

"You and Miss Lynn sure find interesting people to hire," Alexavier said as he opened the car door for Olivia.

Olivia leaned up to kiss him on the lips. She was lucky to have Alexavier in her life. But he was only partially right about the people they hired. The truth was that the diner somehow had a beacon drawing those in need. She and Miss Lynn just happened to embrace them.

Alexavier held her hand as they followed behind Marlow briefly to see that she made it to the boarding house okay.

Hoping the night didn't have anything else in store for the new little waitress.

Chapter Ten

Marlow waved as Olivia and her boyfriend drove past her at the boarding house. She sat in her car for over thirty minutes, deciding to sell the Jag as soon as possible. It would never feel like hers, even though the buttery leather seats hugged her body. The car would always remind her of Royce Chatham.

It angered her thinking about all the time she'd wasted working on wedding plans. Royce focused on work and the expectations from the political world he and her mother belonged to. Suddenly, she realized the wedding had been their way to keep her busy.

Did Royce really yell at her to call her mother? Did her mother put him up to it? Would she honestly expect Marlow to marry him now?

It was probably about the senator's public image. Michelle Ripley ruthlessly guarded the information that got out to the press. Royce's job was perhaps on the line, which made Marlow smirk.

Everyone in Michelle Ripley's world had an expiration

date. If he weren't good enough for Marlow, then Michelle would certainly think he wasn't good enough for her.

Marlow had so much clarity about the situation now, and if she'd only said or done something at the moment on her wedding day, things would be different. Sure, she could talk on camera and had thousands of social media fans, but no one understood how hard that was for her.

She avoided confrontation. On camera, she might pop off with some retort, but afterward, she would replay the incident in her head for days. As she weighed each additional comeback, she wished she'd said to the offender. Insecurity crept into her soul.

Her mother excelled at putting people in their places. She could do it with such poise that it would take everyone a moment to process the rebuttal. But it usually sent crowds clapping and cheering for Michelle. The senator walked into every room with overwhelming confidence, no matter how big or small the crowd. It was obnoxious but a skill Marlow longed to have her whole life.

A streak of lightning flew across the night sky, and Marlow jumped at the loud cannon-sounding thunder. The summer heat caused big thunderstorms, and she needed to get inside.

Had she just wished to be more like her mother? The ending to this day had hit an all-time low as she headed up the porch stairs.

Tomorrow, Marlow would make a new to-do list that included staying in Maisonville a little longer. After she charged her phone, she would check out her social media accounts. They were probably imploding since her wedding day, and she needed to see if she could repair things with her audience.

Of course, while she was busy writing her task list, she

would think up more things she could have said to Royce. Hopefully, his jaw looked as bad as her hand. But thinking of Royce's jaw wasn't enough to distract her from the pain of her swollen hand.

She quietly crept into the dark boarding house as her mood darkened, too. She needed some ice now, and then tomorrow, when she got off work, she would reach out to several influencer friends to discuss collaborating. It was the best way to boost her online business, and then perhaps she could find something steadier in the marketing field.

Determined to make things happen, she looked down at her hand in the dark because it was throbbing like it had its own heartbeat.

She didn't turn on the light because she feared it would shine through the transom above Mrs. Bowers' bedroom door and wake the older woman. But when Marlow saw a large dark shadow nearby, she couldn't stop a scream that erupted from her chest. A warm hand quickly cut off her shriek.

Zachary's voice sounded deeper than usual. "It's okay. It's me. Don't wake up, Mrs. Bowers."

His body was so close to Marlow that his body heat sidetracked her brain for a second. The night air was hot and humid, but somehow, that always cooled Marlow's skin. She bit her bottom lip to stop thinking about his hot body and reminded herself that she didn't like him. "Why are you creeping around here in the dark?"

Before he explained that he was getting some water and didn't want the light to wake Mrs. Bowers, he got a better glimpse of her from the lightning streaming through the kitchen window.

She was holding her hand and looked utterly disheveled.

Zachary gently pulled her wrist closer so he could examine her. "What happened? Are you okay? Who the hell did this to you?"

There was no mistaking the concern on his face and the anger.

"It's nothing. I'm fine."

Zachary grabbed a dishtowel and filled it with ice. "Hold this," he said, giving her the towel as he picked up her injured hand and pulled it under warm running water.

Marlow quickly jerked it back, "Ow. That hurts."

Smiling this time, he was gentler as he eased her hand back under the water and carefully soaped up her skin. "Stop being such a baby. You can't leave this dirty. It could get infected."

Nodding, Marlow leaned against the sink and partially against his chest as she watched him wash and examine her injuries. Once her hand was clean, he used paper towels to blot her skin. "Hold the ice on it," he directed and then began to look her over from head to toe.

"Marlow, you have to tell me if someone hurt you. I'm a police officer, and I can keep this from happening again."

She stepped back and shrugged. "Royce came to the diner tonight."

Without a word, Zachary turned and stormed toward the front door.

Did he have his keys? Marlow ran to catch up to him on the porch. "Wait. What are you doing?"

The thunder rumbled louder as it got closer, but it was nothing compared to the storm on Zachary's face. "He's not going to get away with putting his hands on you."

The rain roared down, and she saw his jaw clenched in anger. Marlow placed her good hand on his face, and when he leaned into her touch, her pulse raced. "He didn't, I mean——"

she swallowed hard before she admitted, "I'm the one that hit him."

Zachary looked like he didn't believe her, so she explained further. "He showed up at the diner and tried to sit in my section, but Olivia waited on him instead. When he finished eating, he lingered outside until we closed."

Zachary's dark eyes looked black, and his expression was hard. The storm that surrounded them on the porch accentuated his anger. "He ambushed you in a dark parking lot?"

Marlow smiled. She couldn't remember anyone acting protectively over her since her grandmother passed away. It felt odd to have Olivia, Alexavier, and now Zachary defending her. She awkwardly admitted the truth. "He didn't ambush me. I knew he was there, waiting. It seemed like the time to face him finally."

The situation with Marlow Ripley grew more complicated by the day, and Zachary had vowed not to get swept up in any more nonsense like he'd experienced in his past. But he couldn't deny how overprotective he felt. While most people would look at beautiful Marlow, who grew up in a wealthy family with a famous mother, and think she couldn't have any problems, he could almost feel the pain behind her blue eyes.

Zachary gently guided her away from the rain blowing sideways. The porch was deep, and for the time being, they could sit on the furniture and not get wet.

Could Marlow talk about what had happened? The electric storm made telling him the truth feel more raw.

They each sat on the wicker sofa but at opposite ends, turning to face each other. Every time the lightning struck, Marlow's hair brightened, but her face was still in the shadows. She didn't look up as she quietly admitted what she hadn't told anyone else. "When we got engaged a year ago, Royce wanted us to wait for sex until our wedding night." Marlow's hands fidgeted in her lap as she paused to let that truth sink in. Zachary patiently waited until she continued.

"He said it would make things special and gave me this story about how he couldn't wait until we were husband and wife. I believed the whole thing." Marlow shook her head and corrected herself. "Well, to be honest, I did have some doubts. Nine months ago, when we went to check out the venue, there was something about how he flirted with my bridesmaids and mother. It happened again six months ago when we met with the caterer and tasted wedding cakes. Both times, we had huge disagreements, and I broke up with him. Michelle flipped out the first time, and the second time, she lost her mind. Both times, I ended up calling him and apologizing."

Zachary reached over to adjust the towel full of ice on top of her hand. She'd held it while she talked, but he was pretty sure her fingers were continuing to swell. He kept his hand on top of hers, holding the ice.

His kindness was going to be her undoing.

"Marlow, I know it's hard to see it now, but realizing he wasn't the man you wanted to marry in time to run out of there was a gift. Yes, you could be in Bora-Bora right now, but you'd be there with him."

Lightning struck, and the thunder rolled as the truth of Saturday's events turned her stomach. Zachary Bowman was right. And Marlow would rather be here with him, on the porch in a storm, instead of paradise with Royce. She just couldn't admit that or talk about Royce anymore.

She used the icy towel to wipe her tears, and there was a clean swipe across her cheek. When she looked up into Zachary's eyes, he grinned at her. "You have a little something right here," he said and then motioned to her whole body, making her laugh.

"You're telling me." Marlow sniffled and shook her lengthy hair, making dry grass fall to the porch. Zachary stared at her. *How had she gotten so dirty?*

"Come on, Marlow. I'll help you upstairs."

Holding her uninjured hand as he led her up the staircase, Zachary refused to admit he was getting involved with her. Marlow just needed a little help, was all, and he happened to be there.

He walked her into the bathroom to turn on the shower. It was the first time he'd gotten a clear look at her. Marlow looked like she'd rolled around in the dirt. There were streaks down her cheeks from her tears, and the bruising on her hand looked worse.

She avoided his eyes as she reached into the cabinet for a towel. Her heart was beating so fast, and she could feel the pull toward Zachary Bowman, which freaked her out a little.

Before he stepped out the door, Marlow admitted, "Tonight, Royce said he missed me."

Zachary turned to look at her again. Royce Chatham had manipulated her for two years and, no doubt, wasn't done yet.

"Then he said he had needs, so I punched him in the face."

Zachary couldn't imagine Marlow hitting anyone. And she hadn't told him exactly what had happened on her wedding day, but he suspected it was terrible. "That's how you hurt your hand? You slugged him, Kung-Fu Barbie?"

Marlow nodded, and right then, he wanted to kiss her more than he'd ever wanted to kiss anyone. She had to feel it, too, because she leaned in close and hugged him. "Thank you for not ignoring me tonight," she said and then turned around to start undressing.

Zachary grinned that she knew he was avoiding her. As she pulled her top off, exposing her back to him, he stared briefly and then forced his legs to move. He closed the door behind him as he said goodnight.

It was one of the most challenging things he'd done in a long time. Marlow was going through a difficult breakup, and he wasn't a rebound kind of guy.

Zachary hadn't had casual sex since he was in college. Sex was serious to him, and he wouldn't take advantage of a lonely woman. But there was no denying Zachary was drawn to her. He had a protective nature, but how he wanted to protect Marlow was primal.

There was also a lot more to her story, and she needed to talk about it. Could he get her to trust him? He shook his head because there was more to Marlow than she would ever tell. And those secrets would be a problem because Zachary believed in honesty.

Chapter Eleven

"Miss Lynn. I can do it. I'm sure of it," Marlow said when Miss Lynn told her that she had to take the day off, maybe two, because of her injuries. But she wasn't sure she could. Her hand was much worse, and the bruises were between dark purple and black. Miss Lynn wouldn't be swayed.

Marlow had gotten up early to try and log into her social media accounts. She needed money and it was the best place to start since she'd been successful. But her hand hurt as well as her heart and she couldn't bear to deal with her followers' disappointment, too. She planned to work on it later when she felt better. Now without work at the diner to distract her, she didn't know what she would do.

When Zachary pulled into the diner parking lot and didn't see Marlow's car, he instantly worried about what else happened. The woman had a monsoon of chaos raining over her most of the time.

Olivia spotted Zachary as he parked and met him at the door. "Her hand looked worse this morning, and there was no way she could carry plates or glasses to customers. Do you think Marlow's hand could be broken?"

Zachary wiped his jaw where he'd shaved extra close that morning. He'd wanted to check in on Marlow before he left for work but changed his mind.

Olivia leaned in, "You still talking to Leonie Ford?"

The question caught Zachary off guard. "What? I haven't talked to her in a couple of days. I still plan to buy a house here if that's what you're asking."

Cutting her eyes at him, Olivia leaned in, "That's not what I'm asking."

Zachary smiled because Olivia had never been someone who pulled punches.

"You should know that I'm team, Marlow," she said, and it was obvious that Olivia wasn't going show him to a seat or offer him any coffee.

"Glad you two are friends," he said as he waved to Miss Lynn across the diner. He wouldn't unpack his dating life with Olivia. She didn't know the details of his last relationship or breakup, and he'd never been one to talk about his personal life. They were friends, but he wouldn't discuss Leonie or Marlow with her.

More than anything, Zachary didn't think he could sit at the diner until he knew if Marlow was okay——so much for avoiding her. They'd only met a few days ago, but Zachary understood her. The first time he saw her all dressed up, he would have guessed she was a privileged, pampered, princess. But he wasn't so sure anymore. Marlow was strong-willed and hard-headed, like him. She wasn't the type to ask for help and tried to do everything on her own.

After all, when she decided to run out on the wedding, she hadn't turned to her mother or bridesmaids. She'd admitted five hundred people were inside the cathedral, yet she didn't reach out to anyone there.

She was upset just thinking about what had happened. It made Zachary never want to ask her about it again. Without another word to Olivia or Miss Lynn, Zachary turned and left.

"He's a man on a mission," Miss Lynn told Olivia as the dark-haired waitress joined her at the register.

Olivia watched Zachary's police cruiser pull onto the road toward downtown. Before returning to her customers, she leaned in and whispered, "I'd say. Mission Marlow."

Miss Lynn continued watching until his car was out of sight. She hoped Olivia was right. But it had been a while since Marlow left, and the young woman was physically injured and emotionally done. Honestly, she wasn't so sure Marlow hadn't finally left them for good.

Zachary tried not to think about the obvious. Marlow had been through a lot in just a few days, and people rarely thought the homecoming queen had problems. She had them in spades.

Smiling that she'd probably give him hell for calling her a homecoming queen like she did over Runaway Barbie, he kept his eyes peeled through Main Street.

Her car was nowhere to be found, so he headed to the most obvious choice, which was Mrs. Bowers Boarding House. Marlow wasn't there either. Mrs. Bowers sat on the porch and waved as he passed by. Zachary waved back at her, working to calm his expression. There was no reason to worry Mrs. Bowers, but Zachary had the worst feeling after how Marlow looked last night.

After exhausting every idea, Zachary made one more pass near the lakefront. It was a long shot, but he tried not to think about her taking the bridge across the lake into New Orleans.

Just as he neared the end of the street, he sighed when he

spotted her car. Marlow was a hundred yards away, sitting on a bench. He pulled in next to her sports car and watched her sitting there. She looked so alone as she held her injured hand and watched the rough waves crashing against the sea wall.

She must not have heard him drive up, but as he walked near, his radio went off, and she turned to look at him.

"How are you doing, Marlow?"

She shrugged but didn't say anything.

"Mind if I sit with you?"

"Suit yourself."

"It's a beautiful day if you like the heat and humidity."

Again, she nodded.

"How's your hand feeling?"

Marlow rolled her eyes as she held it up to show him how swollen and bruised it was this morning. "Can you believe this? It's ridiculous. And to top it off, Miss Lynn is forcing me to take two days off to keep it elevated and iced. She wanted me to go to a doctor."

Zachary examined her hand closely for a minute. "It's probably not a bad idea, Wrestle-Mania Barbie. You might have fractured it." He tried not to laugh because inside, he wanted to ask how hard she hit the guy. He suspected, like with everything, Marlow threw everything she had into it.

Marlow rested her hand carefully on top of her lap. It was apparent it was hurting. She didn't even blink when he called her Wrestle-Mania Barbie. She just looked ahead at the white cap waves hitting the seawall and splashing over onto the sidewalk.

There would be another strong storm that afternoon brought on by the intense heat. Zachary sat next to her as he tried to make small talk. "Did you know that Maisonville was nicknamed Renaissance Lake?"

Marlow shook her head *no*.

"Yup. According to Miss Lynn, people move here to start over again, whether after retirement or other life changes. New residents find friends or the happy life they've always wanted. Most everyone says that there is a little magic to Maisonville. Even Olivia said there was a bit of truth to the story."

The look Marlow gave him was incredulous. After a second or two, she covered her mouth to stifle a giggle.

"What?" He asked.

"Are you seriously telling me this town is magic?"

Zachary didn't answer her. Of course, he didn't think the town was magic. He'd felt bad seeing Marlow so down again and wanted to cheer her up. When Marlow giggled again, it was clear that she was happy laughing at him. He looked into her shiny blue eyes and decided it was worth it. "Have you had any coffee today, Lead-Foot Barbie?"

Marlow was still grinning when she said, "No."

"I have a great place that's walking distance from here. You up for it?"

"Can I call you *Harry Potter?*"

"No."

Sticking her bottom lip out to fake pout, she stood to walk with him. "What about Hagrid or maybe *Professor Dumbledore?*"

He grabbed her by the waist to move her to the other side of him, away from the street. "Not a chance."

Marlow laughed again. He was heavy-handed when it came to giving her nicknames, but she strangely didn't mind it. Whatever was going on between them felt better than him ignoring her.

A few blocks away, she could see the cute little food truck set up as a coffee shop. Espresso to Geaux was still relatively new but was steadily growing in popularity. There was a complete list of coffee drinks, tea, and fruity summer refreshers over ice, along with food items.

"Hey, what can I get you guys?" Evie Mae Shepard asked with a huge smile. She was close to Marlow's age but looked like she had her life together.

"Hi, Evie. This is my friend, Marlow. She just moved here."

"Lucky you." Evie winked at Marlow. "I grew up in Maisonville. It really is a great place."

Marlow looked around at the cool, refurbished food truck. It was painted black with some natural wood touches. Everything down to the signage looked modern and evoked the perfect coffee shop vibe. "This is a great place," Marlow said.

Evie Mae was proud and told Marlow she and her best friend started the business last year. "It was touch and go there for a while, but we've hit our stride."

Marlow and Zachary ordered hot coffee even though it was hot outside. "My first coffee of the day has to be hot," Marlow admitted as Zachary paid for the drinks.

"I think I'd have to quit the police force if I drank anything other than hot black coffee," he admitted. "My father used to tell me that anyway."

It was the first time Zachary gave away any personal information, and Marlow felt it was a moment for them. The smile on her face made her cheeks hurt.

Evie Mae interrupted Marlow's thoughts with her excellent customer service. "Thanks. Y'all, let me know if you need anything else. There's a comfy spot in the shade if you're interested," she said as she pointed them toward the back of the coffee truck. There were several chairs and picnic tables underneath large oak trees with drippy moss. The strands of outdoor lights attached from the trees to the building gave it a relaxed vibe. It was a great spot.

Zachary followed Marlow, and they sat in some cushioned wicker chairs. Marlow sipped her hot drink and then held it to her chest. "Whoa. This is extraordinary coffee."

"I told you."

"Yeah. It's just you don't usually find a lot of coffee food trucks, and then to find one that has coffee this great. Definitely a town bonus." Marlow looked at the plain cardboard-colored cup and thought about how she would brand this business.

Several quiet minutes passed as they drank their coffee, and Zachary watched Marlow looking around like she was cataloging the place. He didn't interrupt her at first but finally had to ask, "What's going on in that head of yours?"

When she didn't answer him right away, he figured it was private. Marlow sipped her coffee, and when her smile returned, he felt energy bouncing off her.

"You have to promise you won't laugh at me if I tell you."

"Promise," he said, and the way he looked into her eyes gave her goosebumps. She'd grown up learning not to trust people, and once she let her guard down for Royce, his actions reminded her again why she needed to be alone. But Zachary Bowman was just so convincing, and without second guessing herself, she leaned in close to him.

"You probably don't know this about me, but I have a degree in marketing. But I blew up on social media in college, and afterward, it took most of my time. I figured it had an end date. I mean, who can be an influencer forever? And so I've been daydreaming about starting my own little company and helping small businesses like Espresso to Geaux with their branding and such."

When she finished explaining her idea, she looked at him and then laughed at herself. "Like I said, I'm just daydreaming. No big deal. I don't know the first thing about running my own business."

"Don't do that."

"What?"

"Don't sell yourself short. You can do anything you set your mind to, and I'm sure of that."

Marlow sat there quietly, and it was evident that something was bothering her. Zachary finished his coffee and then stood to throw away his cup.

When he went to sit down with Marlow, she stood.

"Ready to go?" he asked, and she nodded. They walked back to her car in silence.

Pressing her key fob to unlock her car, Marlow seemed to be in her own world. He stepped ahead of her and opened her car door.

"Thanks."

He couldn't let her leave like that and reached forward to touch her shoulder gently. "I'm not sure what happened back there."

Shrugging like it wasn't a big deal, Marlow looked past him at the waves splashing even higher over the sea wall. "Why did you say that?"

"I'm not sure what you're referring to, Marlow?" Zachary hadn't meant to be heavy-handed. He knew he had high ideals and sometimes came off as overbearing. But the last thing Zachary wanted to do was upset her.

Marlow stared at him like she wasn't going to reply. Finally, she shrugged it off. "You don't know how many times I've failed at things," she said and started getting into her car.

Zachary wouldn't let the conversation end there as he

reached for her waist, making her look at him again. He stepped into her space and saw how her breath caught when he was close. "I see you, Marlow Ripley. I see how hard you work at the diner. How sincere you are when you talk to Mrs. Bowers. Hell, you ran out on your own wedding, which had to be impossibly difficult——that takes a strong person. A woman who knows who she is and what she wants. It takes strength."

The hurt look on her face felt like a punch to his gut. Then Marlow wrapped her arms around him and hugged him. When she buried her face into his chest, he held her tighter.

Two minutes later, she said goodbye and left without another word. Zachary watched her drive off and was even more confused.

He wasn't ready to admit what he'd learned about her already. He knew she'd gone to a private school in the city and was the homecoming queen. Officer Shannon had looked Marlow Ripley up the night she was arrested and told him the gossip she'd found. They didn't have much time that night before the senator showed up. Still, Bea Shannon thought it was curious that Marlow went to the West Coast for college instead of following in her mother's footsteps and attending the family's alma mater in New Orleans.

Since Saturday, Officer Shannon had spent countless hours reading about Marlow online. Bea Shannon was in her early sixties and loved social media. She showed everyone the picture of Marlow and Royce Chatham III from the newspaper announcement of their engagement.

Zachary didn't want to pry because he knew firsthand what it was like to have your private matters shared with the world.

He tried not to be a part of the precinct gossip, especially the buzz about meeting Senator Ripley. And how her daughter was now living in their town. But he did glance at the picture and mentally noted that the couple didn't look happy together.

But anyone looking could see Marlow Ripley was something special. If she wanted to start her own business, wouldn't people in her circle line up to help her get started?

There was more to the mysterious Marlow Ripley, and Zachary vowed to find out why she was still hanging around in Maisonville.

Chapter Twelve

It had been over a week since Zachary talked to Marlow. She still hadn't returned to the diner because of her hand and refused to have it examined by a doctor.

Tenille Fontenot, who he'd only heard about before last week, had filled in at the diner. He'd met her husband, Reaper, last year when he came to St. Marksville to help with Olivia's problem.

Tenille and Reaper happily lived in New Orleans, but she was still a favorite among the diner customers. She was young but friendly and proficient at waitressing. She also handled the final design touches at the boarding house for Mrs. Bowers like a professional.

Another local, Ryan Gentry, completed the floors, moldings, and minor updates earlier that week. His wife was on bed rest because they were having twins, or she would have been there to do a final check, too.

Slowly, Zachary was getting to know all the locals, but still, the summer crowd bustled around town. He felt like he'd moved to a much larger place than the Maisonville he'd visited months ago. But Olivia reassured him that once school started and the summer crowds were gone, things would be boring again.

Zachary wasn't convinced it would ever be boring in the little water town. The Fourth of July was only two weeks away, and things were getting busier. He went out again that morning for a noise complaint on the east side of town.

There were newer homes on that side, condos, and townhomes on the water. The police department got called there almost daily. Zachary had written a dozen parking violations and talked to numerous visitors about playing their music too loud. Most were having a good time and unaware they were disturbing anyone. The steady calls certainly made each day pass quicker.

But getting to know the area better, he decided he wanted a home on the quieter west side of town with plenty of trees and green space. Leonie was determined to get Zachary to buy a new place because she said he wouldn't have time to renovate. She'd shown him three more houses on the east side of town.

"It's just perfect, isn't it?" she insisted as he toured yet another condo. It was three stories, with the ground level as a game room instead of a garage. There were two bedrooms, a kitchen, a great room, and a bathroom on the second level and a large main bedroom with an en suite bathroom on the third floor, along with a home office.

Leonie had gotten more comfortable with Zachary, and when they toured homes, she began to keep her arm intertwined with his. This tour was no different.

"You may not have thought of this yet, but this place would be wonderful for you to grow into with a wife and maybe a baby," she said, and there was no mistaking her wishful thinking.

Zachary was okay with the mild flirting, but she was going too far, insisting he look at properties that weren't for him.

He didn't want to hurt her feelings, but it was time to put his foot down. "Leonie," he said, and she moved in uncomfortably close.

Zachary disentangled his arm from hers and took a step backward. Before he could say anything, she began to talk. "This really isn't it? I mean, are you certain? Your boat slip is right there across the parking lot, and you could be home and, on the water, easily after work."

Admittedly, she had listened to some of his needs. "Yes. I like that, but I've explained that I prefer more privacy. This side of town has the majority of rental properties."

Leonie looked disappointed as she promised to find him more homes to look at on the west side of town. But when he agreed to get dinner with her at Miss Lynn's diner, she perked right up.

When they walked in, Olivia ignored them as Miss Lynn took their order. It didn't matter how often Zachary explained that Leonie only showed him homes——Olivia refused to believe it.

"She's trying to get her hooks into you. I can't believe you don't see it," she said on more than one occasion. "It always ended with her adding in, Team Marlow."

Olivia continued to ignore Zachary, but her son, Lucas, happily walked over to speak to him. "I have more Pokémon cards. Wanna see them?" Lucas proudly held up his Pokémon card binder.

"Sure do," Zachary replied and moved his iced tea to the other side of the table to make room for the book.

Lucas spent fifteen minutes explaining each card and even offered Zachary a few of his duplicate cards.

When Miss Lynn delivered their food and took Lucas to eat some ice cream, Leonie grinned at Zachary.

"Don't bother telling me you don't want any of those for yourself. I can see how good you are with kids, Zach." She reached out and squeezed his hand, and before he could pull it away, Mrs. Bowers, Tenille, and Marlow walked into the diner.

"Hi, Zachary," Mrs. Bowers spoke up first.

He stood and kissed her on the cheek. "We just stopped by to grab a bite," she added, motioning toward Marlow's new cast.

Marlow looked past him, but he was staring at her hard. When he reached out to touch her, she stepped back.

"Broken?" he asked pointedly.

"Fractured," she answered.

Tenille added, "We went to the new clinic. They are efficient over there."

Mrs. Bowers added, "And the doctors are very handsome, right girls?"

"To each their own, Mrs. Bowers," Tenille said. She was happily married and didn't believe there was another man in the world who could compare to her husband. Marlow gave a half grin and then walked off to find them an empty table as far away from Zachary as possible.

When Olivia walked over to wait on them, she leaned down to talk to Marlow. "You okay?"

"Hand just hurts," Marlow said, which was only partially true.

Miss Lynn joined them. "Oh dear, look at your hand."

Mrs. Bowers nodded. "The doctor said she was lucky. If she'd waited much longer, then they would have had to do surgery."

"What?" Miss Lynn looked so concerned, and it made

Marlow uncomfortable. She wasn't used to having anyone worry over her.

"I'm fine, Miss Lynn."

Still, Mrs. Bowers added, "She fractured her hand and broke two fingers."

Olivia winked at Marlow. "Should have seen the other guy," she said, and Marlow finally smiled for real.

It wasn't long before Zachary and Leonie Ford finished eating and left. He stopped at their table to say goodbye, and Marlow smiled at Leonie.

The attractive real estate agent smiled back, proud that she had established some territory over the newest police officer in Maisonville.

He walked Leonie to her jeep, and she held onto his arm. Looking back, she could see all the women at the table watching them, plus Olivia. She leaned forward and kissed Zachary on the lips, and when he stepped back abruptly, she glanced back at the diner. Every single one of the women had looked away. It was a good thing, too, because Zachary Bowman was furious with her.

"Leonie, I don't want to hurt your feelings."

She grabbed his hand warmly and smiled. "Then don't."

He struggled to find the words he needed with her. "I appreciate your help in finding a house, but that's as far as this is going to go."

"You don't have to decide so quickly, Zach. We can see where this thing goes over time. Friends make the best lovers, anyway."

He took a step backward. "It's Zachary, and we will not become lovers, Leonie."

"Is this because of blondie? Didn't she just run out on some guy?"

"This isn't because of Marlow," he said, even though he found himself comparing the two women. "This is because I need a real estate professional. Honestly, I don't do complicated either."

"Well, you are in luck, Zach." She grinned, "I mean Zachary. Because I am absolutely the least complicated person you'll ever meet."

Zachary stared at her for a moment. She had to know that wasn't true. Leonie Ford's reputation preceded her in every circle he entered. Olivia certainly had something to say about her dating record. But he'd learned she had a thing for police officers, too.

Before he moved to town, Leonie had dated two other policemen. He didn't have a problem with that, but she was volatile and prone to showing up at the precinct to yell about whatever issue she thought they were having.

Zachary grew up in a peaceful home and wanted that type of lifestyle now. He and Leonie were not a fit.

She wasn't as convinced as he would have liked as she closed her door and winked at him. "See you soon," she shouted so he could hear her through the window.

When she drove off, he turned and saw that half the diner was watching him. He didn't like being the center of attention, and after his last relationship imploded, he avoided particular personality traits in women.

Zachary would not become the subject of town gossip like in St. Marksville. Climbing into his police cruiser, he headed home to the boarding house without looking back.

Grumbling the whole way there, he thought about how Marlow looked when she saw him with Leonie. Mrs. Bowers also looked disappointed, and he wanted to set the record straight. He was not dating anyone, especially not Leonie Ford.

His frustration grew, and he had to run and burn off some of his anger. He headed for a worn path by the waterfront to push himself harder. He alternated jogging and sprinting until sweat drenched his body. Soaking a shirt was the best way to clear his head, but he was still annoyed.

By the time he showered and climbed into bed, his irritation had climbed another notch. Why was he a magnet for temperamental women? His job put him in the middle of every type of crisis, but he didn't want that in his personal life.

His ex, Chloe Patterson, was a classic troublemaker. With light brown hair and hazel eyes, she pulled him in from the start.

They'd met while still in college with an almost instant attraction. Now, when Zachary thought about her, he felt nothing.

It was hard to believe he'd asked her to marry him. But when she showed up in St. Marksville saying she took a job there with the local news station, he'd accepted her with open arms——never questioning why she'd broken up with him after college in the first place. After all, they were young and still struggling to figure out life.

But he was wrong about Chloe. She swept into town and took everyone by surprise. As a remote reporter, she was masterful at spinning a tale. Zachary discovered that was a fancy way of saying she was a liar.

Kicking off the covers, he stared at the clock on his nightstand. He'd heard Marlow and Mrs. Bowers come in after he'd finished showering. But now, it was close to midnight, and the house was quiet.

He decided to go downstairs and get something to drink. His brain was working overtime, and there was no way he'd get any rest if he didn't find a distraction.

Zachary had struggled with insomnia after his mother passed away. He was an overthinker, his doctor said and prescribed him medication. But he refused to take it.

When he walked downstairs, he saw Mrs. Bowers' bedroom door was closed. But standing in front of the kitchen sink was Marlow. She was attempting to hold a cup of hot tea with her injured hand and stir it with a spoon with the other.

"Here," he said, taking the cup from her hands. There was a jar of honey sitting on the counter. "Want some of this in there?"

"Thanks," she whispered.

He sniffed the warm drink and looked at her.

"It's chamomile. Sometimes, it helps me sleep."

He could tell she was exhausted, but something else was wrong, too. Was she still mad at him over Leonie? "Are you okay?" he asked.

"Can't sleep," she replied without elaborating, which was strange for her.

"Your fingers look swollen."

Shrugging, Marlow took the cup from him and headed toward the porch.

He didn't like her wearing a silk nightgown to sit out there. Quickly grabbing a bottle of water and a quilt, he followed her. "You should probably use this," he said as he handed the quilt over.

Lowering her eyes, Marlow sipped her tea before saying, "Actually, maybe you should cover up with it."

That made Zachary laugh. He was wearing boxer shorts and nothing else, but that pale pink nightgown was sexy.

"Seriously," he said and wrapped the floral blanket around her.

Marlow rolled her eyes but pulled the cotton around her body until she was comfortable.

The silence between them was uncomfortable, and after a few awkward moments, Zachary finally spoke. "You know, I'm not dating Leonie Ford, right?"

"Does she know that?"

Zachary stared at Marlow over that comment. He'd made it clear to everyone that he wasn't interested in dating his real estate agent. But from the outside looking in, it would appear that Leonie was still working an angle to get close to him.

"I'll tell her again."

Marlow stared at him for a second and then back at her tea. "It's none of my business, Zachary."

Her words felt like a punch to his gut. He had just moved to town and was trying to get his bearings. His top priorities were to buy a house and a new boat. So why did he want it to be Marlow's business?

Chapter Thirteen

Marlow finished her hot tea, and Zachary downed his water bottle, but they no longer discussed Leonie Ford.

Zachary's mind hadn't settled down, but he needed rest. Standing, he looked at Marlow, who was holding her injured hand next to her heart.

"Come on, Marlow. Let's go to bed," he said, and as soon as the words left him, he realized his mistake. *Freudian slip?*

"I don't mean together. I can't leave you out here alone." He looked at her seriously, but inside, he wanted to laugh at how he'd worded things.

"I'll be fine. You go ahead."

As usual, she was stubborn, and Zachary, refusing to leave her, sat back down.

Marlow moved her hand with the cast back onto her lap. She didn't mean to sound irritable, but it was aching, and she couldn't stop thinking about the pain. "Don't you have to get up early in the morning for work?" she asked.

"Yes."

Marlow huffed. "Then why are you still sitting here?"

"I don't want someone to pass by, see you out here alone, and get any ideas."

"Like what kind of ideas?"

Zachary shook his head again. Was she going to go there? He lowered his face closer to hers so they were eye to eye. "You know you look sexy as hell, and I don't have to tell you the sexual thoughts it would invoke with most red-blooded men."

Marlow grinned, then slowly stood up and let the quilt fall to the ground. As she leaned over to pick up her teacup, the silk moved across her beautiful silhouette.

She was at the door before Zachary pulled himself out of the trance she'd put him in.

He jumped up to hold the door for her, and his jaw tightened as he worked to keep his hands to himself. Marlow smiled, and he could see the devilment in her eyes. "I have no idea what you're talking about, Zachary Bowman, but it's still nice to know what you think."

Was she teasing him? That mouth was going to get her into a lot of trouble. He followed her up the stairs, which took her twice as long as usual. And it took every bit of patience he could muster as she slowly swayed her hips in front of him.

Such a tease, he thought as she turned back to give him a grin before going into her bedroom and shutting the door.

She was trying to torture him, and he had to admit she was doing an excellent job of it tonight.

He could easily take things too far with Marlow Ripley, and one or both of them would end up hurt. It had been such a long time since he was attracted to anyone. Why did it have to be the runaway bride he'd arrested?

Zachary climbed back into bed and stared at his alarm clock. It was one in the morning, and if he went to sleep right now, he would get a solid five hours of sleep.

Had Marlow's tea helped her drift off?

Kicking his covers to the end of the bed, Zachary turned to face the wall that wasn't attached to her bedroom. That woman may have spent most of her life in the public eye, but she hid more secrets than anyone he'd ever met.

He needed to find a house so he could move. He'd thought Marlow would be gone by now, but it didn't look like her people were coming to fetch her. The rich and famous usually kept their distance from regular folks. But she didn't seem to be going anywhere.

It was also taking him longer to find a house than he'd planned. It didn't help that he was comfortable at the boarding house and had zero sense of urgency about buying a home anymore.

Had Marlow gotten that same homey feeling at the boarding house?

Pulling the sheet and blanket back over him, Zachary tried to stop thinking of the Barbie next door. He was wiped out and counting sheep had never done the trick. So, Zachary counted the boats he considered——*Grady-White, Manitou, Sun Tracker.* Then, the color he preferred, which finally, *gratefully*, helped him fall asleep.

Struggling with insomnia for several more nights, Zachary decided it was his indecisiveness over buying a house that was causing his trouble. Determined to make something happen, he bought a boat. It was bigger than he'd planned but used and still within his price range.

It wasn't an impulse buy, but watching Marlow mope around the boarding house for over a week prompted him to do something drastic. It was either that or seduce her until she smiled. And he had to keep reminding himself why that wasn't a good idea.

There was a lot to do once you purchased a boat, and he'd spent the better part of the week getting it all done. Thursday night, he brought dessert home from the diner to celebrate and couldn't stop smiling when Mrs. Bowers praised him repeatedly for getting such a great deal.

In her youth, her family had a similar boat and would go out for the entire weekend. "It's going to be a work in progress," he said, explaining that the engines were new, but the previous owner had gutted the interior to remodel it.

"What do you mean," Marlow asked, and it was the first thing she'd said to him other than a thank you for the pie. She'd been on her computer and he didn't think she was listening.

"Well, the boat's upper deck is all new, so that I can use it now for fishing. But the living space, kitchen, bathroom, and bedroom are mostly bare walls and need everything."

"Wow. You know how to do all of that?" Marlow asked.

Mrs. Bowers beamed over Marlow's curiosity. The woman couldn't hide how much she wanted them together.

"I've redone floors and some small things. It doesn't look that difficult. It's going to be delivered early tomorrow morning. Why don't you come with me to meet them at the marina."

Marlow hadn't been out of the house all week. He'd watched her open and close that computer a dozen times. She shrugged, and he could tell she was struggling to think up a reason to decline.

"Come on, Marlow. We can take it out for a quick spin."

Looking at him skeptically, she held her injured arm beside her chest. She still favored it, and he thought by now there would've been some improvement. "Don't you have to work tomorrow?"

He was working twelve-hour days until after the Fourth of

July crowd left town, and it seemed like Marlow had missed him. Or maybe she wanted to be alone?

He jumped up to clear the dishes before Mrs. Bowers or Marlow tried to do it while he answered her. "Yes, but we're going at seven in the morning. I'll have plenty of time to get to work by noon."

Mrs. Bowers looked concerned, and he winked at her. "Officer Shannon is going to be off tomorrow, and she usually works the noon to midnight shift," he explained.

"I'm also off Saturday instead of Sunday. Next week, I still have twelve-hour shifts until the holiday ends."

Mrs. Bowers had gotten used to Zachary being there at night. She was a creature of habit like most older people, and he liked to keep her informed of his coming and going.

He winked at Mrs. Bowers as he gathered his things to head upstairs. "Good night, ladies. See you in the morning, Marlow."

Zachary had to get out of there before Marlow came up with another reason why she couldn't go. He suspected she would try and get out of it in the morning, too, but he was ready to carry her out of the house if necessary.

Breakups were challenging, but the only way to combat a little breakup depression was to keep moving forward. It might take all of them working on Marlow to get her out of the dumps, but he was willing to take on the challenge.

❧

As he'd suspected, Marlow hadn't stirred by a quarter of seven. He dressed and then knocked on her door again.

"I'm too tired, Zachary," she said as she cracked the door just enough to peek out at him. "I'll buy you a coffee," he replied.

"Just go without me. I can see it some other time."

He put his hand on the door frame so she couldn't close it. "I'm not going without you."

Marlow stared back at him. "I thought you said you had to be there to meet the driver?"

"I do."

"So you're just not going to get your boat today?"

"I guess not. Thanks."

"You are so infuriating. You don't need me there," Marlow grumbled as she left the door half open and turned to put on a pair of white shorts and a floral tank top.

He was a big fan of her vacation wardrobe.

She slid into her sandals and marched her grouchy self down the stairs without saying anything else to him. When she climbed into his truck, he smiled at her. "I don't need you there, Marlow, but I want you to be there."

She looked at him, and he could see her questioning. He didn't understand it either, but they were friends. Or at least he was trying to be her friend.

Zachary still remembered everything about his breakup with Chloe. He also knew it was essential to have support.

When he pulled into the parking lot of the Coffee truck, she sighed and got out. She was going to pout all morning, but he didn't mind. He found her adorable, and it made him laugh.

They got to the Marina at precisely seven, and the truck carrying his boat pulled in a few minutes later. He was busy watching them navigate the drive, but when he looked over at Marlow, she had a look of wonder.

"That's it?" she asked.

"Yes," he replied, and his brown eyes lit up. It took longer than he'd figured for them to get the boat into the water, but he couldn't think of a time when he'd been more excited.

After signing the paperwork, he and Marlow climbed on board. She looked around and then watched him put in the combination to open the door downstairs.

The code was 54321, and Marlow teased him. "Top-notch security there, Officer Bowman."

"It's so simple no one will think of it, right?"

Marlow shook her head. "I think every kid in town will try it."

Zachary hadn't thought about that and made a mental note to change the code as soon as he read the manual on how to do it.

When he turned around to look at Marlow again, she had her hands on her hips and was shaking her head. "Zachary Bowman. I thought you said you were getting a fishing boat. This looks like a mini yacht."

"So you're saying you like it?"

"It's incredible." Marlow ran her hands along the window ledge trimmed in thick wood. "The possibilities in here are endless. What vibe are you going for?"

That may have been the funniest thing she'd ever said to him. "Vibe?"

She stomped her foot at him, and he was thankful to have stirred the feisty woman underneath those sad eyes. "Don't act like you don't know what that means."

"I just think it's funny you think I have a vibe in mind. This is a fishing vessel, woman."

"So, what, you're going to sit on Yeti coolers in here and use netting for your window treatments."

"Sounds perfect," he replied and walked toward the bedroom. He knew he was pushing Marlow's buttons. It was one of his favorite things to do.

"You are impossible," she said, following behind. "I think

this will take a lot more time than you realize. You're going to need a professional, Zachary."

He turned and stood in her space. She took a deep breath but didn't back away from him. "Are you applying for the job of Decorator Barbie?"

The way her eyes sparkled, he had to admit, he'd missed this side of Marlow.

"I don't know anything about boats, Officer Bowman. But I can figure out what looks good. If you're willing to admit that you need my help." He liked her sass and leaned in until they were only a breath apart.

Marlow took a deep breath, sure that Zachary Bowman would kiss her.

But as he leaned in, a woman's exaggerated voice rang out, "Oh my, Gawd, Zachary Bowman. You went and bought a houseboat?"

Chapter Fourteen

Marlow's mask was instantly back in place as she dipped underneath Zachary's arm to put some space between them.

Leonie Ford walked down a few steps and peeked in on them. "There you are," she said, eyeing Zachary like he was her prize.

"What are you doing here, Leonie?" Zachary didn't hide his aggravation. But Leonie wasn't going to give up so easily. She joined him, passing by Marlow without speaking, and wrapped her arms around one of his. She gave a little smirk like he knew why she was there. "You said you were buying a boat. I came to see what you got, and I have to say, Zachary, it is something else."

When she batted her eyelashes at him, Marlow stifled a laugh. That earned her a glare from the other woman. Seconds later, Leonie grinned back at Zachary. "So, should I be worried that you're planning to move in here?"

Zachary hadn't considered living on the boat, but it would be big enough. "I am still looking for a house."

Leonie wiggled like she was giddy and leaned on Zachary's

shoulder. "You don't know how happy that makes me. I have three great options for you on the west side of town, as you asked."

She talked for thirty minutes about the homes, effectively taking up his time to take Marlow out on the boat.

When Leonie finished, she pulled out her phone to set appointments with Zachary that week. "I'm sorry, Leonie. I have to work twelve-hour days through the end of the week."

"What? Oh no," she frowned again, and Marlow wanted to gag. Didn't the woman have any dignity?

"You're going to miss the fireworks on the river? I hoped we could have a picnic or something to celebrate——your new boat or something."

Was she implying that they had something going on? Marlow looked at her and then Zachary incredulously. She'd had enough. If he wasn't interested in Leonie Ford, then why didn't he shut her down?

The entire situation drove her up the wall, and it was too early in the morning to deal with it. Marlow turned and marched back upstairs and off the boat.

She'd wait by Zachary's truck for a few minutes, and if he didn't come out soon, she'd start walking back to the boarding house.

Zachary locked up his boat and said goodbye to Leonie before walking to the truck. He unlocked the door and watched Marlow climb in without looking at him.

The entire way back to the boarding house, they were silent. It was awkward and the opposite of what he'd wanted to accomplish by asking Marlow to go with him.

"I'm going out on the boat tomorrow morning if you would like to go with me, Marlow," he said as he pulled to the far left of the driveway at the boarding house and parked his truck.

"No thanks. I have plans tomorrow," she said and hopped out of the truck quickly to head into the house. Marlow didn't have any right to be angry at Zachary. She'd been sure he was about to kiss her on the boat, but maybe she'd been wrong. Maybe he was interested in Leonie Ford. Perhaps he was like all the other men in the world, and he wanted all the women——at the same time.

She went into her bedroom and slammed the door. She instantly regretted disrespecting Mrs. Bowers' house as soon as she did it. Flopping down on her bed, she put a pillow over her face and screamed.

She'd read that people acted irrationally when they hit rock bottom. *Was this rock bottom for her?* Her hand still ached as much as it did that first night she injured it——maybe more. She had no money and still couldn't pay Mrs. Bowers after the sweet woman gave her a room and fed her daily. She'd logged onto her social media accounts and saw a video of Royce lying to everyone about what happened. His story was that he was a victim of heartbreak because Marlow left him at the altar. He made her out to be irrational and immature, which her mother was happy to corroborate with a few short comments like, "Marlow, just come home," and "We all love you and can work this out."

Then, to have Zachary act like he cared about her and realize he treated that, what did Olivia call her, that maneater the same way as he did her, which proved she wasn't special, was so infuriating. And to top it all off, her birthday was next week, and she hated her birthday.

There was a knock at her bedroom door, and she froze.

Marlow knew it was silly because everyone on the block could have heard her slam that door. Still, she didn't move.

"Marlow?" Zachary said her name. "I'm heading to work." He paused, and she stood up and stared at the door. "I'm working until midnight."

For just a moment, his voice sounded like he needed her. She put her hand and then her face up to the door and closed her eyes. She could almost feel him there.

"Okay. I'll see you later," he said.

She wanted to open the door. She really did, but this was only temporary. As soon as she had the money, she was leaving there and never looking back. But more than anything, being with Zachary Bowman would never be brief, so this thing between them had to stop.

Listening at the door, she heard him tell Mrs. Bowers goodbye and then ran to the window to watch his police cruiser pull onto the street.

It hurt to see him go, and it didn't matter that he would be home tonight. Swiping at her tears, Marlow laid down on her bed again, letting her emotions take over and crying herself to sleep.

Zachary felt off for most of his shift. Thoughts of Marlow overwhelmed him, and it was more than Leonie interrupting their moment on the boat.

She'd been so down lately, and he knew how hard it was to pull yourself up when nothing seemed to be going your way. But for a second, he'd gotten through to her and made her smile. He would do anything to make her happy, and for that reason, he needed to put on the breaks.

For weeks, he'd dismissed the idea of looking up Marlow or the senator online. He'd told Bea not to share any more information with him, and he didn't have social media accounts personally. But Marlow wouldn't share more about herself, and he no longer just wanted to know. It was more of a need now, and he couldn't do it fast enough.

It was late when he pulled into the diner parking lot. He was surprised there weren't more cars, but it was near closing time. Of course, he'd been there this late before with people forming a line outside to get in.

It was nice to have space for a change, and Zachary sat in a booth where he could pull out his computer and work. Olivia got him an iced tea and a sandwich and continued her closing routine.

Zachary wasn't sure where to start but decided to look up Senator Michelle Ripley first. There were plenty of articles and videos from her early city council days and then her election campaign ads. There was never a Mr. Ripley in the picture, and the woman didn't appear with anyone at dinners or public events.

Seeing videos of the senator visiting her mother in a nursing home, he noted how rarely Marlow was around. She had to be a child at that time. Then he came across some footage that wasn't as polished and realized Marlow must have been behind the camera.

When she laughed and stepped around the video to hug her grandmother, he was fixated. Her blond hair was almost to her waist, and she was slim. But most notable was the way she hid from the camera. Marlow seemed nervous or shy and was completely different from the woman he knew today.

Closing his computer, Zachary was frustrated at the lack of

information. He wasn't a computer guy and never looked into anyone's background this way.

He used a closed system available to him with the police department, but searching through Google was ridiculous. It was against department rules for him to do a background check on someone for personal reasons. And he didn't break department rules.

Olivia walked over and sat down across from him to study his face. "What's going on with you, Zachary? Why do you look so glum?"

He grinned because Olivia was still looking out for him. Zachary had a crush on Olivia when they were kids, and she was a year older than him in school. Now that they were friends again, and she was a mother, she meddled more than ever. He liked that about her and cared for her, too.

"Seriously, what's going on with you?"

"Nothing. I'm good. Just taking a break before I have to go back out," Zachary said.

"You're not telling the truth. Does this have to do with Marlow? I saw you on the computer. Were you looking up her social media?"

Zachary didn't know the first thing about social media. "I was looking up Senator Ripley. It's weird that she hasn't checked on Marlow, right?"

"I didn't talk to my parents for ten years before they died. Is it weird?"

Feeling bad that he hadn't thought about Olivia's history with her parents before he made that comment, Zachary drank the rest of his tea. Had he been judging Marlow?

Olivia knew she'd put him on the spot. "I know you were close to your parents. But you need to realize that we don't all have the same supportive family life or loving relationship. It's complicated for a lot of us."

Standing, Olivia shot him a big smile before giving him more advice. "Your girl rocked social media all through her teens. She's pretty famous online, and although she hasn't logged in since her wedding day, people are clamoring for her to return. I think the answers to some of your questions might be there."

Zachary stood and hugged his friend. "She's not my girl, Olivia." With that, he left the diner and got back to work, attempting to forget about Marlow.

After all, he was supposed to protect the town of Maisonville and didn't have time to learn social media. But mostly, he would have to figure out how to sign up for an account first, and wouldn't that take some time?

He patrolled the quiet town for a few hours, but when he returned to the police station, he asked a couple of interns to help him set up those social accounts. It didn't take them long, and after a quick tutorial, where Zachary took as many notes as possible, he hoped he would remember the details when he got home.

It was after midnight when he got back to the boarding house. The whole place was dark as pitch when he crept upstairs. Marlow's lights were off. Initially, when she got to the boarding house, she would stay up all hours, but lately, she spent most of her time alone in her room. Was she sleeping that much because of her breakup? Perhaps she was avoiding him?

After a quick shower, Zachary climbed into bed. He should have been thinking about fishing tomorrow, but instead, he thought of how his breakup had been rough. If his father hadn't been ill, he might have had a rebound relationship or two by now.

The idea of Marlow needing a rebound relationship made him angry. Picking up his phone and logging into his new Instagram account, Zachary searched for Marlow Ripley. He wasn't prepared for what he found. She was even more stunning on camera, and he grimaced at how effortlessly she wielded her phone or camera around and videoed everything.

He randomly picked one where she was wearing a formal blue beaded dress. Her mother was in the background and looked stunning, too. Marlow was whispering and telling the audience how important her mother's speech was and highlighted how proud she was to be there to witness it in person.

She was good at pulling the audience in, and he noticed how much more he wanted to watch her. He clicked on several videos. More than half were about her mother, and the others were about products or items Marlow liked to use daily. Sometimes, she would say the video was sponsored, but a lot of the time, she was honest and said whatever place she was promoting, or item was her favorite, and she wanted to tell others.

It was apparent why she was so popular. Sure, she was beautiful and engaging, but she had this believable quality, too.

Why did that make him so mad?

Chapter Fifteen

Zachary returned his phone to the nightstand charger and flipped off his lamp. He knew why he was angry. He clearly had a type, and he hated to admit that to himself.

He hadn't lived under a rock and knew most people looked at social media. But didn't they usually post what they were eating or jokes?

His ex complained when videos became popular on social media. She said they looked like low-budget news or commercials. Eventually, she made them, too, but he figured it was part of her sinister plan to take over the news station in St. Marksville. But still, Zachary hadn't considered how similar Marlow's video posts were to a remote reporter. *How had he missed that tremendous detail?*

The camera loved his ex, Chloe Patterson, too. It didn't take her long to woo the town with her weekly uplifting interviews. However, she was never satisfied and pushed for promotions and demanded one of the anchor positions.

It didn't matter to her that the two anchor reporters had been there for years with a rapport she couldn't break.

It was hard to like that side of Chloe, especially when she complained about being more attractive than the current female anchor and more popular. Chloe Patterson actually told him that she deserved the glamorous life.

Zachary sat up in his bed. How had he been so blind? Chloe had grown up in a privileged home like Marlow. He could see it now so clearly. The way Marlow got everyone to take care of her, and Chloe told him that it was his job to do it.

Of course, Zachary wanted to love and care for someone, but he expected that woman also to feel the same way about him.

Marlow Ripley looked like a woman who needed saving. His ex perfected that look in the mirror, including fake tears. Chloe said it was essential to make her audience believe her. Manipulating others was a terrible trait.

Allowing yourself to be manipulated was almost as bad, and Zachary had spent weeks preoccupied with Marlow Ripley. He felt foolish and now regretted it.

There had to be a woman somewhere that didn't need to be famous or have followers. That behavior seemed shallow, and Zachary was deeper than following trends or being famous.

Staring at his clock, he rubbed his face and then eyes. It was two in the morning, and he'd planned to be up in four hours.

The girl next door didn't have the power to keep him up all night anymore. He'd suddenly understood Marlow's behavior because he'd dated her before.

He slid back down in the bed and pulled his sheet and comforter up around his shoulders. Closing his eyes, he remembered how Olivia and her son, Lucas, talked about Maisonville.

When Zachary discovered that his father's old friend Tim

Gallegos was the chief of police there, it felt like things were falling into place.

His dad passed away in early spring. Zachary sold his house and then his parent's home within two weeks of each other. It all worked out so he could start over again in this beautiful little town. He had to laugh because that was the tall tale about Renaissance Lake, and although he didn't believe in magic, he liked to think there was a higher power at work in his life.

When he lost his mother, his dad would say she was their guardian angel. If there was anyone that deserved to be an angel, it was her. Zachary did not doubt that she would look after him from the beyond if possible.

Whatever was at work, he'd made it to Maisonville just in time to join Mrs. Bowers, who was alone, and to meet Marlow Ripley.

Zachary groaned. These past few weeks felt more like a test and less like fate. He turned over and glared at the clock on his bedside table again. If he fell asleep now, he could get three and a half hours of rest.

Flipping his pillow over to the cool side and twisting back around under the covers, Zachary tried to relax. The bed was comfortable, and he could feel his body sinking into it.

Chloe Patterson had a lot in common with Marlow Ripley. Maybe they both were meant to be in front of a camera, but he'd learned his lesson. There was value in a quiet life, and things were never that way with Chloe. It would never be that way with Marlow, either.

It was time for Marlow to go home and resume her social media life, influencer life, whatever it was, and leave him in peace.

He stared at the ceiling and then, after a while, stared at the clock again, calculating how much time he had. If he fell asleep now, he'd get a solid three hours.

He rubbed his face, thinking about beautiful Marlow, who wasn't exactly like Chloe, and the warmth of sleep enveloped him. Somewhere in the recesses of his mind, he heard a loud noise and woke to Marlow screaming. He was instantly on his feet with his gun and ran toward her bedroom as fast as he could get there.

He wrenched open the door at the same time Marlow pushed it open. She ran behind him, and he kept an arm holding her against the back of his body.

"Someone was outside my window looking at me," she said.

Her voice trembled, and she said it so seriously he hated to doubt her. "Marlow, we are on the second floor."

"I-I know."

"Stay here," he commanded and headed toward the window. The lights were still off in Marlow's room, and he scanned the roof of the porch as well as the yard.

He could vaguely make out a shadow across the street, but he wasn't sure if someone could have gotten that far.

"It's okay. I'm going to go check outside."

Marlow looked at him and shook her head. "You're not dressed."

Looking down at his boxer shorts, Zachary winked at her before he bounded down the stairs and out the front door.

It was hard to believe Mrs. Bowers didn't stir from all the noise. Marlow thought about waking her for a second because she was scared for Zachary to go out into the dark alone.

She ran to the front window to watch for him. Hidden from sight by heavy, lined drapes, she peeked out but couldn't see anyone, including Zachary, out there.

It felt like an eternity until he opened the front door.

Marlow ran her hands over his arms and his chest. "Are you okay? Did you see anyone?"

Zachary had to catch his breath, and it wasn't from running outside after a potential Peeping Tom. "I'm fine. I didn't see anyone."

She searched his eyes for a clue of deception. "No one?"

As he shook his head, she stared at him, disbelieving. "I swear. I heard a noise, and when I looked out the window, a man looked back at me. He shook the window frame, trying to get inside."

Zachary nodded as he headed toward the kitchen for a bottle of water. "Sometimes people dream of an event and when they wake up, think it happened." He spoke without looking at her, which felt worse than if he'd accused her directly of lying. It was precisely the way her mother or Royce would have treated her.

"I wasn't asleep. I've been up for hours," Marlow said and then held up her injured hand with a cast. "This thing is very uncomfortable, and I don't like how the pain medicine makes me feel, so I haven't taken it."

"Have you been back to the doctor?" he asked with a tone of condescension.

Why was he acting like this? Marlow shook her head because he didn't care about her arm or whether someone tried to get into her room.

He finished the water and threw the empty bottle into the garbage can. "Well, Miss. Ripley, I don't know what to tell you, but it's hard to imagine someone scaling the side of this house to look into a random window for a cheap thrill at three in the morning."

"A cheap thrill?" she replied.

He knew he'd gone too far with that comment, but he was

tired and didn't want to be the good Samaritan anymore. Avoiding looking at her and trying not to think about how genuinely scared she appeared, he headed for the stairs.

Silently, Marlow walked behind him. When he got to his door, he looked over to see her peering inside her room from the hallway.

"I'm telling the truth, Zachary. And maybe it wasn't random. Someone was looking inside my bedroom window." Marlow wrapped her arms around her body, and he could see she had goosebumps.

He wanted to go back to bed. He should have left Marlow there without another thought. But he couldn't do it.

"Come on, Marlow. You can sleep in my room tonight."

She looked at him and then back at her doorway. If she hadn't been so scared, she would have refused his offer. But she couldn't go back into her room tonight.

It didn't matter if he really believed her or not. She didn't want to be alone. She climbed into his bed without another word.

When Zachary followed her into the room, he shook his head. He'd meant for her to sleep on the sofa in there. But Zachary wouldn't throw her out of his bed. If things had been different, he might have wanted her there for other reasons. They were adults and could handle sleeping in the same room without feeling weird.

He slid under the covers and stared at his clock for what felt like the hundredth time that night. It was almost four in the morning. If he fell asleep now, he would have two solid hours of sleep. It wasn't much, but he could work with it.

He turned over and, in the dark, could make out Marlow's slight frame curled up next to him. He wanted to ignore her and, after figuring out how much she had in common with his ex-girlfriend, planned to sever whatever connection they were building.

But she saw something or someone at her window. At first light, Zachary would check it out. They weren't a good fit, but he'd be damned before he let anyone hurt her.

Marlow Ripley was becoming a full-time job. One he kept making time for over and over again. Perhaps the secrets she kept would be the answer to getting her out of his life.

Chapter Sixteen

Two minutes before the alarm sounded, Zachary carefully reached behind him to turn off the clock. He didn't want to move because Marlow's body was pressed against him. She smelled like coconut and vanilla, and he took a deep breath.

She was beautiful, and he couldn't deny why he was so easily attracted to her. His body naturally reacted when she walked into a room, but now, lying next to her, he had to ignore how they fit together and get out of there.

Twenty minutes later, dressed for work, Zachary went outside to look for evidence. If Marlow saw someone, there would be a way to prove it. Or maybe disprove what she thought happened.

When he pulled himself up on the porch roof, he saw several shingles knocked loose and hanging on the gutter. The guy must have lost his footing and slipped. That would explain the noise that woke him before he heard Marlow scream.

As he examined the window, there were freshly chipped wood shavings. The guy wasn't just attempting to look in on her. He tried to get inside.

He felt worse over his *cheap thrill* comment last night. She'd been in real danger. It didn't take long to get more police officers there to check for more clues.

Marlow slept through everyone traipsing through the upstairs and her bedroom. It wasn't until the officers were finishing up that she walked out of Zachary's room. Her long blond hair was mussed, and she naturally got everyone's attention wearing that pink silk and lace nightie. Zachary possessively covered her with a throw blanket.

"Oh, I didn't know anyone was out here," she said, her cheeks turning pink.

He should have woken her first. "Sorry, Marlow," he said as he escorted her to the bathroom and explained what he'd found.

"So you do trust me then?" She woke up thinking of how he didn't believe her last night, and to find a house full of officers surprised her.

"I might have been a little hard on you last night," Zachary admitted, and this time, he looked into her eyes.

It felt so much better than before, but she didn't want to make a big deal of it. "My clothes are in my bedroom," she whispered, leaning in close. Zachary tried not to react to her sweet breath so close to his skin.

This woman was slowly killing him. "I got you," he said and went straight to her room to grab her something to put on. But when he saw all of her silk and lace bras and panties folded in the drawers and delicate clothes hung neatly in the closet, he had a hard time. Going through her garments felt personal, and he'd sworn not to do that with her.

Zachary pulled a few things together and brought them to Marlow in the bathroom. When he knocked on the door, she had already pulled her long hair up into a messy bun on top of her head. She was stunning no matter what she did, and he worked at keeping a serious demeanor around the other officers.

"Thanks." Marlow smiled up at him sheepishly before she closed the door again.

When Zachary turned around, two officers inside Marlow's bedroom and one standing outside the window all smiled at him.

Of course, they knew Marlow. They hadn't had anything more exciting happen lately. The gossip would reach a fever pitch once it got out that she was staying at the boarding house and in the room next to Zachary's.

He eyed them all and shook his head, hoping to keep them quiet while still in the boarding house. But Zachary knew the teasing would be relentless when he returned to the station.

He didn't care what they said to him. But he didn't want Marlow to feel uncomfortable about the situation.

By the time Marlow dressed, the officers had packed all of their things and put the window and room back the way they'd found it.

Mrs. Bowers had coffee waiting for them, along with some store-bought donuts. She thanked the officers for coming to their rescue and asked Zachary to stay behind to talk for a few minutes.

The older woman was worried, and he could see it. She took her coffee outside to the front porch, and he joined her there once everyone else left.

"Zachary, I'm an old woman," she said before he even sat down. "But not so old that I don't know there are things I should probably be doing to keep this house and its residents safe."

"Mrs. Bowers——" he began to say, but she reached out and touched his arm to interrupt.

"I know this little town doesn't see much crime, but it's time to accept that sometimes trouble comes to Maisonville. What can I do to be ready?"

Zachary loved that Mrs. Bowers wanted to protect her people and property. She was an energetic little woman, and he could only imagine how tough she was when she was younger. He loved older people. "We could install some cameras. Maybe an alarm system. Some companies specialize in home security."

"Alright. That's what I'll do then."

"What are you doing?" Marlow asked as she joined them outside.

Mrs. Bowers reached her hand out so Marlow would walk over and hold it. "Child, I'm so sorry someone scared you while you slept in this house."

"It wasn't your fault, Mrs. Bowers. I'm the one who's sorry. I didn't mean to bring all this nonsense to you or this town. But some people don't like my mother's politics, and sometimes they want to take it out on me."

"That's terrible," Mrs. Bowers said.

Zachary nodded and then asked, "You've had stuff like this happen before?"

Marlow nodded. "Jokes on them. Michelle didn't even take a day off when they last broke into our house."

The anger on Zachary's and then Mrs. Bowers' faces surprised her. "It's not a big deal. Our house in the city has a ten-foot stone wall and an iron gate. Sometimes, people feel passionate about their causes and do whatever they want to get publicity. You know, even negative publicity can help get their voices heard."

"They got into your house?" Zachary asked.

"Twice. Once, I was out of town, and the other time, I called 911 and hid in the safe room until the police arrived."

Marlow didn't want to continue with this conversation. Acknowledging the break-ins made it feel more dangerous. She'd never talked about it before and didn't expect the police to investigate it this time because they hadn't in the past. Her mother wanted it swept under the rug so it didn't make national news, and that was what happened. "I've lived alone for a very long time. I know how to climb out a window or run if needed. Seriously. I'm good." She said and headed to the kitchen to get some coffee.

Mrs. Bowers didn't like the sound of that any more than Zachary. She nodded to him, and he took her half-empty coffee cup and followed Marlow inside.

While Marlow made herself a cup of coffee with cream, Zachary refilled Mrs. Bowers and made himself a cup. Marlow could feel his eyes on her and put on a happy face while she considered her next move.

Zachary wasn't going to let it go. "I'm a cop, Marlow. If you'd told me the danger, I would've been on the lookout."

Marlow shrugged. Her care had been the price of her mother's career, and no one had ever acted like it was a big deal. Why was Zachary so upset?

"You don't always have to act so tough, you know. We all need a little help sometimes," Zachary said.

He always looked in control, and Marlow couldn't begin to think of what he couldn't get for himself. "What do you need help with, Zachary?"

Zachary locked onto her as he considered her words. "Finding a house, furnishing a boat, finding the creep that was looking through your window, the list is endless."

Marlow sipped her coffee. "I thought you were going fishing this morning?"

"Plans change," he said and returned to the porch to give Mrs. Bowers her coffee. He didn't want to tell Marlow he would work because of their attempted break-in. She already tried to act like it wasn't that big of a deal. But her climbing into his bed because she was scared was a big deal to him.

He couldn't go fishing while she was potentially in danger.

A few minutes later, Marlow joined them on the porch. As soon as she sat down, Mrs. Bowers smiled her way.

It was the only warning Marlow got before Mrs. Bowers shared her business with Zachary.

"Did Marlow tell you she went back to see Dr. Nash at the clinic yesterday?"

Zachary looked at Marlow and then Mrs. Bowers. "No, ma'am. She didn't."

"It's not a big deal. It's just healing slower than expected, and I can't go back to work for another week." Marlow drank more coffee and looked off in the distance.

Why did she minimize things about herself? Like she wasn't important? His ex, Chloe, never behaved that way. Whatever happened in Chloe's world was the most important thing happening anywhere.

It surprised him that he might have been wrong about Marlow. But more importantly, he was wrong to judge her.

Finishing her coffee quicker than usual, Marlow seemed to have something on her mind. Before she went inside, she told Mrs. Bowers, "Tenille is going to work for me, and I thought I might take some pictures around town. I used to post pictures on my social media back in the day." She smiled, and Zachary stared at how beautiful she looked. "Have any suggestions for me? Places I should photograph first?"

Zachary didn't like the idea of her walking around town alone after what happened last night. But Marlow Ripley had made it clear that this was her life, and she rolled with it. He was going to have to be quick if he wanted to intervene. "I'd say the lakefront and possibly the state park," he answered before Mrs. Bowers could gather her thoughts. He added, "I bet Mrs. Bowers would like to go with you today."

"Oh. That's a good idea," Mrs. Bowers replied. If Marlow was suspicious, she didn't let on. Instead, she looked happy about it.

While Marlow went back inside to gather her things, Zachary set up tracking on Mrs. Bowers' phone and showed her how to use it, too.

Mrs. Bowers would spend the day with Marlow, and he could easily see where they were at any time. At least it gave him peace of mind as he went to work for a few hours. He could absolutely find reasons to run into them, too. Perhaps they'd even get a coffee, or all three grab dinner together.

The possibilities were endless, with Mrs. Bowers setting the schedule. She was calculating and seemed to like the idea of Zachary watching over Marlow even more than he did. He only hoped whoever had tried to get into the house last night was scared off for now.

Unlike the times in her past, Zachary and the Maisonville Police Department would not forget about this case. Marlow Ripley was one of them now. They had some fingerprints and would follow every lead they could so the town residents wouldn't have to worry.

Word in this town would spread fast, and Chief Gallegos would want answers more than anyone. Marlow may not believe it, but they would do everything possible to track down that intruder.

Chapter Seventeen

It took longer to get out the door because Mrs. Bowers suggested packing a picnic before they were tourists for a day. A few sandwiches, chips, and cookies later, they were on their way.

Mrs. Bowers was excited to ride in Marlow's sports car and giggled when she put her seatbelt on. "I've never been in a Jag before," she said and then told Marlow that she didn't learn to drive until she was married. "Times were different back then," she said and smiled on the ride over to their first stop.

The trail head, which took up an entire city block was exceptional. An outdoor market was going on, and Mrs. Bowers explained the town held it every Saturday morning. There were also regular outdoor concerts, picnic tables, and a splash-fountain sprinkler system for kids to play.

Next to the area was a hiking and biking trail called The Trace. It used to be part of an old railroad system that had since been paved over and spans twenty to thirty miles long.

Marlow took pictures of Mrs. Bowers in front of a tower,

holding a flower bouquet, and sticking a foot into the fountain next to some children.

They laughed and had a great time as Mrs. Bowers played along, always being a good sport. Once they finished, they drove to the lakefront, where Marlow photographed trees or water splashing over the sea wall. Her options seemed to be endless around there, and Mrs. Bowers silently observed the incredible talent Marlow had for photography.

From the lakefront, they made their way over to Espresso to Geaux. Surprisingly, Zachary was there getting coffee, too. He sat with them while they sipped their coffee, and Mrs. Bowers doted on Marlow's skilled camerawork.

When Marlow showed him a few that she'd taken, he, too, was impressed with the pictures. He casually called her Photography Barbie, which made her laugh.

While Zachary bought another pastry, Mrs. Bowers bragged about him teaching her how to find friends with her phone tracking. Marlow immediately offered to be friends with her too and quickly set it up. When Zachary returned, he could tell they were up to something but didn't ask.

"We were just making plans and will head to Fontainebleau State Park next," Mrs. Bowers told him.

"That sounds like fun," he replied and then added, "It's a little out of my jurisdiction."

"Well then, I guess you'll have to take off and join us today," Mrs. Bowers said and elbowed Marlow lightly to get her attention.

"That's right," she agreed. "We could use some pictures of Maisonville's finest."

She stared into his eyes for a beat too long. Marlow could feel the heat on her cheeks and stood up to do something with herself. She headed over to Evie Mae and began taking photos.

It was getting harder to stop flirting with Zachary, and she didn't want to embarrass herself.

Zachary watched Marlow shamelessly as she took multiple pictures of the coffee truck. He liked her calling him Maisonville's finest. Zachary liked it a lot. But he needed to get going before he got himself into trouble. Having her in his bed last night was intimate, and it was hard to understand how a little human touch could change things. He'd underestimated Marlow and possibly hadn't treated her as well as he should have. She had similarities to Chloe, but she was not his ex-girlfriend. It didn't matter that Marlow didn't know his thoughts last night. He owed her an apology or at least owed her a better side of himself.

Finishing his coffee, he walked over to throw the cup away. Mrs. Bowers and Marlow followed behind him, and he told them he'd see them later. "You two ladies have a good time but be careful out there. If you need me, you have my number."

"You be careful too," Marlow said, and the words seemed to rush out of her mouth before she could stop them.

"Always am, Marlow." Zachary tipped his head at her but didn't break the stare into her baby-blue eyes. He wanted to pull her into his arms and kiss her. But this wasn't the time.

"See you both later," he offered and, with that, turned and walked to his car.

Marlow watched until he was out of sight, and when she turned around, Mrs. Bowers had a massive grin. "That young man has a nice little swagger to him. Don't you think?"

Putting her hand over her mouth, Marlow stifled a laugh. Mrs. Bowers had a way with words. "He definitely has swagger," Marlow agreed.

They didn't talk about Zachary again on the ride to the state park. It was about a twenty-five-minute drive over, and

Mrs. Bowers asked Marlow why she didn't pursue photography full-time.

"My grandmother was an artist. She painted the most incredible pictures, and I guess I never considered my photography real art. I mean, I did make money at it when I was in school. Mostly, I sold print rights online, but I moved on to bigger things."

She explained what it was like being a social media influencer and how that had been her full-time job. But she avoided admitting her mother was always against Marlow selling her photographs.

As she pulled into the parking lot at the state park, she confided in Mrs. Bowers like she had Zachary about wanting to start her own small marketing company.

"Why, I think that is a fine idea. Truly, dear, you have so much talent."

As soon as they exited the car, Marlow marveled at the scenery. There were tons of giant oak trees with hanging moss, and the water lapped the shore. The two didn't seem to go together, and she could imagine people thinking she'd photoshopped the scenery. After all, she'd grown up only a half hour from here and had no idea it existed.

Quickly, she snapped pictures of butterflies near wildflowers as the breeze off the water pushed them from plant to plant. Next, she focused on the multitude of oak trees with their limbs dipping down to the ground before turning back up toward the sky.

The afternoon storm clouds slowly moved in and gave her a play with the sunlight. It was easy to take moody-looking pictures with the added clouds and shadows.

Marlow was lost in her art as Mrs. Bowers sat in a lawn chair. The older woman enjoyed watching Marlow in her element as she dropped to her knees to capture different angles of things. She tilted her head one way or another as she wandered all around, more carefree than Mrs. Bowers had ever seen her.

She'd been a little busy herself, preparing a surprise for Marlow a little later. By the time she checked her watch, it was way past lunchtime. Mrs. Bowers sent a text message to Zachary, advising him they were still at the park. She told him they would head to the riverfront next, where they would have lunch. She instructed him to wait for them, and he laughed at the pushy woman's style.

Not giving anything away, Mrs. Bowers asked Marlow if she had gotten everything she needed at the park. "I'm famished, child."

"Oh, I didn't realize the time. We could find a picnic table around here somewhere, I'm sure," Marlow offered.

Mrs. Bowers' face must have gone pale since Marlow reached for her. "Are you okay?"

"Yes, dear. It's just that I have a better spot in mind," she said and tried to reorganize her thoughts. She wasn't an actress, and she wasn't as quick as she was in her younger days.

They packed up the lawn chair and headed to the riverfront. Mrs. Bowers told her about a spectacular spot by the draw bridge where they could sit and eat their sandwiches. "That way, when the bridge opens, you can get a great shot of it or the boats passing by," she said, and Marlow smiled.

It was a great reason to picnic at the riverfront, and Marlow hadn't suspected a thing. As they parked and carried their picnic basket to a concrete table, Mrs. Bowers said they should call Zachary to join them.

It was still a pleasant day with lower humidity, and the rain had held off, although the clouds were overhead. When

Marlow nodded, Mrs. Bowers whipped out her phone like a professional.

Marlow smiled as the older woman sent a text almost as quickly as Marlow could. Then, while Marlow took a few photographs, Mrs. Bowers put a tablecloth down and real silverware.

"I thought we were having sandwiches?" Marlow asked as she walked over to help.

Mrs. Bowers gave her a sly smile. "I might have packed some extras for a special lunch."

Marlow watched as Mrs. Bowers put potato salad on the table along with cold fried chicken. When had she done all of that?

Next, she pulled out three pieces of pie, one strawberry, one chocolate, and a coconut, which told Marlow that Miss Lynn was in on this picnic too.

As soon as Zachary walked over and whistled at the amazing spread for lunch, Olivia drove up and honked her horn. Mrs. Bowers leaned over and kissed Marlow on the cheek. She then said she was too tired to stay and eat but insisted Marlow and Zachary enjoy their lunch together. Then she used her cane to get out of there as fast as Marlow had ever seen her move, getting into Olivia's car.

Zachary watched the whole exchange and shook his head, confused. When he looked at Marlow, she laughed. "I think we've just been hoodwinked."

"Hoodwinked?"

It was an expression Marlow had learned from her grandmother years ago. "Look at this food. I helped her make sandwiches and put chips in a bag."

Zachary laughed. "We could learn a lot from older people."

"You're telling me. I think those women are aiming to set us up, Zachary. I'm sorry. I want you to know I had nothing to do with this."

He felt like he should come clean. If Marlow didn't want to have lunch with him, he had to let her off the hook. "Marlow, I asked Mrs. Bowers to stay with you today because I was worried about you going out alone. But I didn't know anything about this picnic, and you don't have to stay and have lunch with me if you don't want to."

Marlow rolled her eyes. "I was worried you would think it was me."

Zachary leaned closer to her. "We are in over our heads with Mrs. Bowers and possibly Miss Lynn. I'm okay with pretending this is a lunch date if you are, but I call dibs on that strawberry pie."

Marlow laughed that they each had worried the other was in on this lunch date. "You can have all of this food if you want it."

If she were honest, she would admit that she had a crush on the handsome police officer. She'd barely been there a month but couldn't deny how she felt. The feelings slammed into her as he held her last night as she slept beside him. There was comfort in his arms, and she hadn't known how much she needed it. She would go along with this pretend lunch date because she wanted to be there more than anywhere else. But if any of this ever got back to her mother or Royce, they would never let her forget it.

They twisted things like that all the time. They'd say that Marlow had been seeing Zachary Bowman all along. He'd get the blame for being a marriage-wrecker or worse. Destroying his reputation would be their priority. It wouldn't matter that she'd just met him. Lies like that had a way of ruining people. And she wouldn't let them hurt Zachary.

She had crazy, mixed-up feelings for Zachary and the way he kept protecting her. Her duty was to protect him from Michelle and Royce, the ugly side of her world.

"A pretend picnic date sounds great," she said and sat next to Zachary so she could pass him the plate of cold fried chicken. He bumped his shoulder into hers and handed her a bottle of sparkling water. It would be the best date she'd ever had, pretend or not.

She just knew it.

Chapter Eighteen

Marlow drank her water while watching Zachary eat a healthy portion of everything. It was impressive how much food it took to keep him going.

When he noticed her watching him, he grinned and added another piece of chicken to his plate. He was the most self-assured person she may have ever met. Her mother was confident on the outside, but her meanness always made Marlow suspect she was hiding a lot of insecurity behind that bravado.

"You know a ton about me, and I hardly know anything about you. Where did you grow up? Do you have any siblings? Did you always want to be a police officer?"

"That's quite the list of questions, Marlow."

"You know all those things about me," she said.

Zachary wasn't used to being asked personal questions, but he didn't mind telling her. "I grew up in St. Marksville. Olivia and I went to school together, but she was a year older than me in school. St. Marksville makes Maisonville look like a metropolis. I'm an only child. My mother was a pianist who mostly played for our church and taught lessons. My father was the town chief of police. Did I cover everything?"

Hearing Zachary talk without real emotion behind the details of his life felt oddly familiar. "I guess you became a police officer because of your dad?"

Zachary nodded as he put a scoop of potato salad on Marlow's plate next to the chicken she hadn't touched. "I'll make a deal with you," he said, and she smiled until he told her that he would talk if she would eat.

"I'm not hungry. Besides, I usually only eat dinner."

"And exactly why do you do that?" He finally asked what he'd wanted to know for a while.

"It's just how we did it in my house growing up, and I never really thought about it." Marlow left off the part where it had been that way since her grandmother entered a nursing home. She knew the way her mother acted over food was odd. But she didn't like to talk about it.

"Well, I don't like to talk about myself, and that's the deal I'm offering."

Marlow looked at the food and grimaced. Slowly, she picked up her fork and moved a potato around on her plate before taking a bite.

"Don't make it look so painful. You never eat, and that is not healthy."

"Thanks, Dr. Bowman. Is that your professional diagnosis?"

He smirked at her sass and finished off his chicken. Then he leaned in and said, "We can play doctor anytime you want, Marlow."

It was the first time he flirted brazenly with her, and she was surprised. When was the last time a man had done that? Marlow's cheeks turned pink, and he laughed. She immediately got that stubborn look that he liked so much. "You are not a doctor, Officer Bowman. And I hardly know anything about you."

That made him laugh even harder, and he could see she was proud of herself. Zachary handed Marlow the fork she'd set down and encouraged her to take another bite. "You eat, and I'll talk." He encouraged.

As soon as she ate a mouthful of the potato salad, he nodded. "I was very close to my folks. They thought they couldn't have children and didn't have me until they were older. By the time I was three, my mother had taught me to play the piano, but my father was my hero. I wanted to be just like him and never considered doing anything else."

It hurt Marlow's heart to hear him talk about them in the past tense. Zachary could almost see the wheels turning in her head as he put a slice of bread on her plate.

She didn't say anything but looked over at him. Zachary didn't miss a beat as he put butter on her bread. "My mother passed away when I was a sophomore in college. She had cancer. My father was diagnosed with COPD two years after I started working for him. He'd always smoked like a chimney. He wasn't supposed to make it as long as he did, especially since he couldn't give up the smoking. He died a few months ago, but he'd been in and out of the hospital for months and on hospice care for ten weeks."

Marlow's eyes watered, and she reached out to squeeze his hand. "I'm so sorry, Zachary." She hadn't heard from her father since she was a kid and certainly didn't have a traditional mother-daughter relationship with Michelle. To hear that Zachary lost his whole family and how close they were made her sad for him.

Taken aback by her sincerity, Zachary stopped talking. He

pushed back his plate and picked up the generous slice of strawberry pie. It was getting harder to remember this was a fake date because Marlow was a great listener and genuinely sweet.

After he ate half the dessert, he nodded her way. "They were good parents and good people. It was harder to stay in my hometown after they both were gone."

Marlow certainly understood how that felt. She didn't want to stay in her house after her grandmother went into the nursing home. But she was a kid and didn't have any power. Her mother wouldn't hear of moving.

She took her fork and slowly stuck it into Zachary's strawberry pie. When she scooped some onto her fork and into her mouth, he watched every second of it.

She felt the way he looked at her, and it made her a little desperate to be closer to him. Struggling to act like it didn't affect her, Marlow ate another bite.

"Where is your dad, Marlow?"

The question instantly distracted her physical reaction to Zachary. "Good question. He left when I was five, and I haven't heard from him since. My mother said he didn't want to be a father. It was right before Christmas, and I was in kindergarten. He just walked out for the proverbial pack of cigarettes and never came back."

Picking up the chocolate piece of pie, Zachary sat it in between them. Without being prompted, Marlow grabbed the first bite. "I didn't win the genetic lottery when it came to parents," she said as she took another bite of the creamy dessert. "What does Miss Lynn put into these things? They are decadent and possibly sinful," she said and then closed her eyes as she appreciated the sweetness.

When she opened her eyes and saw Zachary staring at her,

she set her fork down. It was time to change the subject. "It's only fair since you know about my ex that you tell me about yours. Does she still live in your hometown? Give me some gory details."

"Is that fair?" he asked as he finished off the chocolate pie while she watched.

"What? Mine was filmed for the whole world to see and is still being rated on the World Wide Web. So tell me." she asked, making light of her situation, which he found admirable since it had to hurt still.

"I'm sorry that people are still talking about you and your wedding on the internet?" he said, and the look he gave her made her stomach have butterflies. He was too good for her.

"I don't care what people think about me. Besides, those posts are only words, right?" she said matter of factly.

She continued to amaze him, but he didn't want to talk about Chloe or admit that people saw his breakup, too. Realizing that Marlow had more in common with him than his ex-girlfriend, hit him hard.

He stared at her, trying to see what else he'd misjudged her for until she cleared her throat. "Gory details, sir."

"She is still in my hometown, at least she was when I left, but that is all I will say about that."

She watched Zachary take a bite of the coconut pie before she began cleaning up their picnic. He jumped in there to help get it all picked up and into the basket.

"I might have to give you a new nickname," Zachary teased.

Marlow rolled her eyes but didn't stop gathering items. She rolled the used utensils into the cloth napkins and stowed them inside the basket. She would wash it all when she got back to the boarding house.

Zachary leaned in close. It got her attention, and she

stopped cleaning to look up. He was incredibly handsome and genuinely a good person. Precisely the kind of guy her mother would have approved of Marlow dating before Royce Chatham came around. Senator Michelle Ripley would have quickly wrapped one of her campaigns around Zachary Bowman, the public servant and all-around good guy.

"Hey. I was only kidding. Besides, the only thing I ever say is that you're a Barbie."

Marlow smirked. "You know Barbie is an independent woman. She owns her own home and car, plus a fabulous wardrobe. She can afford all that because she's a professional lawyer, doctor, jet airplane pilot, elementary school teacher, and even President. It isn't an insult."

Zachary gently lifted her chin with his finger and leaned in until they were a breath apart. "It was never meant as an insult, Marlow."

When he said her name and stood too close, it felt like he was going to kiss her.

He didn't. But he did stare into Marlow's eyes for a minute, and she was frozen there, counting the golden flecks in his brown eyes. The entire pretend lunch date had felt surreal. It was almost like they were the only two people in the world.

When he reached around her to carry the picnic basket, her breath caught. If Zachary could tell, he didn't let on but walked her to her car and put the basket into her passenger seat. "Thanks for the fake lunch date. Best one I've ever had."

"Me too," Marlow replied. But nothing about their lunch date felt fake to her. She'd slept in his bed last night, and they didn't even discuss it. She was confused because she wasn't supposed to like Zachary, and he didn't like her. Did he?

Chapter Nineteen

Zachary could feel Marlow's reaction to him standing too close. He'd felt that same way as soon as Mrs. Bowers left them alone for lunch. He'd had to work hard to hide his feelings since he woke up close to her that morning. Watching her sleep curled next to him had gotten to Zachary. She wasn't someone who trusted easily, and he'd picked up on that the first day he'd met her. And after she'd been scared to death last night and he'd discounted her fear, she still trusted him.

The pull to tell her how much that meant to him was strong, but he thought better of it. Marlow Ripley didn't get close to people, and he would earn that trust she'd freely given him. She deserved it more than anyone he'd ever met. Kindness went a long way with her, and it hurt to think that she wasn't shown more tenderness in her life.

She'd pretty much admitted that, hadn't she? He would show her gentleness, and they didn't have to date for that to happen. Marlow deserved it.

He smiled at her as he opened her car door. "I don't have to work tonight. I'll see you at home?"

Was the boarding house starting to feel like home?

"Sure," she replied as she climbed inside her car, already lost in her thoughts. Maisonville had quickly pulled her in with genuine friendships. Mrs. Bowers felt more like a relative. The fake date picnic with Zachary had confused her because she understood a little more about him, plus he'd been honest and sweet.

"Hey, Marlow." Zachary startled her as he got her attention again.

She looked up, and her cheeks were pink as she answered him. "Yes."

The way she looked at that moment made him want to yank her out of that car and kiss her breathlessly. He took a deep breath to maintain his composure. "Would you do me a favor and not go out anywhere alone until we figure out who was outside your window last night."

"Okay," she said, and he closed her door before forcing himself to walk away.

Marlow watched every step he took back to his police car, smiling that he had swagger like Mrs. Bowers said. When he looked over at her, she waved before she drove off toward the boarding house.

What was she doing falling for Zachary Bowman? She'd just broken up with Royce Chatham, and the whole world knew it. She wasn't sure what the time constraints were for dating again after planning a wedding for fourteen months. Forget about whether or not you loved that person or if he treated you like nothing. "And that's because you aren't supposed to date anyone, even pretend to date anyone for a long time," she said aloud to herself.

When she laid awake over the past few weeks reading some of the posts written about her running away from her wedding, people boldly gave their opinions on the subject. Some argued that she had to stay single until everyone forgot about her ex-boyfriend. But others argued that wasn't reasonable because no one would ever forget her long, drawn-out engagement to Royce Chatham.

Marlow had only partially told a story to Zachary about not caring what people thought about her. She did worry a little about public perception that she'd left Royce high and dry. But she didn't know what to do about it.

At the moment, other influencers were posting bets on who would show up in public with a date first, her or Royce. At the moment, speculations were higher for it to be Marlow because Royce had spent a night online guessing all the reasons she left him, *as if he didn't know*, stating that he loved her too much.

Many of her followers were still intact, but the majority said they felt sorry for Royce. He was playing up the pity card in public as often as possible.

He was a *snake* and would get away utterly unscathed because Marlow was too embarrassed to talk about the truth of what had happened. Plus, it was her social media accounts filled with the wedding-palooza over the past year. There were thousands of women following her so they could emulate Marlow's choices for colors, flowers, music, and the like. She understood this would follow her for the rest of her life. Even if it weren't her fault, she would shoulder the blame.

The fantasizing over Zachary Bowman, no matter how handsome, protective, and capable he looked in his police uniform, didn't matter.

As she pulled into the driveway at the boarding house, she still couldn't get the way Zachary looked at her out of her mind. It felt like he was drawn to her, too. This couldn't just be her, could it? And didn't he say he would see her at home? The words felt so personal, and why?

She knew why. It was hard not to really like Zachary. He was the first man that had been nice to her in a very long time. He was also a very handsome, sweet, considerate man who also happened to be the police officer who arrested her on her wedding day when she tried to escape the press and her mother.

Marlow took deep breaths as she got out of her car. No matter how hard she tried to talk herself out of it, she cared about Zachary. Sleeping next to him, she'd felt safer than ever before.

"Are you okay, dear?" Mrs. Bowers' voice was off in the distance. "Marlow?"

Marlow looked up and smiled at Mrs. Bowers, who was now standing in front of her rocking chair on the porch instead of sitting. She nodded to her sweet older friend as she carried the picnic basket up the porch stairs with her.

"How was lunch?" Mrs. Bowers smiled knowingly.

Marlow grinned like a fool and then tried to stop. "It was great, Mrs. Bowers. But don't think I don't know what you and Miss Lynn are up to, and possibly Olivia," she said as she took the basket inside to clean it out.

Mrs. Bowers followed her into the kitchen and tried to help her put the leftover food away. Once they finished, Marlow leaned over and hugged the older woman she loved dearly.

"I'm going to take a short nap," she told Mrs. Bowers before heading upstairs. Marlow was suddenly exhausted, but as she stood in front of her bedroom, she couldn't go inside. It still didn't feel right. She looked next door, and without second guessing herself, she crawled into Zachary's bed and, within minutes, was sound asleep.

It was dark when Marlow woke up and looked over at the

clock. It was almost nine, and she sat up straight in the bed. Marlow looked around the room, lit only by a night light, and saw Zachary's wallet, keys, and watch on the nightstand. He'd draped his uniform over the sofa and tucked his shoes neatly inside his closet, which she could see since it was ajar.

She pulled the covers up to her neck and thought about how to handle this. Zachary had obviously come home from work and found her in his bedroom. In. His. Bed.

Burying her face in her hands, she heard the door open slowly and didn't want to look up and face Zachary. He sat on the bed next to her. "Everything okay, Marlow?"

She nodded. *This was embarrassing.* "I'm sorry for intruding," she said. "I was exhausted when I got in, and for some reason, my room felt-" she couldn't find the words.

"How did it feel, Marlow?" he asked, and he looked genuinely concerned for her, which made it worse.

How could she tell him she'd felt alone in there but didn't in his room? It wasn't like she hadn't spent the majority of her life that way, and even though she'd dated Royce Chatham for two years, it hadn't changed the amount of time she'd spent by herself. "I don't know. I didn't think I'd fall asleep in there, especially since the peeping tom and all those policemen touched everything in the room, too. Then, when I opened your door, your room was dark, and it was cooler than anywhere else in the house." There was a large tree outside of Zachary's room that kept it shaded all day.

"It looked inviting, and before I thought better of it, I climbed in and fell asleep."

Zachary leaned forward and kissed her sweetly on the forehead. Marlow leaned into him, and her heart squeezed tight. He was the most considerate man she'd ever met and proved to be more kindhearted than most people.

He nodded. "It's fine. I don't mind. Listen, Mrs. Bowers and I already had dinner. Are you hungry? She insisted on heating some soup for you. She was sure you weren't feeling well when you got in."

"Thanks. I'm good now. I think I'll go downstairs and get that soup," Marlow said, avoiding his eyes again. How could she have slept that long without waking when he came home?

She got up and went straight downstairs, unsure what she would do tonight. The idea of going into her room alone made her uneasy. What if that guy came back? What if, this time, he was successful at getting to her?

She tried to put it out of her head as she found the bowl of soup Mrs. Bowers left for her and some crackers. No one had done that for her since her grandmother passed away. Maisonville was a wonderful little gem of a place, and while her mother loved to scold her and say, "Everything that glitters isn't gold, Marlow," she knew this town was totally golden. She wasn't sure she could leave this shiny goodness behind.

But then again, was she ready to face Michelle Ripley when she decided Marlow had been punished enough? Her mother had sworn to disown her so many times that Marlow had lost count. The longest she'd gone without speaking to Marlow was when she was fifteen. It lasted five weeks and was one of the many hurtful things the woman had done to her.

Even when Marlow went through her bad behavior years, Michelle always returned to collect her because she needed to control everything about her daughter's life.

It was hard to gauge how much time she had left because running out on a $75,000 wedding was a doozy. But based on her past, Marlow figured she only had another good week or two before Michelle or one of her minions came to town, and she sure didn't want to be here when they showed up.

Wiping her eyes, it didn't make sense that Marlow was still tired. But her throat was a little scratchy, and her nose a bit stuffy. Generally, if she went without sleep, her immune system took a beating. Was she getting sick? She didn't have time to be ill. She needed to work and save some money. Prepare for the next time she has to run.

She washed her bowl and dragged herself back upstairs. Zachary's door was ajar. Had he left it open for her? When she peered inside, he was sound asleep. He looked so peaceful, and she watched him for longer than would be socially acceptable.

Marlow could not intrude, so she closed his door and went into her own bedroom. To be careful, she slid the highboy dresser in front of her window. Someone would have to break the glass before pushing the dresser out of the way.

When she crawled into bed, her bones felt achy, and she had a chill she couldn't shake. There was so much on her mind, and she felt like she would never truly relax until she had a set schedule and a permanent place to live. Right now, she just needed more sleep and hoped that when she woke tomorrow, her head would feel clearer.

Her last thoughts were of sleeping with Zachary the previous night and how warm his skin was to the touch. It was just one innocent night of comfort, but she longed to have that again someday.

Chapter Twenty

Mrs. Bowers and Zachary had breakfast on the side porch. He had another late shift today but wanted to make them pancakes. Mrs. Bowers happily made the coffee and put some bacon in the oven.

Both were surprised that Marlow wasn't up because she never slept in. "That cast is giving her a lot of trouble," Mrs. Bowers said. "I think I heard her up late last night."

Zachary thought about Marlow sound asleep in his bed when he got home. It felt right having her in there, but he knew things were complicated for her.

It was ten when they finished off the rest of the coffee. "I know a little lady that is going to be dragging if she doesn't get her cup of Joe this morning," Mrs. Bowers said. She remarked again that it was strange for Marlow to be still asleep, especially once she smelled the first pot of coffee brewing.

Zachary carried in all the dishes and offered to check on the sleepy head. When he got upstairs, it was eerily quiet.

Could someone have gotten in while he was sleeping? He

knocked on Marlow's door, but she didn't answer. When he tried the door handle, it was locked.

With a little force, he yanked the door open. It took a few seconds for his eyes to adjust to the dark. He immediately saw that Marlow had pushed the giant chest of drawers in front of her window. She had her blankets pulled up over her head. Only her blond hair showed, and he was taken aback by how small she looked curled up there.

"Marlow? You okay?" he asked, but she didn't stir. Zachary gently pulled her covers back and pushed her hair off her face. She was so hot he withdrew his hand at first.

When he placed his palm on her forehead again, she blinked a few times but didn't fully wake. "Hey," she said, but he was sure she didn't know what she was saying.

Zachary wrapped her blanket around her body and scooped Marlow into his arms. Downstairs, he told Mrs. Bowers not to come close because Marlow was sick with a high fever, and he didn't want her to catch whatever it was, too.

Promising to call her once he knew anything, he had Marlow in the back seat of his car and was off to the new medical clinic within minutes.

The clinic was only a few miles from the boarding house, but Zachary was nervous that he should have called an ambulance instead. Marlow was talking gibberish in the back seat, and he was furious that he hadn't checked on her sooner.

He carried her inside and realized he wouldn't be able to answer most of their medical or personal questions about her. Thankfully, they tended to Marlow first and said they would get the information once she was stable.

Stable? Holy Mother, the thought that she needed to be stabilized felt like a punch to his stomach.

"Are you her husband or boyfriend?" the nurse asked, and without hesitation, Zachary said yes.

The nurse had seen family members worried like that before, so she didn't ask him which one it was; she just let him stay with Marlow. It took a few minutes for the doctor to determine that Marlow had the flu and, with the high fever, became dehydrated. He tried to reassure Zachary but warned him that because she was so thin, her immune system succumbed to it quickly.

They pushed intravenous fluids and medicine to her, and in an hour, she was finally conscious enough to ask what had happened. Zachary was in the hallway talking to Mrs. Bowers at the time.

"Mais Cha, your sweet boyfriend carried you in here unconscious. He was so worried he couldn't even fill out paperwork," the nurse said as she fanned herself. "I think he's smitten for sure."

Marlow nodded at the adorable Creole nurse, who then stuck a thermometer in her mouth and a blood pressure cup on her arm while she explained to Marlow that she had tested positive for the flu.

Marlow muffled the words, "In summertime?"

The nurse smiled. "We see dat flu year 'round now, just worse in the winter."

It took Marlow a few minutes to put it all together in her head, but she finally figured it out. She'd gotten up in the middle of the night to throw up and was shaking from being chilled to the bone.

After brushing her teeth, she thought about waking Zachary but didn't want to disturb him. He'd only gotten a couple of hours of sleep the night before, and she knew he probably needed the rest.

So she added an extra blanket to her bed and crawled under the covers, planning to get up in a little while if she didn't feel any better. That was the last thing she remembered.

When Zachary returned to the room and saw Marlow awake, he rushed to her bedside. His phone rang, but he ignored it. "Hey," he said and swept her hair off her forehead. "How are you feeling?"

"Better. Sorry I worried you."

"Don't apologize, Marlow. I should have checked on you sooner. I knew you weren't feeling well last night."

The nurse leaned in and winked at them. "You two are just so cute together. I will let you have a few minutes, but your blood pressure is back to normal, and your fever is down to one hundred. It was 105 when you got here."

"Thank you," Marlow said, and Zachary stood up to open the door for the nurse. "Thank you, ma'am, for everything."

When he closed the door, Marlow watched as he wiped his brow before sitting back on her bed. "You okay, Zachary?"

He silenced his phone that went off again, and looked relieved as he picked up her hand and held it close. "No. You scared me to death, woman."

He leaned forward and kissed her forehead. "It's so good to see you sitting up. The doc said you were pretty sick when we got here."

When Marlow nodded, he still seemed worried. "The doctor also said you're underweight, which was why you got dangerously dehydrated so quickly."

"I threw up last night and should have gotten some water or Gatorade. I apologize for worrying you and Mrs. Bowers."

"No, Marlow. I think you're missing the point. Skipping meals isn't healthy. Your bones aren't healing properly, and your immune system is weak. You need to take care of yourself."

He was overreacting. She ate lunch with him yesterday and dessert. "I normally work out and take supplements. I've just been a little distracted."

Zachary kissed the back of her hand and held it warmly against his chest. It was sweet, but made her nervous by the way he looked at her. "You can tell me the truth, Marlow. I'll do everything I can to help you. Do you have an eating disorder?"

"What?"

The doctor walked in and interrupted their private exchange. "I was worried about the same thing, but her bloodwork came back good, Officer Bowman. She's healthy."

Marlow didn't appreciate them talking like she wasn't there. She cleared her throat, and the doctor immediately looked remorseful.

"Sorry, Miss Ripley. We were rather shaken when you got here. I had to run several tests to treat you properly. You were extremely dehydrated, and of course, you have that cast from the broken hand. Coupled with the fact that you were unconscious and frankly frail-looking, it caused some concern. I had an anorexic patient when I was a resident and didn't catch it until her kidneys shut down." She could see the regret on the young doctor's face. His patient must not have made it.

"I was under a lot of stress these past few months. That's all. Maybe I neglected to eat here and there because I was too tired to cook or order meals. I substituted a lot with protein shakes. I'll be more mindful."

"At least get your weight over a hundred, okay? A hundred and fifteen would be even better, but I know it takes time."

Marlow nodded. She thought her clothes fit a little loose

but had no idea her weight had dipped below one hundred. *Michelle would be thrilled.*

"Make Officer Bowman cook dinner some of the time. All that eating out will catch up to him, too." The doctor laughed. He leaned in and added, "Don't you dare tell Miss Lynn or Olivia I said that about the diner. Okay?"

Marlow and Zachary laughed but agreed to keep the doctor's comments a secret.

"Alright, Miss Ripley, we have some paperwork and instructions to ensure you get better quickly. Then we will spring you. Okay?"

Minutes after the doctor left, the nurse returned with paperwork and instructions that she went over with Marlow and Zachary. "Now you take good care of her, you hear?"

Zachary promised that he would take good care of Marlow, and they headed back to the boarding house.

Tenille had swooped in and helped Mrs. Bowers strip Marlow's bed. They disinfected the room, remade the bed with fresh linens, and turned on an air purifier.

Next, Tenille swabbed the bathroom upstairs, steam mopped all the floors, and sprayed Lysol on every light switch and doorknob in the house.

By the time Marlow and Zachary got home, every surface in the boarding house shined. Everyone tried to warn Mrs. Bowers to keep her distance, but she laughed and assured them that she was up to date on her flu shots.

She made a large pot of chicken noodle soup, and Zachary hauled a tray up to Marlow's room with soup, crackers, electrolyte drinks, and medicine to keep her fever down.

He'd called in late to work but had to get going as soon as he dropped off her food. She was already drifting off when he walked in with the tray.

"Once you eat, you can sleep for a few hours," he said, a little bossier than usual.

Marlow followed his orders, and once he was sure she was comfortable, he kissed her on top of her head. "I won't be back until after midnight. But call me if you need anything." Being thoughtful was so natural for him, and Marlow couldn't stop thinking of how attentive he had been at the hospital.

Once he was gone, Mrs. Bowers took over, checking on Marlow every hour as well as giving her medication as needed. She slept most of the afternoon, and, by evening, was strong enough to shower and put on fresh pajamas.

When Zachary got home, he found her wide awake, watching a movie in bed. The smile she gave him was like a beacon pulling him into her room.

He climbed on top of her bed to sit next to her. "I'm sorry, if I made you late for work today. I hope you didn't get into too much trouble."

"So, you admit you are trouble?"

"Of course not," Marlow bit her bottom lip struggling not to laugh. "Maybe a little bit of trouble."

Zachary nodded at her admission and settled in next to her. It felt natural when Marlow snuggled closer to him, and he ran a warm hand over her hair.

"Thank you for caring for me this morning," she whispered.

Zachary kissed the top of her head. "You're welcome. I'm glad I was here to do it."

"Mrs. Bowers told me you were supposed to look at houses this morning before work today. I assume it was Leonie Ford blowing up your phone at the hospital?"

"I don't know what you're talking about," he said before winking at her.

"I'm afraid Leonie Ford isn't my biggest fan."

"She doesn't know you."

"Trust me, that doesn't matter. I could tell by how she looked at you that day on the boat that she was interested in being more than your real estate agent."

"Is that so?" Zachary found this information very amusing. "And did that bother you, Jealous Barbie?"

Marlow swatted at him playfully. "I felt sorry for her because I already knew you had a thing for me."

She kept a straight face for a second, and then they both laughed. "I think I might start calling you Comedian Barbie."

Marlow cut her eyes at him. "I already told you I am not offended by being called a Barbie."

"I wouldn't tease you if I thought it upset you."

Marlow locked eyes with him. He was so sincere sometimes that it took her breath away. She nuzzled her head next to him.

Zachary leaned down and kissed her on her forehead. When he spoke, this time his voice sounded serious. "You had me worried today."

Marlow smiled up at him and he moved to lie next to her so he could hold her in his arms.

"Thank you for worrying over me," she said, and he leaned in and kissed her lips. It was warm and sweet, which made her melt into him. But he didn't take it further. He pulled her body into his and stroked her back soothingly.

After a minute, Marlow found her voice again. "Why are you so good at taking care of people? And everyone here already adores you. Half the town already knows your name. It's like you've worked on the Maisonville Police Force your entire life."

"You're pretty impressed with me, aren't you?"

Marlow shoved his chest with her hand. "I'm trying to give

you a sincere compliment, Zachary Bowman. Why can't you take it?"

Zachary wanted to tell her how much it meant to him, but he was already overstepping the boundaries he'd set with her. He tried to thank her without giving too much away. "Thanks, Marlow. I care about people and like to help. It doesn't seem like anything special. It's just the way I am."

"Trust me, it is special. Don't let it go to your head, but you're pretty special, Officer Bowman."

"You're not so bad yourself, Miss Ripley."

They lay there staring into each other's eyes until Zachary forced himself to move. "I'm going to let you get some rest," he said, but before he left, he kissed the top of her head again. It was getting harder to keep his hands off her, but somehow, he made his way to the door. "I'm going to leave my door open, and your door cracked so I can hear you if you need me, okay?"

"Okay. Goodnight, Zachary."

"Goodnight, Sleepy Barbie."

Chapter Twenty-One

By midweek, Marlow's fever was gone, and she felt better. She was up early and sitting at the dining room table with her computer. She posted her Jaguar for sale and already had three offers when Zachary got downstairs.

"Morning," he said, and she looked up and smiled at him.

"Good morning," she replied, raising her cup of coffee.

A few minutes later, he sat next to her with a giant bowl of cornflakes and a banana. He was dressed in his uniform, ready for work. "You look like you feel better?"

Marlow nodded. "Much. Thought I would get some things done today." She showed him the ad for her car and then the messages from interested buyers. "I've been looking through my photographs from the other day, and I'm trying to decide which ones to post."

"Please don't meet anyone interested in the car unless I'm with you, Marlow."

Marlow shrugged. "I know you aren't online, but it's been my thing for a long time now."

He reached out and touched her hand. "That may be true,

but I have been a police officer for a long time. An expensive car like that can bring out the worst in people."

"Fine. I'll have any interested buyers meet me at the police station to look at the car."

He seemed pleased with that response. So, Marlow explained about the social media business, too. "It's a good way to make some money. After college, I worked for my mother posting political things, but in the beginning, I sold photographs, and it fed my creative side." She leaned forward. "Literally. I bought groceries and paid for rent with the money I made. I love photography, and people seem to enjoy my pictures." She didn't explain how her mother disapproved of her choice of colleges and refused to pay for more than tuition. It was a way for her to get Marlow to quit and move home but she'd found a way to make money.

Zachary hadn't looked back that far in her social media accounts and only saw the videos she did for her mother or for products she endorsed. "I'm not judging you, Marlow. It just seems like a slippery slope."

"How is that?" she asked as she watched him eat.

He felt her eyes on his food and grinned at her. "Want a bite?"

"No thanks." She didn't want him to worry about her eating anymore, so she added, "I'll eat something after my coffee. But you should know, cereal is more of a dessert."

"It's fortified with vitamins plus the banana and milk, so it's great for you." He showed her the picture on the box that said it was fortified with vitamins.

"We'll have to agree to disagree about your breakfast choices." She smiled at him and then went back to her computer.

After Zachary drank the milk from his bowl, he leaned in to look at the pictures Marlow pulled up. "You do have a good eye with that camera. But if you did it before and ended up doing mini ads for products or selling your mother's agenda, what will stop you from doing it again? That's the slippery slope I was talking about."

"Well, first of all, I only endorsed products I liked. And Michelle isn't talking to me. I doubt, after what happened with the wedding-palooza, she will want me at any of her speaking engagements."

Zachary nodded. He could tell Marlow felt rejected by her mother, and it was hard for him to imagine growing up without parental support.

"While I don't understand posting things for the world to see, I like your pictures, Marlow." He stood and took his bowl back into the kitchen.

When he returned, he stopped short of kissing her. He'd gotten carried away the last few days with hugging or kissing her and needed to take a step back. "Have a good day, Marlow. I'll be late tonight," he said and headed toward the front door.

She noticed he'd held himself back today after snuggling with her over the past few nights. Marlow had a huge crush on him but she could wait until he figured this thing between them out. In the meantime, she would enjoy watching him because Zachary Bowman looked fine in that blue uniform.

Besides their private talks at night were special to her and if this was all there would ever be between them, then she would enjoy the moment. It was a fact that things never stayed peaceful like this in her world, and she'd learned to find happiness in the small moments because they weren't small to her.

As she daydreamed about Zachary, her computer pinged again because another person was interested in her car. She promptly replied to those interested, giving them the address to the local police station like Zachary wanted. She hoped to get it sold as quickly as possible so she could put yet another thing with Royce behind her.

Having money for most of her life made the instability of not having it amplified in Marlow's heart. She would feel much better once she paid Mrs. Bowers and Zachary, although neither had asked her for money.

Secretly, it would be her birthday gift to herself. She would never go as far as to celebrate the day, but over the years, she learned that doing something for others helped her cope.

It would take a few more hours to post her prints online, and she hoped the energy she got from completing the task, plus the caffeine boost from her coffee, would bolster her for the following items on her list.

Marlow had avoided posting anything on social media regarding her wedding or Royce, especially since he'd flagrantly posted his version. But it had been a month since anyone heard from her online. Once they saw her new photographs, there would be even more questions. It was time for her to say things in her own words without the negativity. Her online followers didn't need the brutal details, and she could take the high ground here.

Setting up her camera on the porch where the morning light was perfect, Marlow pulled her coffee cup into her chest as she began filming.

"Hi, everyone. It's me, Marlow Ripley, coming to you live from a new Zen location. I know it's been a minute since we chatted, and I honestly needed a little time after the colossal wedding fail. You guys too?

"I Hope you guys can forgive me but accepting that something I spent over a year planning wasn't going to work out was hard to face, especially after bringing you guys along with me for every meticulous detail of the wedding-palooza.

"My gut kept telling me it wasn't what I wanted, and every time, someone close to me insisted that it was and that I couldn't stop the motion of this freight train after I chose to get on board.

"Dumb analogy? Yeah, I thought so, too. Still, I kept going even though I've always told you guys to follow your instincts."

Mrs. Bowers was unaware of Marlow's filming and brought the carafe of coffee outside to refill both their cups.

Once she was in the frame, Marlow laughed and introduced her to everyone on the live feed. "If you're going to jump from a train, may I suggest you find yourself a wonderful safety net friend like mine. Her name is Mrs. Bowers, and she makes great coffee."

Mrs. Bowers caught what was happening and waved to the camera before telling everyone, "Hello." She bumped her coffee cup gently into Marlow's, and they both said "Cheers" before taking a drink. Then Mrs. Bowers stepped out of view to sit in her rocking chair and listen to Marlow continue filming.

"Look, I know I could——should have handled things differently. And I hope that you guys can learn from my mistakes. But Royce Chatham did not love me. After a lot of soul searching, I've decided not to share the details but just know he gave me the sign I needed to make a better decision. One day, I'll have to thank him for being an example of what I didn't want in my future.

"I hope you guys can understand that I would never intentionally mislead anyone, and I fully take responsibility for what happened.

"I am an intelligent, independent woman and should have put the breaks on as soon as I had doubts. And for that, I am fully accountable for my actions.

"But for now, no hard feelings, just moving onward and

upward. If you are in a tough spot, remember you have to take care of yourself if you want to be there for others.

"Those of you that have been dying to tell me what you think, once I stop filming, the post will be open for comments.

"Give me your best or your worst.

"Until next time, cheers."

Marlow blew a kiss to the camera and then turned it off. When she opened the post for comments, they flooded into her account.

"I might break the internet today, Mrs. Bowers," she said as she shut off her phone and joined her older friend to finish their coffee.

"Well, I think that sounds like a great idea. This world could do without a little internet."

Marlow laughed at how true that comment was and how refreshing she found Mrs. Bowers.

She spent the rest of the morning editing her photographs before finally posting them on her website and advertising on her social media accounts that they were available. It had taken a lot of time to crop and edit, but she was proud of her work.

That afternoon, Marlow went to Espresso to Geaux and talked about marketing to Evie Mae and her best friend, Felicity, who co-owned the coffee truck. Marlow explained that she was starting a marketing company to help small businesses like them.

"I'm afraid our marketing budget is minimal at this time, Marlow," Evie Mae explained.

Felicity added, "We would love to be a part of a woman-owned marketing company, but right now, the only way to keep us in the black is just to do a little social media advertising and word of mouth."

"I get it, and honestly, any marketing company worth their

salt should help bring in more money than they charge for their services. And I am just getting started and haven't earned your trust." Marlow said and paused for a moment. "What if I put together a plan and see if you like it? Then we could track my changes to see if it's profitable?"

"How can you do the work without getting paid for it?" Evie Mae asked. "Well, I'm broke right now, so there is no place to go but up," Marlow laughed. "Seriously, I've been an online influencer for several years. I just had a brief break and hope to get that rolling again, so it will pay the bills. All you have to do is let me do a mock-up of what I'm thinking, and then we can figure it out." She looked around and said, "Maybe a free coffee each week?"

"Sounds fair," Felicity agreed and then introduced Marlow to her black and white Siberian Husky dog, Winston, who'd not so patiently waited for them to finish. As they all stood up so Evie Mae could go back into the truck, Marlow could head to her next appointment, and Felicity could walk Winston before she drove across the lake to her office, Winston threw his nose into the air and howled.

"Great dog," Marlow said as she got on her knees to hug him. Winston nuzzled under her chin making Marlow laugh. She was going to need a dog really soon.

Back in her car, she was thankful that had been so much easier than she'd thought. It helped that Evie Mae and Felicity were close to her age and hungry for success. They'd proven how comfortable they worked outside the box by starting their coffee shop out of a food truck. They were her perfect first clients. Next, she pulled into the medical clinic.

But before she could walk inside, Zachary pulled in behind her. "What's up?" he asked, looking concerned.

Marlow walked over and hugged him. She was so excited

about her last meeting that it seemed natural. But Zachary stepped back as if she'd done something wrong.

"Um, Nothing. What are you doing?" Marlow asked, sounding a little exasperated. Wasn't Zachary the one who was affectionate toward her first? When he crossed his arms in front of him, it was a sure sign of rejection.

"I was driving by and saw your car. You didn't mention a doctor's appointment this morning," he said now with an accusatory stare.

"I'm fine. Just stopped by to talk to Tobias and Asher." Marlow didn't like the way he looked at her.

Zachary locked onto her as she referred to the clinic doctors by their first names. When the hell had she gotten so friendly with them? She was hiding something, and he knew it. It was the whole reason he'd been careful with this friendship because he needed honesty.

"You don't want to tell me what you're doing here, Marlow?" He couldn't help sounding snappy.

Marlow shook her head. She'd wanted to surprise him, but now she wasn't so sure she wanted to share anything with him.

"Okay then. See you later." Zachary got back into his car without another word and drove off.

What just happened? And why was he mad at her? She wasn't hiding anything from him, not really. Remaining single was her only option in life because she couldn't handle constantly feeling like she was doing something wrong.

Feeling a little more deflated than before, she headed inside to meet with the two brothers who had started the new clinic together.

Chapter Twenty-Two

Dr. Tobias Nash and his brother, Dr. Asher Nash, smiled when they sat in their small break room to meet with Marlow Ripley.

The last time the doctors saw her, she was delirious with the flu. But today, Marlow Ripley was all business and undeniable charm.

The brothers had moved to Maisonville six months ago after building their new medical clinic. Tobias was two years older than his brother Asher and waited for him to finish medical school before beginning this venture.

Marlow asked them why they chose Maisonville for their clinic and why they wanted to own their own place when so many doctors joined existing medical groups. She wasn't prepared for how excited they were to tell someone their story.

Dr. Tobias Nash started first. "We're Greek on our mother's side, and our family is made up of restaurateurs. We helped our uncles in their restaurants, and neither wanted to do it long term. Besides, women love doctors, don't they?"

Tobias was handsome, with dark hair and blue eyes. He was

flirting and made her laugh. His brother, Asher, was more serious and elbowed Tobias over his last comment.

"Our dad's family is Irish and settled in New Orleans in the 1800s. He went to medical school but decided to teach instead of practice. That's where our love of medicine comes from. And both of us are single. Women may like doctors, but doctors don't have time to date, especially when they start a medical clinic. Right, Tobias?"

Marlow smiled at the brothers, who seemed to be communicating telepathically as they looked at each other instead of her. "And Maisonville was a good choice even though it's small?" she asked.

Tobias answered her. "We used to spend our summers here as boys with our grandparents. They had a place on the lake, and we both loved the quiet pace of this town and its proximity to the city and the rest of our family."

"We have a lot of first cousins living along the Gulf Coast and like to stay close to each other. We get together every couple of months. Maybe you'd like to come to one of our family parties?" Asher said, surprising her since he hadn't been the one flirting.

"Well, I don't know," she said, stumbling over an excuse.

Tobias hit his brother in the arm this time. "You're making her uncomfortable. Don't you remember she's dating Officer Bowman?"

"Sorry, Marlow," Asher said.

"It's fine. Seriously," Marlow's face flushed at the handsome doctor's flirting. It took her a second before she pitched her marketing plan to them. But once she got going, she was extraordinary. Tobias and Asher listened to every word, and although she wasn't quite sure how she would handle their account, the doctors were thrilled at the idea.

"We've truly wanted to hire someone to handle marketing. We just hadn't taken the time yet." Tobias admitted. "But we know we should invest 20% to 25% of our annual revenue to make this successful."

Marlow nodded, but before she could tell them they didn't have to commit a large budget up front, Asher spoke. "He put it off because he didn't want to have to do another thing for the business side of our clinic. I, however, love business, and we both have money. So, sign us up, Marlow."

"I didn't even bring a contract," she laughed. "This was supposed to be an exploratory meeting to see what your needs were, but okay, I'm ready."

She stood, and both men stood, too. "Email us the contract, and we'll get it back to you," Tobias said.

They walked Marlow to the lobby to give her their business cards and then opened the front door for her.

"Absolutely," Asher added. "And if you and Bowman aren't serious, I'd love to take you to dinner sometime."

Tobias wrapped an arm around his brother and pulled him back into the building. "Don't mind him. He doesn't get out much." Tobias gave her a short wave, and then she could see him scolding his younger brother in the lobby.

Marlow was flattered if not a teensy bit embarrassed over their flirting. But more importantly, had she just sealed her first two clients before she legally set up her company? Marlow waited until she got down the road before she squealed with excitement. As the only traffic light in town turned red, she pulled out her phone because her first instinct was to call Zachary and tell him the good news.

But suddenly, she thought better of it. Zachary had stopped and questioned her before she walked into the clinic. At first, he seemed worried. But then he acted as if she was hiding something from him. Marlow still had things she hadn't told Zachary, but that didn't make her dishonest.

Something was going on with Zachary, but she didn't have time to worry about that now because she had to meet people back-to-back at the police station so they could look at her car.

Zachary had asked her not to meet with anyone alone, but she couldn't call him now. Not after the way he'd acted. So, she went to the police station and asked Officer Bea Shannon if she had a moment to help her.

The first man was close to her age and kept telling her how much he loved the car, but it was too expensive. He didn't have the money, and she couldn't afford to give it away.

He was hostile when she told him she didn't think it would work out. But as Officer Shannon stepped forward and explained to the young man that he needed to move on, he called Marlow a rich bitch and stormed off.

It taught Marlow that she should never meet anyone from the internet without someone there to watch her back.

The next man was in his late thirties or early forties. His name was Abe Johnson, and he smiled at both Marlow and Officer Shannon. Abe had done his homework and knew what the car was worth.

He asked if he could test drive it, and Officer Shannon offered to ride with him. They were gone for twenty minutes, and when they returned, he agreed on the price but needed to get a money order.

They made plans for Mr. Johnson to drop it off with Officer Shannon, and once he left, Marlow hugged the older woman tightly. Officer Shannon was proud of how things were working for young Marlow and agreed to let her treat her to coffee later in the week for her help.

Selling her car was the best way to end her mostly fantastic day, and Marlow couldn't wait to tell Mrs. Bowers everything.

Officer Shannon told Marlow about a title company downtown where she could get her car title notarized for the sale. Marlow stopped there first before heading to the boarding house.

She was excited and a little exhausted when she got home, but Mrs. Bowers wasn't there. There was a note on the fridge telling Marlow that she was playing cards with her friends until late.

The older woman had a busy social life with friends, but with Zachary gone too, Marlow felt more alone than she'd been in a while.

No one knew that her birthday was tomorrow, the fourth of July, and Marlow had planned to pay them all back with the money she got from selling her car.

It would be a celebration, just not a birthday gathering.

Marlow's mood dropped as she walked into the kitchen to make a sandwich. For a moment, she considered going to the diner, but she needed to meet Mr. Johnson back at the police station any time now. So she ate alone at the kitchen counter, waiting for the phone call.

An hour later, Officer Shannon sent her a text that Abe dropped off the money order. But he needed his brother to drive his car home when he took possession of the Jaguar. He would reach out tomorrow so they could meet up.

It was a half hour before the Bank closed and Officer Shannon offered to meet Marlow there. She would open a new account with the funds and withdraw the cash she needed to pay back Mrs. Bowers and Zachary.

Returning to the boarding house, Marlow happily planned to work on her new business strategy until someone got home.

But, before she could get started, she peaked at her social media.

She hadn't expected people to go easy on her, but the comments still hurt. Several accused her of staging the whole engagement and wedding for ratings. Then others believed Royce's heartbreak story.

Marlow was the villain in both scenarios. She knew people could be brutal and thought she could handle the fallout. She wasn't.

Closing her computer, she headed upstairs to shower and go to bed. Tomorrow, she would get rid of that ridiculous car, pay her debts, and officially begin her new business.

If she could forget that it was the day she was born and all the miserable things that usually happened to her on that unlucky day, she might get some sleep tonight.

It was normal for Zachary Bowman to work twelve-hour shifts or longer when needed. It came with the territory of being a police officer. Each day was different and brought along challenges and moments where he could make a difference in helping others.

The Fourth of July was his first holiday-shift with the Maisonville Police Department, and things were not going well. He'd helped the State Police with a near-fatal car accident involving a family, arrested a husband and wife for aggressively fighting in front of their children, and just assisted another officer who tried to pull over an older man for speeding who pulled a gun on him before taking off. And he had four hours left in his shift.

He should have known it wouldn't go well after receiving a

phone call from his ex-girlfriend at the start of his workday. Chloe wanted to meet with him and insisted it was necessary. He shouldn't have taken the call, and after refusing to see her, she poured on the waterworks.

There had been a time in his past that a crying Chloe would send him into action. Today, it just made him angry.

It was why he was short with Marlow in front of the medical clinic. Zachary wasn't a jealous man, but Marlow was wearing that pink sundress that he liked so much and had clearly spent time on her hair and makeup. He should have told her she looked beautiful, but he'd heard about the handsome doctors from Mrs. Bowers, Miss Lynn, and even Olivia. All the women in his circle said repeatedly how both doctors were a catch. When Marlow said she felt fine, he couldn't help but question why she was there.

He owed her an apology. He'd practically accused her of being dishonest and the way she'd looked at him haunted him all afternoon. When Bea Shannon told him that she'd stood with Marlow as she met with potential car buyers, he felt even worse.

Neanderthal behavior wasn't usual for him, and he needed to explain why and ask for forgiveness in person. But he wouldn't get home until the early morning hours and had to be back at work early, too.

As he headed out for yet another assist call, Zachary picked a handful of flowers in front of the police station so he could leave them for Marlow in the morning. The garden club seniors were going to yell at him, but if Marlow would forgive him, it would be worth it.

Chapter Twenty-Three

Unlike most of her birthdays, Marlow woke up to flowers and breakfast. Mrs. Bowers was off with her garden club friends until later, but she'd left Marlow coffee and a sweet note.

Zachary made pancakes and set them on the counter next to a giant bouquet of wildflowers that he'd picked from somewhere. He'd handwritten a note, too, telling her he was sorry for his behavior yesterday.

She couldn't stop smiling because they didn't even know it was her birthday. But things were turning around for the best, and she could feel it.

Carefully counting out the money she owed Mrs. Bowers and then Zachary, she left each of them an envelope with cash and a thank you note for helping her out in a jam.

The morning went by quickly as she stopped by the diner to talk with Miss Lynn. Miss Lynn had been a successful diner owner for a long time and Marlow needed some guidance on starting her new marketing company.

Olivia cheered Marlow on as she filled out paperwork

online. When Mrs. Bowers and a few of the garden club seniors showed up, she had a celebratory lunch.

"Did you hear that someone vandalized the gardens in front of the police station?" one of the older women asked Marlow. She thought her name was Velma but wasn't sure.

"No, ma'am," Marlow answered as the woman added. "There has never been any landscaping over there, and we spent several days planting a wildflower garden. The afternoon rains keep it watered, and it was maintenance-free until now."

When Marlow looked over at Mrs. Bowers, who was struggling to hide her smile, she suddenly knew where Zachary had found the bouquet he'd left for her.

Mrs. Bowers shook her head. "Velma, you can't even tell if any flowers are gone. Some poor man probably had to make amends for something."

The other ladies parted down the middle, half agreeing with Mrs. Bowers and the other half grumbling along with Velma.

After lunch, Marlow took a taxi across the lake to pick up her baby blue Bronco. It had been parked in the garage at her house in the city for months. Michelle and Royce were in Washington, DC, and she didn't have to worry about seeing them.

The moment she sat in her grandmother's old car, her heart was whole. Selling the sports car was the right decision and getting this one back into her life felt right.

The drive home gave her the time she needed to gather her thoughts. First, her hand felt much better and had to be healing properly. Second, things were going well in Maisonville, and she felt comfortable for the first time in years. And finally, Zachary Bowman was right, and she could do anything she set her mind to doing.

It took a couple of hours for Marlow to get to the city and back to Maisonville. She was proud to have accomplished so much before dinner. The holiday traffic in the small town was a beast, but as she drove over the draw bridge, she realized the boats on the water outnumbered the cars on the road.

The weather had been sunny and beautiful for most of the holiday, and boaters were making the most of it. As she pulled into the driveway of the boarding house, Abe Johnson sent her a text message.

"Miss Ripley, I'm sorry for getting back to you so late. My brother and I were at a barbecue. Would it be too much trouble to meet?"

As she began to type out her message, he sent another.

"I understand if you need to wait until tomorrow, especially since Officer Shannon isn't at the police station today."

Mr. Johnson had been pleasant to do business with, and Marlow was ready to check this last item off her list. Besides, she didn't have any other plans and told him it wasn't any trouble at all.

They agreed to meet in the bank parking lot because it was closer to her. It would take her about five minutes to drive there and only ten to walk back home.

Mrs. Bowers stepped outside to sit on the porch with her afternoon tea as Marlow got out of the Bronco and into the Jaguar.

They waved to one another as Marlow backed out of the driveway. She was happy to get the car over to its new owner.

She also grinned because that sweet older woman would sit on her porch in the afternoon even if it was two-hundred degrees.

When Marlow pulled into the parking lot of the bank

branch, she didn't see Mr. Johnson's car. She watched the marina across the street and the various boats on the river.

Clouds were slowly forming, and it looked like the fireworks show might get rained out tonight. Just as she wondered where Abe Johnson was, he sent her a text asking the same thing. Abe had been there all along, parked in the lot, directly facing the riverfront.

Marlow pulled around to the other side of the bank, immediately seeing his car facing the water. It was late, but still daylight outside. She hadn't thought about the bank being closed for the holiday, and for a split second, thought she should probably have him follow her to the police station instead. But she'd already cashed his check and knew Mr. Johnson was serious about the car.

It wouldn't take a couple of minutes to give him the title and the keys. Plus, she wasn't exactly alone because there were plenty of people on the river that could see them.

Abe smiled at her as she parked the car and got out. He introduced Marlow to his brother, Aaron, who shook her hand. She couldn't explain why Aaron made her feel uncomfortable. Perhaps it was the way he slid his hand into hers or when he held her hand too long. But the chill bumps on her arms told her she needed to hurry up with this transaction.

"You look familiar," Aaron said as she turned away from him to face Abe. He was a few years younger than Abe, and she suspected he'd been drinking. Quickly pulling out the paperwork, Marlow showed Abe where she'd signed and had the title notarized, so he could get the car put into his name.

"Are you sure we don't know each other?" Aaron asked, attempting to get Marlow to pay attention to him again.

"No, I'm afraid I don't know you," Marlow replied as she thanked Abe for buying the car, handed over the keys, and began walking out of the parking lot toward the boarding house.

She pulled out her phone to call Zachary, knowing it would make her feel better. He would lecture her for going alone, and she would have to agree that he was right again. But before Zachary answered, someone grabbed Marlow from behind, sliding a firm hand over her mouth when she tried to scream.

Fear wound through her, and Marlow kicked and squirmed until she fell onto the pavement. When she looked up, she was surprised to see it was Abe and not Aaron who'd grabbed her.

"I told you she wouldn't go easy," Aaron told Abe. "She ran last time."

Marlow stilled as she examined Aaron's features again. He'd worn a black hoodie the night she saw him outside her window. This time, it was Aaron's turn to grab her, and she kicked wildly, hitting him in the chest and chin.

Abe was more determined. "You spoiled little girl. I don't give up so easily." He grabbed her legs as she kicked and bucked, then yelled to Aaron to get her arms.

When Aaron grabbed her shoulders, she swung her cast into his head, and he dropped her again. But Abe dragged her along the concrete toward the old car. The trunk was open, and she fought with everything she had to keep from being put inside.

Thunder cracked across the sky, and lightning flashed, but still, Marlow couldn't believe no one heard her screaming.

Huge raindrops roared down from the sky, but Marlow saw two boats full of people going by as Abe tried to shove her into the back of that car.

"Wildcat," Aaron called her, and she could see he wasn't getting close again after she'd bloodied his face. Marlow fought

Abe, who was losing his grip in the rain. As he made one last attempt to haul her into the trunk, she kicked him in the groin and cracked her cast over his head. She felt the blow in her bones, and when Abe let go, her face hit the tailgate.

With blurred vision and pure determination, Marlow ran toward the marina. There had to be someone around that could help her.

The further she went, the more deserted it looked. The sun had gone down, and daylight was waning. The storm was thrashing outside, and the only thing in Marlow's sightline was Zachary's boat. As she slid on board with wet shoes, Marlow peered back to see if Abe and Aaron were behind her.

They were arguing and shoving each other, but she didn't think they saw where she went. As she punched in the code for the cabin door, it didn't open. Her heart sunk, *had Zachary changed the combination?*

Her hands shook as she tried it again. She could hear Abe cursing his brother for not helping get the senator's daughter into the back of the car.

This time, the cabin door opened, and she fell inside, locking it behind her. The cabin was empty, and there wasn't anything to hide under. Marlow's mind raced as she pulled her knees into her chest and tried to make herself as small as possible.

It was darker in the cabin, but she could see their shadows as they got closer. Suddenly, she heard Abe curse and then the sound of their heavy footsteps running away. Something or someone scared them off, but she was too frightened to come out of hiding.

Her entire body trembled as she tried to keep quiet and stop the terror from overtaking her. Marlow's heartbeat filled her ears as she tried to control her breathing. When she felt someone pushing on the cabin door, she thought she might have a heart attack.

"Marlow?"

When she looked up, it took her brain a second to register that it was Zachary. She scrambled to her feet as he reached for her and pulled her into his arms.

"It's okay. It's okay. We got them," Zachary said, he said, kissing the top of Marlow's head and holding her so tight she could barely breathe. But she didn't care. Zachary was there. He'd gotten to her in time.

He picked her up, carrying her to the upper deck, to a bench seat. From there, Marlow could see police cars and flashing lights, but she didn't see Abe or Aaron. She didn't want to either.

Zachary covered her with his raincoat as he examined her. She hadn't realized she was even hurt until he said something. "You're going to be okay," he said as he gently eased her wet hair off her face. Marlow didn't speak but nodded as he worked to keep her calm.

"I got your call, and guessed you dropped the phone because I heard rustling and what sounded like it hitting the ground." He hugged her gently before kneeling in front of her. "Thank God, I heard boat horns in the background and prayed you were at the riverfront and not the lakefront because it was closer. I saw the Jaguar in the bank parking lot."

Marlow nodded as she tried to sort out what he was telling her. It was difficult because her mind was still overwhelmed with how fast things went wrong.

"I'm so proud of you, Marlow. You fought hard, and I heard the whole thing."

A paramedic joined them on board and asked Marlow if she could walk to the ambulance. "No. I'm good. I want to go home," she said and then repeated herself a second time. "I'm good. Seriously. I need to go home."

Zachary held her hand. "Marlow. I'll follow you to the hospital. Let them check you out."

"I'm fine. I just want to go home," she repeated firmly.

The paramedic asked if he could clean her wounds and opened his first aid kit when she agreed. Zachary watched over her as the man cleaned and dressed all of her cuts and scrapes. She'd destroyed the cast on her hand, and the paramedic said he'd never seen one broken like that. He gently removed it and put a brace on her hand instead.

The police chief walked over as the paramedic finished and asked Marlow a few questions. Marlow explained to him what had happened, but when she told him that Aaron had been the one at her bedroom window, Zachary stormed off the boat.

She watched him go to the end of the dock to get control of himself. When he walked back over, he still looked angry. He stared at the chief of police who calmly continued to talk to Marlow.

"Do you have any idea what this was all about?" Chief Gallegos questioned.

Marlow shrugged. "Abe did give me the money for the car, so that wasn't a ruse. But I think they must not like my mother's politics because they referred to me as the senator's daughter."

The chief nodded and told Zachary to get Marlow home. After everyone left, he sat beside her on the boat, almost as upset as she was.

Chapter Twenty-Four

Marlow watched as anguish washed over Zachary's face. He was angry, and she wasn't sure what to say, so she apologized. "I'm sorry, Zachary."

"What are you sorry for?"

Marlow had screwed up, and she knew it. People were superstitious and talked about Friday the 13th being bad luck. For her, it was the Fourth of July, her birthday. From the time she'd turned thirteen, not a single good thing had ever happened to her on that day.

It felt like the tectonic plates of her world shifted on that day, bringing as much crazy into her life as possible. She should have stayed home and hidden under the covers until the day ended. But she'd tempted fate.

"I should have listened to you and met them at the police station again. But Abe had paid for the car already, and he was super nice when Officer Shannon and I met with him yesterday. I didn't think-"

"You didn't think. But you also didn't deserve what happened to you, Marlow. I don't know what to say about it. I don't want anything to happen to you, but you impulsively do these things, and I can't protect you if you won't listen."

"Who told you it was your job to protect me?" She asked defiantly. *Sure, she was wrong. Later, she would tell him that, but right now, she didn't need a lecture.*

Zachary wanted to yell at her. At the same time, he was grateful that he'd gotten there in time. But he wouldn't fight with her.

"Let's go, Marlow. I'll drive you back to the boarding house." He stood and waited for her to follow.

They didn't talk on the way back to the boarding house, and when they walked in, Mrs. Bowers flipped out. "Oh, my heavens. What happened?" She said with tears in her eyes as she put a gentle hand on Marlow's face.

"I'm fine, Mrs. Bowers. Truly." Marlow didn't stop to talk or explain. She headed upstairs and straight to the shower.

As soon as she was out of earshot, Zachary told Mrs. Bowers what had happened. The older woman hugged him fiercely and told him he was a hero.

He didn't feel like a hero. His mind went back to when he'd met Marlow Ripley. She'd argued with him about pulling her over, and not once since she'd been in the house had she asked for assistance. She was suspicious when he tried to help her get her car.

Zachary had said she was trouble from the start, and he didn't want that in his life, but he cared about Marlow. Her independence was admirable, but the secrets had to end. He needed to know that she wouldn't do things like meet creeps in a bank parking lot without telling him first. No more surprises, he'd already lived that life with Chloe. It was no life at all.

He went to his bedroom and changed out of his wet uniform. Marlow was in the shower, and he was pretty sure she was crying in there. Part of him wanted to storm through the bathroom door and hold her close. But the other side, the rational side, said she needed time to process everything. But the weight of what had happened tipped the scale of their relationship. He felt it the moment he heard her screaming over the phone. They couldn't just be friends anymore.

The thought of him not getting to her in time almost broke Zachary. It would torment him for the rest of his life.

His rules had to be followed and that stubborn woman had to accept it. Changes would be made so they could move forward. "There are rules," he said aloud——Knowing good and well, Marlow marched to the beat of her own drum.

They each needed time to calm down, and then would have a serious conversation. Zachary was still crazed over those two men going after her. He'd tackled the older one that ran out of the marina first. The other man had been so scared he immediately fell to his knees on the ground. It took two officers to pull Zachary off the man, and he'd never lost control like that in his entire life. But after hearing Marlow's terrified screams over the phone, he could have ripped the man apart with his bare hands.

He was too angry to have a civil conversation tonight with Marlow. But when his phone rang and he saw who it was, he certainly picked it up.

MARLOW CRIED the entire time she stood in the shower. She'd learned to hide her emotions that way when she was younger. But this time, she'd really messed up, and it almost cost her everything. Maybe her life. She hadn't let her guard down like that, but one time in high school and once in college, and those were hard lessons back then.

At least in NOLA, she had a panic room and a panic button that would send off alarms and alert law enforcement to help her. In college, she called her mother, who sent in the troops.

Having someone like Aaron peeping in her bedroom at the boarding house had sent her running to Zachary. But still, she hadn't felt like she was in danger in Maisonville. But in the past, that would have been more than enough warning.

Shivering at what those men might have done to her, Marlow turned the hot water up. It didn't help. It was going to take time for her nerves to settle.

Wrapping herself in a fluffy towel, she wiped the mirror clear with her hand. The bruise near her eye looked bluish-green now, and by tomorrow, she might have a black eye.

Carefully drying her body, Marlow was shocked at how many cuts, scrapes, and bruises there were. She had fought for her life.

Slipping into her nightgown, she stared at herself and then sniffled. "You look like Mauled Barbie," she said and then half-heartedly laughed. That's what Zachary would have told her if he hadn't been so upset. But she knew he had every right to be mad at her. It showed how much he cared, and that friendship was starting to mean the world to her.

She wiped her eyes again and slowly pulled on a long floral silk robe. The silk was light, but still she felt everywhere it touched her skin. As she shivered, her muscles ached. She was bone tired, and it took her longer than usual to clean up the mess she'd made in the beautifully appointed bathroom.

Living in this lovely old home, next to super cop Zachary Bowman, and having coffee on the porch with Mrs. Bowers had utterly messed with her sense of survival.

Crawling into bed with Zachary had messed with her heart,

too. If she were honest, she wanted to sleep with him tonight but wasn't sure she could muster the nerve to knock on his door.

After everything that had happened, he might not even be in there. Marlow tip-toed out of the bathroom and saw a dim light shining underneath his door.

Maybe she could talk to him for a few minutes? As she got closer, she heard him on the phone. "I wouldn't say we're friends, and trust me, there will never be more," he said.

Marlow had never heard him sound more bitter.

"Because I don't like lying, and omitting the truth is the same."

Was he talking about her? Frozen in her tracks outside his bedroom door, Marlow regretted being there at all but couldn't stop eavesdropping.

"I will never understand the desire to be famous. Putting stuff out there to build a fan base or to get likes and comments is a shallow life to me."

Tears filled Marlow's eyes again. This was the birthday that kept on giving. He was talking about her. He thought she was shallow?

"I don't know what else to say, but I'm not looking for a plastic talking head. The only people I want in my life are honest, authentic people who care about others and less about popularity."

Marlow covered the sob that was building in her chest. She backed down the staircase until she was halfway, and then ran down the remaining stairs. She didn't stop as she picked up her purse, computer, and keys on the entryway table, went out the front door, and climbed into the Bronco.

How could Zachary talk about her like that? Who was he discussing her with, and what were they saying on their end of the phone? She'd only ever seen him talking about personal stuff to Olivia and Leonie Ford. Olivia wouldn't let him get away with talking about her like that. They were instant friends and Marlow had always suspected it was because they had similar family drama. Why would he talk about her to Leonie Ford unless he genuinely was interested in his real estate agent?

Looking down at her bruised body, she didn't have the strength to fight. Marlow wasn't even sure she could go back inside. How could she face him knowing what he thought about her? And why would he pretend to be her friend when, in actuality, he didn't like anything about Marlow at all?

Frantically swiping at her tears, Marlow tried to get herself together. She'd woken up that morning blissfully unaware of the disastrous way this day would end. But all her birthdays were awful.

Sitting there in the driveway, she began to think about everything she'd done since stopping, or rather being stopped, in Maisonville.

She'd learned about generosity and how to be grateful from Mrs. Bowers, who'd opened her house to Marlow without question. Miss Lynn reinforced those traits by giving her a job as a waitress just because she needed one. Olivia had been an example of how hard work and perseverance could help you overcome any obstacle to make your own happiness.

Then there was Tenille, Evie Mae, and Felicity at the coffee truck, Doctor Tobias Nash, and his brother, Doctor Asher Nash, who were all kind to her.

Marlow had nothing when she got there except a car, a suitcase, and the generosity of others. She'd taken amazing photos and posted them for sale online, apologized for misleading her followers after she ran away from her wedding, sold the sports car so she could pay her debts, and started her own marketing company with two great clients.

She wasn't a plastic talking head or shallow.

How dare Zachary Bowman say all those awful things about her. He had no right to judge her so harshly when all she'd done was try to be a better person. She had made some real friends here, and she'd done all of that after being in town for only a month. Marlow needed to find her moxie and march back upstairs to set that know-it-all Officer Bowman straight.

She dried her face and breathed deeply just as her phone rang. Had Zachary heard her running down the stairs? It didn't matter. She was ready for him. She jerked up her phone, with all the gusto she had inside her, and pressed the answer key ——at the same time, it registered in her brain that it wasn't Zachary.

It was her mother, Michelle Ripley.

Chapter Twenty-Five

"Marlow Maxwell Ripley, I have had enough. Are you ready to stop this foolishness," Michelle's voice was tight, but she was articulate and cutting as usual.

Marlow wanted to hang up, but she couldn't. She'd always felt small when her mother scolded her. It took a moment for her to answer. "Missing me, mother?"

"I don't miss the drama of your immature behavior. I am a busy woman and don't have time to clean up your messes."

"That's right, you have people for that, don't you?"

Michelle was about to lose it, and Marlow could feel that anger building up on the other end of the phone. They pressed each other's buttons like no one else.

"Don't you take that flippant tone with me, young lady? I heard what happened in that little town you've been hiding out in. What has to happen so you will finally understand that your actions have consequences?"

Marlow was attacked through no fault of her own, yet her mother acted as if Marlow had done something wrong. "I don't know what you're talking about, but I did nothing wrong here."

Michelle was clicking a pen as she spoke. It was her equivalent to a fidget spinner when she was frustrated. Marlow had watched her mother click away like that most of the time when they argued. "Really? Not your fault? I've heard that excuse so many times that it holds zero weight in my book."

Marlow wanted to tell her it didn't matter how she felt about it, but as usual, her words fell silent in her head. She'd never stood up to Michelle the way she wanted. Her mother had a way of making Marlow second guess herself in every situation. And Marlow already knew she shouldn't have met those jerks alone today. But there was no use in explaining that to her mother.

"How dare you film a video called 'Coming Clean' and show up on camera looking like that. You have me to thank for that social media career that made you famous, and I can take it away too."

So she wasn't talking about the brothers who attempted to kidnap her? Marlow's mind was reeling as her mother hurled insults her way.

"Do you hear me? And I presume you've been eating your feelings. You looked fat, Marlow. And your hair was a mess. Do you understand the ramifications of your actions for all of us and after what you put Royce through."

"Wh-What I put Royce through?" Before Marlow could say anything more, Michelle cut her off.

"You have played around in that town long enough. I am done with this nonsense. You will return to work for me, posting social media content I approve of and nothing else. No more foolish posts about small-town life in a boarding house like some pauper who had to claw her way to success."

Wasn't that the back story her mother tried to sell to everyone? Even though she had a famous artist mother who provided more than enough for both of them.

"You will pack up, move home, and follow the program as usual. Do you understand me? If I hear one more word about you mooning over Officer Bowman, then I will end his career. Have you forgotten how I bailed you out the last time?"

"Officer Bowman and I aren't even friends." It was a ridiculous thing to say, but the only thing that came to mind.

"I'll expect you to report to me first thing in the morning, and I won't take no for an answer. Enough is enough."

Before Marlow could reply, her mother, the senator, hung up. The entire phone call felt like a slap across the face. Michelle Ripley had nothing if she didn't have perfect timing. After hearing Zachary put her down and being reminded of her past transgressions, Marlow had to stop fooling herself.

She made mistakes all the time and didn't have what it took to run her own marketing business. Besides, she did know what her mother was capable of, and she couldn't let her hurt Zachary.

Looking down at her battered body wearing that thin silk gown and robe, Marlow shook her head disapprovingly. Michelle would flip if she saw her sitting in the Bronco looking like that without any clothes or shoes. But Marlow had bought everything in the boarding house for her honeymoon. There was no need to go back inside and get anything because she didn't want to see it again. She would throw the silk away as soon as she got home, too.

Slowly backing down the dark driveway, Marlow pulled onto the deserted street. With only a single glance back at the boarding house, she headed toward the bridge that would take her back to New Orleans and the hell that was her life sentence.

She would miss everyone. Even though Zachary hurt her feelings with what he said about her, she would still miss what she thought they had.

Her mother didn't make hollow threats. She meant every single word she ever said. She would brag that she earned people's respect, but everyone feared the backlash of a disapproving Senator Michelle Ripley.

Marlow certainly didn't respect her, but she feared what she'd do to people close to her. If only she could explain to them that she'd left for their own good and not her personal well-being. But she knew she'd never be allowed to see any of them again.

It was late when she pulled into her driveway in the city and punched in the code to the iron gates. As she slowly drove forward, all she could think about was how she'd almost escaped this life.

Marlow went inside, turning on all the lights as she went. Her mother was still in DC, but she would expect a video call first thing at six in the morning, which was seven for Marlow. It was their usual meeting time.

Marlow went to the front of the house to double-check the locks. She couldn't help wondering what Zachary and Mrs. Bowers would think once they realized she was gone.

She wished she'd given Mrs. Bowers one last hug. Her hugs were the best. But running out of the house had been her first instinct.

The need to run from her problems was genetic, her mother would say. It was programmed into her DNA from her father since he ran out on them.

Marlow walked to her bedroom and pulled out pajama shorts and a tank top. She wadded up the outrageously expensive silk nightgown and robe, then tossed it into the garbage.

Sitting on the floor, Marlow opened her computer. It was a force of habit, but she went straight to her social media pages. There were now over a hundred thousand comments to her video, and perhaps it was masochistic, but she wanted to read them.

Of course, the mean comments were still there, but now that Marlow looked again, she wondered if they hadn't been from Royce or someone in Royce's office. It was her mother's office, too, but it still seemed plausible. Especially since those messages all sounded the same as they insulted her personally and told Royce he could do better. There were twenty-five posts like that, and then every remark afterward was from someone that said they still loved her and would continue to follow. Some said they prayed for her because Royce had an untrustworthy look about him.

For years, her mother, who considered herself an expert in dealing with the public, said people mostly followed celebrities or pseudo-celebrities like Marlow to watch them make mistakes. At the Maisonville Jail, Michelle told her that she'd provided more than two-hundred-thousand followers plenty of fodder to torment their family for years.

Marlow had worried herself sick over becoming a joke to everyone online, but her mother had been wrong. And that was one of the biggest issues in their relationship. Michelle Ripley said everything as if it were a fact——barring anyone from ever questioning her. It had never occurred to Marlow that this time she was right.

She'd confided in Royce that it felt like her followers were rooting for her most of the time, and when she talked to the camera, it felt as if she were talking to all of them. He smirked and told her that was crazy because those people weren't her friends because they didn't know her.

But as Marlow sat alone on the floor reading testimonials from women who admitted they hadn't gone with their gut feelings and married the wrong man, her heart poured out for them. One woman admitted staying for forty years because her family wouldn't accept divorce. Another stayed for ten years without having children because she didn't want him to be terrible to their kids as he had been to her. The stories went on and on, and Marlow wanted to hug every person that had taken the time to share.

Her mother and Royce had been entirely wrong. Marlow felt the warmth from those messages, and she truly cared about those women, too. She knew better than most how hard it was to admit the truth about your struggles. Having online friends made it easier to say what you couldn't say in person. Sure, lots of people were meaner online, too, but Marlow mainly had seen the good in others online. It was Michelle and Royce who didn't know her.

Marlow had allowed Michelle to bully her into returning home. But honestly, Marlow needed a little space to deal with the overwhelming feelings she'd developed for Zachary Bowman.

Thinking back to her mother's comment about how fat she'd looked on the video, Marlow almost laughed. The truth was that Marlow never had an eating disorder, but her mother sure did. The woman ate like a bird, and on the rare occasions she had an event dinner and a few glasses of wine, Michelle would force herself to throw it all up. Marlow had caught her enough times that Michelle had to twist it around onto her. If Marlow had been weaker, she might have fallen into an eating disorder, too.

Marlow spent the next few hours responding to every

message online. It was worthwhile to her, and she wanted her followers to know it.

This arrangement with her mother was temporary. Marlow lay in bed and mentally mapped out a plan. She would break free of her cliche, poor-little-rich-girl existence. After all, Marlow could do anything if she set her mind to it. Someone she was once close to told her so. And there would never be another reason to run away because she would have the power to so whatever she wanted.

She wanted to be in Maisonville because the town and the people were wonderful. It didn't matter if Zachary Bowman dated Leonie Ford. He could jump in the lake for all she cared. He had no more claim to Maisonville than she did because he'd only been there a week or two longer than Marlow.

Pulling her covers up over her head, she admitted that she would be bothered if he dated someone else. But he'd said some awful things, and she couldn't forgive him. She needed to stop giving badly behaved people her time.

But still, she wondered if Zachary noticed she was gone yet.

Chapter Twenty-Six

Zachary shouldn't have answered that phone call. After the day he'd had and how he worried about Marlow, nothing good could come from a conversation with Chloe.

He threw on a pair of shorts and a tee shirt and headed downstairs. Marlow's lights were off in her bedroom, and he figured she was probably asleep. But when he turned the front porch lights off, he immediately noticed her light blue Bronco was gone.

He jogged back upstairs to check on her, her bed was made, and her things in order. Where would she go this late at night alone?

After what happened, didn't she understand it wasn't safe for her to go out on her own? He'd planned to talk to her in the morning, but she was going to force him to lay down the rules tonight.

He paced for a few minutes and then grabbed a bottle of water. Mrs. Bowers walked into the kitchen, still pleased with him. "I figured you went to bed," she said, smiling at Zachary. "Can I make you something to eat?"

"No, ma'am. I came down for water. Do you know where Marlow went?"

Mrs. Bowers looked confused. "I thought she was upstairs. I figured you two got to talking."

Had Marlow listened to him while he was on the phone? It wasn't his best moment, and he'd been harsh with Chloe. Had that upset Marlow?

"Goodnight, Mrs. Bowers," Zachary said and kissed her on the cheek before he headed back upstairs to get his phone. Something didn't feel right, and he wouldn't be able to clear his head until he talked to Marlow.

When she didn't answer, Zachary sent her a text. His conversation, taken out of context, could have made him look judgmental and cruel. He wasn't proud of losing his temper and said some things that he probably shouldn't. He needed to explain himself.

Of course, he'd been out of sorts since the incident at the marina. He'd been out of his mind worried about Marlow and thought that was clear.

His first inclination was to get in his car and look for her. But he needed to calm down and act rationally. Perhaps she needed to clear her head. He still wouldn't like her out of the house alone, but it would give him a way to ease into the conversation of how to keep her safe.

"Marlow, please text me back and let me know you're okay."

Who was he kidding? Zachary couldn't relax until he knew where she was and how she was doing.

Minutes later, Marlow responded. "I moved back home."

Would she truly move back home? The incident had shaken her, but he never would have thought she'd return there.

"How can I be sure this is really you?"

It took several minutes for her to respond again. "Trust me, it's me."

If she would fuss with him, then things weren't too bad. "Isn't that what a kidnapper would say too?"

"Wow, too soon, Bowman."

He didn't like her in New Orleans alone, but at least she replied to his messages. "Tell me something that only Marlow Ripley would know."

"Zachary Bowman, this is Runaway Barbie. Now, let me get some rest."

It wasn't an ideal situation, but at least he knew the senator's house in New Orleans was safe. He didn't send another text but went to bed just as angry as before.

In New Orleans, Marlow turned off notifications on her phone and plugged it into her nightstand charger. Although she'd asked him to let her sleep, the fact that he didn't text anymore hurt her feelings. She might be overreacting, but her emotions had been all over the place since she'd almost been kidnapped.

Marlow got out of bed to double-check the locks and alarm system in the house. If she were honest, and she wasn't at that moment, she would admit that her emotions had been out of wack since she'd conceded to work for her mother.

Climbing back into bed, Marlow thought about Zachary racing to the marina to find her. How could he act that way and then say those awful things about her? Marlow knew a lot of politicians who said one thing and did another, but she'd never thought buttoned-down, straight-as-an-arrow Zachary Bowman would act that way.

She rechecked her phone and there weren't any more messages. Why couldn't Marlow stop thinking about him? She checked the clock and then calculated how much sleep she could get if she fell asleep now. But the silence in that big empty house was louder than ever before, and Marlow missed Zachary being a single wall away from her.

Tears filled her eyes, and she ended up crying herself to sleep. She would wake up feeling stronger; she just knew it.

EARLY THE FOLLOWING DAY, Marlow threw on a long sleeve tee shirt and some jogging pants. Her mother kept the house set on Artic temperatures, and Marlow always thought it was to match the woman's cold heart.

She sent a text to Mrs. Bowers, thanking her for her hospitality. Then she asked her to donate the suitcase, clothes, and toiletries that she'd left behind.

Next, Marlow sent a short message to Miss Lynn and Olivia, thanking them for everything and apologizing for not helping more at the diner.

She missed them all terribly, but she had woken up with a renewed sense of what she needed to do to protect all of her new friends from Michelle Ripley's rage.

The video call with her mother went as expected. Michelle scolded Marlow for not being presentable, meaning showered and picture-perfect, then had one of her assistants give Marlow the social media schedule Michelle wanted for the rest of the month. It included two trips to DC, highlighting Michelle's planned speech and a pretend surprise dinner for Michelle's birthday. She always wanted the world to see how beloved she was and humble.

Marlow circled her own notes, while the assistant recited a thirty-day list of events. Getting Marlow's followers hooked on daily segments was of the utmost importance to her mother, and it made Marlow cringe.

People weren't dumb, and if she only posted things about her mother and politics, they would see right through it. Michelle had never understood the importance of being an honest voice.

As soon as the video chat was over, Marlow closed her computer. Her phone vibrated, and she frowned when she saw it was another video chat. This time, it was with Royce.

"What?" she asked, staring at the jerk she'd almost married. Royce still had a bandage on his nose. *Served him right.*

"Mar, I wanted to reach out and talk about your upcoming trip to DC."

"I don't have anything to say to you, Royce."

"You're going to have to find a way to forgive me, Marlow, if we are going to work together."

"Who said I was going to work with you?"

"It's what Michelle wants." He didn't finish the obvious second half of that sentence——*and what Michelle wants, she gets.*

"Sorry, no deal. You can tell that to Michelle. She wants to pretend she doesn't have any culpability in what happened, and she absolutely does."

"No one meant to hurt you, Marlow."

That was the biggest lie he'd told so far, and Marlow shook her head before she hung up on him.

She'd have to fly out of town tonight to be in DC to video her mother's super-fake surprise birthday party. But she couldn't bring herself to book the arrangements or pack yet.

If she'd kept to herself instead of making friends in Maisonville, her mother wouldn't have had any ammunition to use against her. Marlow had to play this smarter.

She had to make sure that Michelle would never want her back. Of course, she would have thought running out on her wedding would have been enough, not that she'd planned to do it. But it had been humiliating for Marlow and she certainly thought for her mother. Half the guest list were people Michelle invited. A public embarrassment plus wasting close to a hundred-thousand dollars should have been enough to get Marlow exiled for good.

Why would Michelle force her back there?

She could only think of one reason and that was to make her pay for how much she embarrassed Michelle and Royce. Saying their name in the same sentence made her sick to her stomach.

Marlow had to keep focused on what she needed to do to get what she wanted. First, she wanted to be financially independent. Gaining access to the money Michelle had no right to take from Marlow's bank account was key. Her mother's lawyers and accountants oversaw everything, and it was time to remove their access.

It didn't take Marlow long to set an appointment with the attorney's office. As usual, she could never reach any of the lawyers by phone. But she told their assistant it was urgent and would meet the head attorney at three that afternoon.

The accountants were kinder, and she spoke to them over the phone, asked for some advice, and then received the documents via email for her signature to make the changes official.

She was able to have her online business direct deposit funds into her new bank account. Once she received the money Michele had taken, then she would deposit it in the bank too. Michelle could no longer touch it.

When Marlow returned home, she made herself a smoothie and went through more photographs to add to her business page. She offered digital copies for download and also print options that were printed, packed, and shipped by a third-party company for her.

When she checked her sales page, she realized that her projections had been way off. She refreshed her computer and was amazed that it was correct, over five-hundred pictures had been downloaded or bought.

Marlow put her hand over her mouth and laughed. That was a ton of money, and she could make a living off it alone if she kept adding more photographs.

It felt good to feel some control over her future, and she picked up her phone to call Zachary. Before it went through, she hung up. He'd told someone they weren't friends. Actually, he didn't stop there, and she would never forget the tone of his voice either.

She was tired of being naive. But every smile that man gave her felt real. He was charming and had that goody-goody attitude down pat. He'd tricked her so completely.

Marlow was a magnet for awful people, and she was sick of it. She had to wake up. Walking in on a cheating Royce minutes before they were to be married had to be the turning point in her life.

She wasn't perfect and had made plenty of mistakes, but she would never treat anyone like that. Turning that heart-wrenching moment into her golden ticket to a new fulfilling life was her goal now.

It was time to toughen up. See people for who they are and stop letting them walk all over her.

When Marlow finished going through her online contracts and obligations at the attorney's office, she had to hustle home and pack. Her flight was in three hours, and it would take time to get to the airport in rush hour traffic.

The good news was that she better understood her business and what to expect as an influencer in the way of income. She took the paperwork with her and then fired all of the attorneys handling her business. It would take a little time, but she'd find someone who represented her best interests. And that person would not be affiliated with Senator Ripley.

Marlow arrived at the busy airport with just enough time to grab a giant coffee and water for the plane ride. She wasn't looking forward to seeing her mother or pretending they got along during the birthday event.

As she took her seat on board, she realized there was no reason she had to stay at her mother's house. Marlow called Michelle's assistant and had her book a hotel room. This way, Marlow could keep things professional or at least keep up the charade.

The flight to DC was a little over two hours, and Marlow charged internet services to her mother's credit card. It was a business trip, after all, and the offices of Senator Ripley could afford it.

She responded to another thousand messages on her social media account and saw that Miss Lynn, Olivia, and Olivia' son, Lucas, had sent her a video. They told her that she was already missed terribly, but they would see her soon. Before signing off, Miss Lynn and Lucas blew her kisses, and Olivia winked into the camera. It made Marlow laugh. She sure hoped she would see them soon.

There was a voice text or at least an attempted voice text from Mrs. Bowers. She kept asking, "Is this thing on?" and then would talk to Marlow as if she were on the phone. She loved that woman.

Zachary tried to call her once and then sent a text message. He wanted to talk to her and said it was important.

She wanted to believe he was sincere, but Marlow understood integrity could be faked. She'd watched Michelle and Royce fake it for years.

She didn't trust herself to talk to Zachary and ignored the text. There was plenty to do as she planned several posts she would make over the next few days.

Michelle didn't own her, and it wasn't up to her to approve or disapprove of Marlow's social media accounts.

Once she landed and checked into her hotel, Marlow ordered dinner and a piece of pie from room service. She felt like she was a million miles away from Maisonville and decided eating pie would ease her lonely heart.

Being the tougher version of herself was taking its toll. Marlow watched as the bedside alarm clock clicked to midnight and felt that little voice inside her head doubt her ability to follow through with this plan.

She pulled out her computer and reread some of the messages from her social media followers. One, in particular, mentioned that she had been in a terrible relationship for most of her life. But she'd found true love at sixty and promised it was worth the wait. She added that you have to remove all the bad things and people from your life so that you'll have room for the good stuff.

Marlow swiped at the happy tears she felt for that sweet woman and wished she could tell her in person how much her words meant.

At that exact moment, she received a text from Zachary Bowman.

"Are you still awake?"

"Yes."

Instead of sending another text, he called her, and Marlow stared at the phone for a second. She shouldn't answer it because his voice would wear her down. But after reading that post online, she felt like it was a sign. Did she even believe in signs?

"Hello."

She heard him exhale into the phone before he spoke. "Nice to hear your voice, Marlow."

She nodded but didn't speak. How could Zachary say ugly things about her yet talk to her like she mattered?

"Are you still there?"

"Yes."

"It's quiet without you here, Marlow."

"I guess that's good for you." She wanted to say since you don't have a plastic talking head in the house.

"What I mean to say is that it's not the same here without you."

That sounded like he missed her. But she knew better. She had to reminded herself that when he didn't know she was outside his door, he said she was shallow.

"Marlow?"

"Yes."

"Why would you go back to work for your mother?"

"You and I aren't friends, Zachary. And trust me, there will never be more."

"What?"

"I'm a plastic talking head. Isn't that what you said?"

"Marlow, you don't understand. I wasn't-"

"Don't. Just don't try and take it back, Zachary. I heard you. I didn't mean to, but I did, and you can't take it back." Marlow didn't want to get emotional, but it hurt to admit she knew how he felt. She may not have meant anything to him, but Marlow cared about Zachary.

"The worst part is that you could have been honest with me. You could have just told me you didn't want to be my friend. You didn't have to eat lunch or hang out with me at the boarding house. I didn't ask anything of you. And I never pretended to be something that I'm not. I was honest with you. My heart was open, and you stomped on it. And even worse, you couldn't say that to my face but had no problem telling all those terrible things about me to someone else. So, I am back working for my mother and Royce because they don't pretend to be good people. They are awful and say the worst things to me, but at least I know where I stand!" Marlow hung up and then screamed into her pillow. It was the first time she'd ever found the exact words she needed to say to a person at the same time she needed them. And it felt absolutely horrible.

She turned off the lights and turned on thunderstorm sounds to match her turbulent heart, and hoped sleep would take her soon.

ZACHARY FELT the boarding house rumble from the thunderstorm outside. It matched his mood. How had things gotten so messed up with Marlow?

He should have gone with his first instinct last night and followed her into the city. If he could have seen her, then he would have explained this misunderstanding.

Now, she probably wouldn't speak to him again.

He had to work tomorrow, but he needed to fix things with her. She belonged in Maisonville, didn't she know that?

He couldn't sleep with the storm and his thoughts. By sunrise, Zachary was dressed and out the front door. He went to the station first, but by 7:30, he was taking a coffee break at the diner, waiting for Olivia to arrive.

Miss Lynn could read Zachary's mood when he walked into the diner and called Olivia to come in early. When Olivia saw Zachary's head down staring into his coffee cup, she knew it was over Marlow. She put her hand on his and gave him a sympathetic smile when he looked up at her.

"I messed things up, Olivia."

His childhood friend was about to let him have it when he came in today. When she and Miss Lynn received the text from Marlow that she'd left town, they figured it had to do with him. But seeing his heart broken made her question everything. "Did this have anything to do with Leonie Ford?"

Zachary shook his head. He didn't want to talk about it

but needed some advice. Before he could say another word, a soft hand touched his shoulder. "Zach?"

Olivia looked up to see an attractive woman wearing a tight-fitting sleeveless dress looking longingly at Zachary.

He'd only been there for a month. How many women was he seeing? When the woman sat down close to him, brushing her body against his arm, Olivia was furious at Zachary. She shook her head and stormed off. He didn't deserve Marlow Ripley if he was going to play games.

Zachary saw Olivia's angry expression, but he was too shocked to see Chloe Patterson to stop his friend. He took a deep breath and turned toward her. "What are you doing here?" he asked.

"Zachy, you can't stay mad at me."

He hated it when she spoke in that baby voice. "I'm not mad. I don't feel anything."

Olivia and Miss Lynn watched the exchange between Zachary and the mystery woman. She was rubbing her body against him, but he didn't look happy.

"Your words hurt me, Zach. I'm not a bad person, and you know we belong together. I just needed some time to work things out professionally. I've already been interviewed at a news station in New Orleans." Chloe wiggled with glee and hugged him as if that made everything all right. "I'll be so close. She ran a long fingernail up his arm and then slightly scraped it back down. "We always had so much fun, and could move back in together."

Zachary stood up. He'd had enough of this nonsense. "After you called me last night, I got in touch with your old boss. He told me, you were fired."

Chloe rolled her eyes and shrugged that off as if it didn't matter. "You know he always had a thing for me, and when I told him that you were my one true love, he replaced me. Me. The most popular reporter that station had ever seen. Whatever. I knew I should have told you before you moved, but I'm here now. We can forgive our youthful transgressions."

Zachary set cash down on the counter and waved at Miss Lynn and Olivia. He headed to the door without another word to Chloe.

That was when Leonie walked in. "I heard your housemate moved back to NOLA?" She wore a black tennis dress, and her hair was messy like she was striving to be casually sexy. "Maybe you could come over for dinner at my place tonight?" As Leonie sidled up closer to Zachary, Chloe walked over.

"Who exactly is this?" Chloe demanded, and Leonie wrapped her arms around Zachary possessively.

Leonie stared at Chloe. "Who exactly are you?"

"I'm his girlfriend," Chloe said.

"Ex-girlfriend," Zachary replied.

Leonie smiled. "Well, I'm his future girlfriend."

Zachary stepped clear of the two possessive women and held his arms up so neither could wrap a hand around him again. "Go home, Chloe. I don't want to see you." Chloe began to turn on the waterworks. That had always gotten to Zachary in the past. But he'd toughened up.

Leonie smiled until Zachary locked eyes with her. "We are never going to date Leonie, whether Marlow Ripley is here or not."

"Who is Marlow?" Chloe demanded.

Leonie and Chloe began arguing, but Zachary didn't miss a beat. He opened the diner's front door and eased the two women into the parking lot where they could quarrel with each other.

When Zachary got in his car, he locked the doors behind

him and rested his head on the steering wheel. He needed to get back to work and sort this mess out later. He'd made himself clear with Chloe before and again today. He was direct with Leonie from the beginning.

How did either of them misunderstand his intentions? He hadn't dated anyone in a long time. He smirked. He hadn't dated anyone except for the fake date with Marlow.

Marlow Ripley was the only woman he'd made an exception for because she was extraordinary. He had to find a way to see her. As soon as he got off work tonight, he would drive into the city and find a way to make her understand.

Miss Lynn watched as Zachary pulled out of the diner parking lot. Leonie and the other woman stopped arguing when he left.

Olivia rang up another customer and then smiled at Miss Lynn, who came over to help her. "That was interesting," Olivia said rolling her eyes.

"I sure thought Zachary would sweep our girl Marlow off her feet. But I guess he's a player?" Miss Lynn looked so disappointed, and Olivia had to help her.

"Miss Lynn, you haven't lost your touch. Zachary Bowman has it bad for Marlow. He dated that she-devil Chloe Patterson before I went back to St. Marksville. My neighbor in St. Marksville pointed her out because she used to be a reporter on the evening news."

Olivia picked up the coffee pot so she could do refills, but before she walked away, she leaned in and said, "You can see all about her antics online. Someone put a compilation of her reporting on social media."

Miss Lynn whipped out her phone and typed in 'news reporter St. Marksville' and began watching Chloe Patterson's terrible behavior. How could Zachary have dated that woman?

She watched until Olivia came back to start another pot of coffee brewing. The younger waitress then turned and explained what she thought had happened. "The way I see it, Marlow Ripley is a strong woman who needs a strong man. Zachary is strong, but he let his compassionate side win out. He gave Marlow space to get over her break up, when our little Marlow needed him to stake his claim." She smirked, "I mean, if Leonie still thinks she has a shot, then he didn't make his intentions known."

Miss Lynn nodded. It would take a grand gesture from him to win Marlow back, and they would have to make sure he understood what that meant.

They wanted their girl back in Maisonville.

Chapter Twenty-Eight

It took Marlow an hour to figure out how to cover her bruises and scrapes from the attempted kidnapping. Her mother hadn't mentioned her blackeye when they spoke on the video chat and thankfully, it wasn't swollen. It just made things easier if she didn't have to deal with it.

She spent the first half of the day with one of the senator's assistants getting the surprise birthday party dinner ready. Marlow had to check lighting and make sure she had microphones set up to catch her mother's perfectly timed surprise reaction to the event and then enough sound clips of her thanking everyone.

In the afternoon, Marlow had a one-on-one meeting with Michelle. Beforehand, she coached herself mentally to keep her calm. There was one way out of all of this, and she had to play her part perfectly. But her mother was going to push her to her limits.

"Sit down, Marlow. You had to know that my attorneys would call me as soon as you met with them."

Marlow shrugged because she did know, and she didn't care.

"I also know you talked to the accountants."

Without much emotion, Marlow replied. "You swiped all the money out of my bank account, Mother. What did you expect me to do?"

"This was never about the money. You know that. Once you returned, the money would have been put back into your account."

The difference between Marlow and her mother was that Marlow knew precisely where she stood in this relationship. "Well, I have the money now, so that task is off your to-do list."

Michelle leaned forward with both elbows on her desk, staring at Marlow. "Don't let that little escapade in Maisonville ruin what we have here."

Locking eyes on her daughter, Senator Ripley needed to remind her who was in power. "This is a mutually beneficial setup between us. I need positive press, and you need content to make you look *'connected'* and *'in-the-know.'* Her mother used air quotation marks for the words connected and in-the-know.

Marlow kept her serene demeanor, matching her mother's. "Royce told me that you refused to work with him."

Marlow smiled as she stood up. She wanted to make sure her mother understood to tread lightly when it came to her ex. "I will not ever discuss Royce Chatham with you. That is non-negotiable. I worked with your other assistant, and we have everything ready for tonight. I'll see you there."

As she began to head for the door, Marlow heard her mother laughing. It was the evil laugh she likened to the villain Cruella Deville.

It took everything in her to turn around. She couldn't mess

this up. Her mother was now clapping, and her face was pure disgust. "My-my, you're confused, my darling." Michelle stood and put her hands on her hips. She thought it made her look menacing, but it accentuated how thin and frail she was now. "Have you forgotten the incident on the West Coast? The one that I made go away? You don't get to tell me what is nonnegotiable in this arrangement or any other. I made you. And I can break you. It's as simple as that. You will fall in line tonight and from here on out. Royce will be at the birthday party, and I expect pictures of him and you, you and me, the three of us smiling, laughing, and getting along. The rest of the world must know there is nothing gossip-worthy to see here. Got it?"

Marlow's pupils dilated as she swallowed her anger and pride. There was a time when what happened in California might have hurt her, but not anymore.

Controlling how the information got out was powerful, and she would take that away from her mother. Just not yet.

Marlow gave a curt smile. "See you tonight, Michelle," she said, and walked out.

Meeting with her mother was the hardest thing she would have to do on this trip. The party would be full of people, and she would be busy taking photos and videos for online posts. Plus, her mother and Royce must be on their best behavior. Marlow could handle it. Then, she would fly home on Sunday to continue organizing her next move.

Several hours later, Marlow and her mother's most recently hired assistant, Sheila, met in the private room where the party would soon start.

"You look amazing," the auburn-haired woman said, looking over Marlow's navy-blue evening dress. It was a simple fitted silk dress with skinny spaghetti straps and an Audrey

Hepburn neckline. The modest heels she'd borrowed from her mother.

Sheila still had on her dress suit she'd worn all day at the office because her boss hadn't given her time to go home and change.

"I brought another one in case someone else wore this same dress. My mother is so fussy about that sort of thing." She winked at Sheila. "About most things, right?"

The poor woman, older than Marlow but only by a few years, looked like she might cry. Marlow grabbed a bottle of Champagne from the bar and pulled Sheila into the ladies' restroom with her and the extra dress.

"You can't let them see you cry, Sheila. It feeds their monster powers," Marlow said as she popped the cork and drank straight from the bottle.

Sheila looked nervous when Marlow handed the dress and bottle over to her. "Don't worry, I won't tell if you won't."

Marlow laughed before she locked the door and sat on the settee in the swanky bathroom to drink a little more.

When Sheila looked at herself in the mirror, Marlow could tell she felt better. She was a little taller than Marlow and built differently, but that was the great thing about a wraparound dress: it could go up or down two sizes if necessary.

Marlow grabbed a couple of rhinestone barrettes and pulled Sheila's hair up on one side. "You look amazing," she said, and Sheila hugged her tightly.

"No one has been kind to me since I started here four weeks ago. Thank you. Thank you so much."

"I'm sorry it's been terrible. I want to tell you that it gets better, but I'm afraid it doesn't. You either learn to run faster or they will trample you."

Sheila drank more champagne and then handed it back to Marlow. "I plan to quit after tonight."

"Good for you. Seriously. Don't look back."

It was time for them to get back out there, but before Marlow unlocked the door, Sheila leaned in and whispered, "I've heard your mother and Mr. Chatham talking about you. They were pretty upset you didn't get married. Senator Ripley said it would take the attention off them, and you messed it up. I didn't know what that meant, but I thought you should know."

Marlow understood. She'd suspected it wasn't a one-time thing. "As long as I'm telling all the secrets I know——" Shelia took another drink of courage before handing the bottle to Marlow and continuing. "Your mother's advisers told her she'd dropped in all the polls since you were no longer posting videos of her. They told her she had to get you back here, or she might not win her next election."

Marlow threw the rest of the champagne into the garbage. That was the best news she'd heard in a long time. She hugged Sheila and pretended to zip her lips up and throw away the key. Both women laughed and prepared themselves for a long night.

Two hours into the dinner, Marlow saw her mother and a security guard corner poor Shelia. The little assistant had run around striving to make everyone happy, but it wasn't enough. Michelle had her sights set on the poor woman from the moment she got there, and while everyone else was served drinks and given a place at the table, Sheila was fired.

As the security officer escorted Sheila onto the elevator, Marlow slipped inside, too. She hugged Sheila and told her to keep or sell that dress because it was vintage and worth some cash. They exchanged phone numbers, and Marlow held her fingers up to her lips at the security officer to keep quiet that she'd been there.

Most of the senator's help didn't like Michelle Ripley, so there was a chance he wouldn't tell.

Another hour later, after the party guests finished dinner and dessert, the crowd moved to a lounge area.

The lighting was smoky and low-lit to make everyone look better as they drank too much. Marlow knew all the tricks and smirked that there wasn't enough dark to keep Royce from looking like a snake.

After dessert, Marlow followed Michelle to the ladies' room. As she'd expected, her mother went in there to throw up all the decadent dinner she'd indulged.

When Marlow slipped back out of the restroom, Royce cornered her before returning to the party. "What are you up to, Mar?" he asked.

She shrugged him off. "I should ask you the same thing."

As she walked away, she switched the memory card out of her camera for a new one. The night was still young, and it didn't look like things would wind down before midnight or later. Marlow continued photographing or videoing guests as Royce seemed to follow her around the party.

It was one in the morning when the last guests left, and Marlow was relieved to pack her equipment. Michelle was the gracious guest of honor, walking everyone to the door or handing out gift bags for attendees.

But as Marlow headed for the door, Royce took her camera bag. "What do you think you're doing, Royce? Give that back." She tried to wrestle it from him, but it was no use.

He unzipped her camera bag and took the memory cards.

"I have to edit those and get them posted."

"Right. Not until I go through them, you don't." He threw the bag at her feet. "You have to earn our trust back, Marlow."

She zipped her bag and pulled it over her shoulder. "That's rich coming from you, Royce. I didn't think you had the word honesty in your vocabulary."

As she headed for the exit, Marlow knew he was watching her go, and for the first time, she had swagger.

Back at the hotel, Marlow pulled the memory cards she'd used all night out of her bra. She would never trust Royce Chatham and figured he would try and take her evidence. It would be like him to confiscate her things to show he had power over her. He might have brute strength, but she was the brains in this operation, and he wouldn't get the drop on her again.

"Fool me once, shame on you," Marlow said as she opened her computer and downloaded everything from the party. She made some quick edits and then posted the event on her social media accounts, including the unflattering pictures of Michelle, Royce, and the guests.

Her mother lost her temper over anyone taking a bad picture of her. But Marlow was ready to play the game. She wrote a heart-felt birthday message to her mother that was a complete lie—then she posted the rest of the pictures. Marlow would use the excuse that she had to get their version of the surprise party out before guests posted their pictures. Her mother believed they controlled the narrative if they were first and Marlow would lean in to that theory.

Royce would see right through it. But Marlow hoped to get on a plane to NOLA before he realized what she'd done.

Chapter Twenty-Nine

Zachary was irritable at the lingering crowds of people still in Maisonville. His day was filled with writing noise violation tickets and towing cars parked illegally. Having to arrest an elderly woman, driving a golf cart under the influence of alcohol, had to be the icing on the cake of his day.

He was still upset over his conversation with Marlow. And by the end of the day, he bent the rules by having someone look up the senator's private address in New Orleans. He didn't feel an ounce of shame over it either.

As soon as his shift ended, he headed for the bridge and called Mrs. Bowers to tell her he wouldn't be home until late.

When he got to the large home, he laughed because it looked like a New Orleans version of a Barbie Dream House, including a third story. The button on the gate was supposed to call the house, but no one answered. He texted and called Marlow twice, but she wouldn't pick up the phone.

He camped in her driveway for an hour before he finally gave up and went back to the boarding house. Mrs. Bowers was out late playing cards, so he ate a sandwich and went to bed early.

Frustrated, he picked up his phone and looked at Marlow's social accounts. It made him feel closer to her, and he wished she would give him a chance to talk about what had happened.

While looking through her old posts, he got a notification that there were new videos. The anger that flew through him when he saw she was at a party made him sit up in the bed. She looked stunning but seemed different in how she spoke to the camera. And it wasn't because she was acting professionally. He'd already watched enough of her videos to know.

Marlow had filmed a surprise birthday party for Senator Ripley. But the way she said *surprise* made him question its validity.

There were a lot of people there, and the senator seemed to talk more freely than usual. He figured she'd been drinking and then tried to remember if he'd ever seen an unflattering picture of the senator. Hadn't Marlow mentioned how vain she was and how she didn't like candid shots?

If Marlow was working for her mother again, then she was going to catch hell over some of these pictures.

The camera panned the room, and there was Marlow's ex, standing next to her mother. There was something in his stance that made Zachary suspicious, but he couldn't put his finger on it.

Senator Michelle Ripley would not be happy over the way she looked in this post. Didn't Marlow say there wasn't anyone there she could trust?

Marlow was an incredible photographer. Looking at those photos, she was clearly sending a different kind of message. Perhaps it was a message that she didn't want to work with them anymore. But whatever it was, when the Senator found out, there would be trouble.

IT WAS seven in the morning when Marlow heard banging on her hotel room door. At first, she'd thought she'd overslept. The idea of running through an airport with everyone staring at her made her sick to her stomach. But her flight wasn't until five, and she'd paid for a late checkout.

The banging didn't stop, and she stumbled into the bathroom to find a robe to put on. When she opened the door, Royce barged inside. "Get out, Royce."

"Have you any idea what you have done?" He was angry, really angry. Marlow had never seen him that mad before.

"I did my job. I went to a surprise party for my mother and took pictures and videos all night."

He crowded her against the wall, and she was pretty sure he was snarling. That was when her door pushed open, and Zachary Bowman stormed over to Royce like he was about to end him.

Marlow blinked and then blinked again. She had to be dreaming, right?

When Zachary pulled Royce up on his tiptoes by his jacket collar, she realized this wasn't a dream. "If you ever put your hands on her again, I will break them off. Do you understand me?" He said, and she was a little afraid of that side of Zachary. Not that he would ever hurt her, but the fact that he could be so menacing was a surprise. It was sexy on him.

But Royce was terrified. *She liked that, too.* "Get out," Zachary ordered, and Royce practically ran out of her room.

When Zachary turned toward Marlow, his face softened. "Are you okay? Did he hurt you?"

His large hands were on her face as he stared into her eyes. Then he ran his hands over her arms and body to ensure she wasn't injured. His warmth surrounded her, and she almost leaned in.

He was more handsome than she'd remembered. But then she thought of the mean things he'd said about her, and she had to be strong. She stepped out of his circle of heat and took a deep breath. "What are you doing here, Zachary?"

"Really? That's the thanks I get from saving you from that sleaze you almost married?"

Marlow's hands waved around as she spoke. "I didn't need saving. I can handle Royce."

"I saw how you were handling him. He was all over you when I walked in." That wasn't what he wanted to say to her, and he needed to get control.

But Marlow was fighting mad. "I've handled him before."

Zachary smiled at her. "Yes, you have, Kung Fu Barbie."

Marlow smiled back at him and then rolled her eyes. She was angry at Zachary. But at that moment, Marlow was a little bit happy to see him. Deep breaths, she mentally told herself. "I'm still not talking to you, Zachary Bowman. And how did you know where to find me?"

She crossed her arms over her chest.

"I went to your house in New Orleans last night to talk with you and when I got home and told Mrs. Bowers, she showed me your location on her phone."

Marlow had forgotten about sharing her location with sweet Mrs. Bowers at the lake front that day. And she couldn't believe Zachary had *gone to her house in New Orleans?* But at the moment she was focused on her anger. "I heard you say we aren't friends and there would never be anything between us." The hurt in her eyes was much deeper now, and it pained Zachary that he'd hurt her even unintentionally.

He wanted to pull her into his arms, but he needed to set the record straight. He needed to feel her close to him, but it was time to tell her the truth.

"You aren't the only one with a messy past, Marlow." Zachary took a deep breath as if he needed it to clear his head. "Those things you heard, the things I said, weren't about you. They were about my ex-girlfriend. You overheard me talking to her."

"What?"

He nodded. "Chloe Patterson. She was a reporter in my hometown. Our breakup was public, not as public as yours, but still a big deal in my life. She called to tell me she was taking a job in New Orleans and wanted to get back together."

Marlow had never considered he'd had a bad breakup or, honestly, any negative relationships in his life. But Zachary Bowman didn't freely talk about himself or share his past.

She leaned against the desk in her room. Leonie Ford was interested in Zachary, too. He had women practically lining up for him, but what did he want?

It took Marlow a minute, staring at his expressionless face had her confused. "Are you considering getting back together with her?"

Zachary stepped closer. "Are you considering getting back together with Royce Chatham?"

His comment sent her into a frenzy like he knew it would. She raised her voice and waved her arms as she spoke. "How could you ask me that? Especially when you walked in on him attempting to intimidate me. Of course, I'm not considering getting back with him. I wish I'd never met him. He's the worst-"

Marlow's words were cut off as Zachary crowded into her space. His glorious body heat surrounded her, and she could barely breathe. When she looked up, he kissed her like he meant it. He pulled her body against his and ran a hand through her long hair. One large hand was under her shirt, stroking her back like he couldn't get enough.

Her whole body responded to him, as he kissed her temple and then dipped his head to kiss below her ear and then neck. She thought this moment would never happen and she'd wanted him so badly.

But this kiss was worth the wait.

Zachary's body was all muscle and hard ridges and when he lifted her, she wrapped her legs around him. It was the hottest kiss Marlow had ever had, and she wasn't sure she could get enough of Zachary.

Time stood still as their excitement became incendiary. His strong hands held her close, and she felt surrounded by the scent of sandalwood and him.

Marlow could barely catch her breath, and when Zachary slowly pulled back, he was panting too. The smile he gave her melted her insides as he sat down on the bed with her still in his lap.

He looked at her and she understood things weren't going any further, and she'd wanted it to more than her next breath. "Zachary?" she said, and her breathy voice surprised her. It was a plea, and she didn't do that.

"I know," he responded. "I've wanted to do that for longer than you know."

Marlow could feel the 'but' coming and nuzzled her head under his chin to enjoy the closeness for a second longer.

Zachary kissed the top of her head. "But we need to talk about what's happening here in DC."

The last thing she wanted to do was talk about her job or her mother. It was something she had to do, and she couldn't explain it to him.

He would interfere or get hurt in the process if he knew what she was really doing. How could she tell him and keep the closeness between them?

"Please," he said and gently lifted her chin so she would look into his eyes. Why was it so hard to resist telling him the truth about things?

"Do we have to talk about this place?" If she could buy herself a little more time. "Besides, you have a story to tell me first."

The knowing grin he gave her calmed her nerves, but she still wasn't sure he would tell her what she wanted to know unless she pressed him. "You've had a front-row seat at my wedding disaster. And you've met my mother. It would be nice to know that I'm not the only one."

"You're not the only one, Marlow." Zachary looked around. "What time does your flight leave? Perhaps you should get dressed, pack, and we could get some coffee and talk?"

Caffeine always made things better, and it had become their thing easily. But climbing off Zachary's lap would take some determination because Marlow had wanted Zachary longer than she could admit.

Ever so slowly, Marlow leaned in and kissed him sweetly on the corner of his mouth. "Coffee sounds great, but are you sure?"

The way his body reacted toward hers told her that he wanted to do so much more than coffee. But time was not on their side.

If Royce had already shown up, her mother would be next, and the last thing she wanted was a confrontation with Michelle in front of him.

Still, Zachary gave her another warm, lingering kiss, and it was clear one of them would have to move toward getting out of there before things went precisely where they wanted them to go.

"It'll take me a few minutes to jump in the shower," she said, wishing she could ask him to join her.

"Okay," he replied, and she swore his voice sounded deeper. How he looked at her told her that he was struggling to follow through with his plan, too.

"Let me grab my clothes, and I'll be right back," she said, slowly climbing off his lap, making sure to rub her body against his again.

Zachary stood as soon as she did and gave her a wolfish grin. "You are the most tempting woman I've ever met," he said. "Go shower, and I'll pack the rest of your things."

Smiling the entire way to the bathroom, Marlow couldn't believe Zachary Bowman was in her hotel room in DC. He'd come for her, and no one had ever done that in her life. It changed things between them in every way. Did he already know that? Could she admit that to him?

Chapter Thirty

Zachary had been to Washington, DC, as a kid. His mother and father made time to go on vacation every summer, sometimes just going to a cabin at the lake or a condo at the beach. Other times, they took bigger vacations like the Grand Canyon, Glacier National Park, or tours in the nation's capital. Still, he was fascinated to have Marlow show him her favorite places.

Before they headed out, he changed his return flight so they could be together. Then Marlow stowed her luggage with the hotel bellman.

Grabbing coffee was first on her list, and they headed to Peregrine Espresso. There was a line, and she assured him it was worth the wait. They sat outside with their coffees and pastries, but when someone from her mother's office walked by, Marlow hid behind Zachary.

They weren't going to talk if she was worried about being seen together. So, they walked until she found an out-of-the-way bench. She admitted that she didn't like politics, but she did enjoy the historic background of the area. Marlow was an artist at heart and saw things through a different lens. She showed him those extraordinary spots.

They held hands while walking around the Washington National Cathedral. She told him it was the highest point in the city and she had tons of pictures she'd taken there. They didn't have the time to take a guided tower tour, but she pointed out stained glass and gargoyles, promising to show him her close-up photographs. Zachary liked the cathedral, but he loved how excited Marlow was to share it with him more.

They walked past monuments but didn't get close because of tourists, then ended up at the Watergate Hotel rooftop bar appropriately named, Top of the Gate. From the bar, they could see Rosslyn, the Potomac, and Georgetown.

By the time they stopped by her hotel to grab her luggage and then took a taxi to the airport, they had a little more than an hour before their boarding time.

Marlow showed him the perks of travel credit cards and frequent traveler experience when she led him to a private corridor and elevator.

There was a cozy lounge with comfortable seating, snacks, and a bar. "This is close to our gate and more private, so we can hang out and talk," she said.

Zachary pulled her chair next to his. "I like privacy."

One beer and a cocktail later, Zachary told her that Chloe Patterson wasn't just his ex-girlfriend, but they had been engaged to be married.

"I would've never guessed." Marlow couldn't imagine a woman who was good enough for Zachary Bowman. "How long were you together?"

He explained how they met in college and got back together when she moved to St. Marksville.

"So, this is a pattern for her? Moving to town and getting you back?"

He had never thought of it that way and laughed at how sharp Marlow was over the situation. "I guess so. I was surprised when she showed up in St. Marksville, but we fell into place as if we hadn't skipped a beat."

"Would you say it was true love?" Marlow was admittedly fascinated with the idea of lifetime commitment.

"I cared about her and was comfortable. But in the end, I questioned whether it could have ever grown into what my parents had."

Marlow told him she'd never seen love like that up close and would love to hear the story of his parents even more than his story with his ex.

Later, Zachary would tell her that was the moment he completely fell for her. "I'll tell you about my folks on the plane," he promised. "As for Chloe, she liked the idea of marriage, but she will always expect to come first before anyone else in her life."

Marlow considered how much that sounded like her mother.

"After we were engaged, I found out why she'd broken up with me after I graduated college."

Marlow leaned in and whispered, "She met someone else who could get her what she wanted?"

Drinking the rest of his beer, Zachary looked at Marlow. "Are you Psychic Barbie now?" he asked.

Marlow leaned forward and kissed Zachary. He was a good man and didn't have any selfish people in his life. "I wish. It sure would have saved me a lot of trouble."

Zachary lowered his eyes at this beautiful woman. He couldn't understand anyone not finding her completely lovable or fascinating. "Well, you guessed right. Chloe met someone whose father ran one of the big networks. She used him to get her foot in the door, but when that didn't work out, she decided she would use me for a while."

Marlow knew love from Zachary Bowman would be a gift.

He explained how Chloe was a remote reporter and had done a great job promoting the town and writing positive stories.

Marlow added details for him again. "But she wanted what she wanted and would sell her own kidney to get it, right?"

Zachary laughed because she wasn't wrong. He opened his bottle of water and offered her a drink first. It wasn't that big of a gesture, but it touched her heart. Zachary was a sweet man. "I promise I won't interrupt again," she said, and he kissed her that time.

"You can say anything you want, Marlow." And he meant it.

The determined look in his eyes told Marlow he was about to tell her the crux of what happened. "Chloe wanted to be a news anchor before she was thirty and felt like it wasn't happening fast enough. She would throw a fit over how she was more popular at the station and more attractive than the woman who had been there for years. I tried to tell her that her time would come. She needed to be respectful because one day she would be the older anchor, and she wouldn't appreciate a new younger reporter taking her spot."

While he drank some water, Marlow took a moment to admire the thoughtful man before her. He wore athletic shorts that showed off his muscular legs. Zachary Bowman looked powerful, and she was attracted to him like no one ever before.

"That was our first big argument," he said, and the comment pulled Marlow out of her lust-filled trance.

"A few weeks later, she apologized and asked to go ahead and set a wedding date. It felt like things were on track, but then my father was diagnosed with pulmonary disease."

Marlow reached out and held his hand. "You'd already lost your mom in college."

He nodded. "It was tough to accept that I would lose my hero. He'd coughed for years but refused to give up smoking. It would kill him, and the doctors didn't know how much time he had left. He refused to tell anyone and continued working. I tried to support him and watched as he worked at giving up cigars and cigarettes. He wore a nicotine patch and tested using a vape device. But nothing helped. It was too late.

"When I told Chloe that I couldn't celebrate with wedding showers or a big wedding while my father was dying, she lied and said she understood. But behind my back, she told everyone that I postponed things indefinitely so they would all feel sorry for her."

Marlow looked mad when she shook her head. "Like you were doing something to her instead of something for your father."

"Exactly," he said. How had he ever thought Marlow was anything like Chloe? "Chloe was gifted at playing the victim, and since my father insisted no one find out that he was ill, she had all of her coworkers and friends believing I was abandoning her or too busy with work to care for her.

"She walked around town like a celebrity because she got that promotion to news anchor. The woman who'd been at the station for twenty years was booted back to working Chloe's remote reporting job."

Marlow squeezed his hand tighter. It was clear how hard this was for him to admit.

"I disapproved of her getting that position, but she kept her head high as she continued getting more airtime and building her audience. Suddenly, Chloe was given longer segments every week and began interviewing professionals like lawyers, doctors, and therapists to discuss whatever would get her bigger ratings."

Marlow nodded. As an influencer, she saw others promoting things they didn't like but would make them more popular. "Controversy equals attention," she said and grimaced.

Zachary had spent hours combing over Marlow's social media videos and posts. She promoted her senator mother, but never put anyone down or went low to get noticed.

He kissed her hand as she leaned into him. "She gave me hell for not appreciating what she was bringing to our relationship and how the money she made would help our future. I was truthful with her. I told her I didn't think it was right the way she grilled people once they were in what she called the *hot seat*. But I never discussed it with anyone else. It was between us."

Zachary Bowman was a private person. Marlow could see that from the start.

"No matter what I said or did, whenever we were alone, Chloe ranted about what she didn't have. She wanted to be famous or to have a bigger house or better car. More fans. I hoped it was a phase from all the added pressure at work or even our relationship." He rubbed the stubble on his chin and jaw, and Marlow realized she'd never seen him the least bit scruffy. He was handsome that way, and she wanted to tell him. But she encouraged him to go on.

"I usually caught Chloe's broadcast with other officers during our dinner break. It was a Wednesday night, which meant she would have one of those hard-hitting interviews. Everyone knew that Chloe worked for ratings and asked pressing questions. She had a relationship coach there, and it felt different. She pushed the man to discuss open marriages or whether breakups were inevitable if a person cheats.

"The doctor tried to be professional and diplomatic, but as Chloe bullied him on the air, he finally broke and asked her directly if she was talking about her relationship. She locked eyes with the doctor and then the camera when she said, yes."

Marlow put her hands over her mouth, shocked to hear what had happened to Zachary.

"When her producer quickly went to commercial, it was obvious that Chloe had been unfaithful. Everyone knew it. I paid for my dinner and headed straight to the station.

"Chloe's boss, the station manager, and her coworker apologized when I walked in. She'd slept with them both. Chloe didn't apologize, and I didn't care to hear the words from her. I asked for the keys to my house back and gave her until the end of the week to stop by and get her things."

Marlow jumped up and hugged Zachary for the longest time. He'd been embarrassed on the evening news in his home town and in a million years, she would have never thought he'd been through anything similar to her.

Of course, he'd handled it better, but still, they'd been through similar humiliation. "I'm so sorry, Zachary," she said as she kissed the top of his head, nose, and lips. A few people in the lounge were watching them, and Marlow sat back in her chair. "Sorry," she whispered.

Zachary smiled at Marlow's pink cheeks. They'd been in their bubble for thirty minutes or more and hadn't realized more people were in the lounge now.

"I didn't speak to Chloe again for a long time. My father hung on for eight more months. I told him before he passed away that I wasn't going to stay in St. Marksville after losing both of my parents there.

"Olivia and her son were in town briefly and talked about Maisonville. I thought it sounded perfect for my fishing habit."

Marlow understood what he wasn't saying. The ghosts of his past were haunting him in that town, and he needed to get away just like her.

"After my dad passed away, Chloe started coming around and used my job as a reason to see me. She would set up an interview with a group of officers, requesting that I join them. Then my father's sisters, who he hadn't spoken to in years because they were rude to my mother and didn't come to the funeral, moved back to town. They would show up at the house under the pretense of helping me with donating some of my parents' things but wanted me to give them the house. Of course, Chloe met the aunts, and together, they all would show up wherever I had dinner or at church, aiming to get me to spend time with them."

Marlow shook her head. "Wow. Talk about pressure."

"I work well under pressure, Miss Ripley." He gave her that grin that made her clothes want to melt off.

He seemed lighter now as he told her the rest. "I put my parents' house up for sale and my townhome. I got the job in Maisonville lined up and, within a couple of weeks, sold the houses and moved. I hadn't talked to Chloe again until you overheard me that night."

Marlow's eyes watered as she thought back to the other night. She had to stop running, and this was her lesson to make that change. Marlow was going to tell that to Zachary but before she could do it, the lounge manager walked over and asked if they were Marlow Ripley and Zachary Bowman.

"I'm afraid your airline has already boarded, and they are calling your names before they close the doors," the manager said.

Marlow and Zachary thanked him and then, much to her horror, they ran through the airport to make their flight.

Chapter Thirty-One

The flight to New Orleans was one of the best Marlow ever had. She and Zachary held hands, which to someone else may seem trivial but to her felt significant. They talked mostly about little things, like how she didn't know how to cook but wanted to learn. He explained how he loved to fish but also enjoyed being outside in nature. It felt personal, even though it was simple, small, glimpses into each other's interests.

At one point, Zachary leaned in and whispered to her, "The small things aren't really small."

Marlow had always felt that way and leaned up to kiss him sweetly.

The way they had met was fast and furious, and living in the boarding house seemed to rush them through the usual way people got to know each other.

But this trip from Washington, DC cemented a bond that neither of them had with anyone else.

Zachary had his truck at the airport and gave Marlow a ride back to her house in the city. "Are you sure you don't want to come back to the boarding house with me?" he asked. It didn't feel right leaving her in the city.

Marlow leaned over in the seat and kissed his cheek. "I would love to go back to Maisonville with you. But I have some things I have to take care of first."

She still hadn't admitted that her mother made threats against him and implied threats against everyone else Marlow was friends with in Maisonville. It would take more time before she was completely free of her mother and her abusive power. But Marlow was ready to do whatever it took to protect everyone.

The large house didn't look like it fit Marlow anymore, and Zachary didn't want to leave her alone. He walked around the truck to open her door and carried her luggage to the front door.

Did he know how much she'd fallen for him?

They stood at the front door of her house, staring into each other's eyes without saying a word. Finally, Zachary ran a hand through her beautiful blond hair. He kissed the top of her head, and when she looked up at him, he warmly kissed her lips.

His hands were now wrapped in her hair at the nape of her neck, and the kiss became fevered. It was going to make him leaving so much more complicated. But as they both leaned into the moment, the front door swung open, and Senator Ripley stood there with her hands on her hips.

Instinctively, Zachary pushed Marlow behind his body before it registered who was there. Michelle Ripley didn't like that one bit and glared at him and then her daughter.

"What exactly do you two think you are doing out here where anyone could see you."

That seemed like an odd remark since there was a locked

iron gate and a tall concrete wall surrounding them.

Marlow then moved to put her body in front of Zachary. "Officer Bowman was giving me a ride from the airport, Mother. What are you doing here?"

The senator, who always controlled her reactions, didn't seem to have the strength tonight. She rolled her eyes and shrugged dramatically, mocking Marlow. "Officer Bowman was giving me a ride, I could see what he was doing. And maybe you have forgotten this is my house?"

Zachary wanted to defend Marlow from her mother, but when he began to speak, Marlow gave him a warning look.

"Don't play innocent with me, little lady. You know exactly why I am here. We will discuss that video you posted and so much more. Good night, Officer Bowman," Michelle said, dismissing him.

When she opened the door wider for Marlow to walk through, Zachary grabbed Marlow's hand. "You can still go with me."

Marlow turned and hugged him. "Don't worry about me. I need to make sure you're safe," she whispered and then told him goodbye as Michelle impatiently tapped her foot.

He watched Marlow walk away with the senator right behind her. Michelle turned just for a second to glare at him again before she slammed the door.

Leaving Marlow with the senator felt wrong, just like that first night they'd met. He knew it in his gut. *How could he walk away?*

He sat in his car for fifteen minutes, battling about what to do. When the front porch light went off, he got a text from Marlow that said she would call him in the morning.

It was going to be a long night, but he pulled out of their uptown neighborhood thinking of her words. *I need to make sure you're safe.* What in the world did that mean? Safe from what?

Inside the house, Marlow walked into an ambush of Royce Chatham and her mother. They had printed still pictures of the video Marlow posted and went through each one, telling her what was wrong with it. "Look at the way my eyes look in that photo." Michelle wouldn't sit down. She was furious and getting more worked up with every step she took. "You have been in this political world your entire life and know I must play both sides. How dare you post a video without clearing it with Royce. Certain groups support me that won't like that I'm friends with anti-weapons lobbyists. This can't be undone."

Royce tried to calm Michelle down and talked to her intimately where Marlow couldn't hear him. Watching them together made the hair on Marlow's arms stand up.

But Marlow knew what she was doing and was ready to defend the online video. She sat on the sofa with her legs crisscrossed and wore a calm demeanor. It was what being close to Zachary had done for her. She may not be able to control what others do or say to her, but she would control her reaction. She cleared her throat so they would both look at her. "First, this is my world, and I'm an expert. No one would think twice about that picture of you, Mother. It's more about the fact that so many people came out to celebrate you. It looks like you have a ton of friends that would pull together to surprise you, which isn't an easy thing."

Her mother lowered her eyes, and then Royce pulled out the next photo. "Why would you use this unflattering one where she's eating that huge steak? Or this one where she's eating a giant piece of cake? Neither are flattering, and you know how she feels about pictures of her eating."

"Thanks a lot, Royce," her mother said as she grabbed the photos and scrutinized how she looked even more. Marlow knew her mother had a distorted view of her own body. It took years to figure out that it was part of her mother's eating disorder that she projected onto Marlow. Michelle had redirected that self-hatred toward Marlow since she was a teenager.

"That is a picture of the Senator, a real woman, who is eating dinner with seventy-five of her friends. And because it was a video and not stills, that second one doesn't portray the whole picture. The video shows the stunning cake her friends and coworkers surprised her with on her special day. You two are acting like maniacs."

Michelle looked exhausted, and Marlow knew that she needed weekends to recharge. As her mother got older, it was getting harder for her to continue acting like she was twenty-five and had endless energy.

"I thought you had an event tomorrow afternoon in DC?" Marlow asked, wanting to change the subject.

"Royce was able to change it to next weekend. I'm speaking to a women's group in the city tomorrow, instead. I expect you there Marlow making up for this nonsense. This is an election year, and I don't need any negative press."

Yawning, Marlow could see every line on her mother's ordinarily over-botoxed face. "I can only capture what's there, Michelle," she said, knowing that her mother hated when she used her first name in private.

"Don't think I don't know what you are up to," Michelle said, pointing her finger at Marlow.

Her mother had no idea, and Marlow planned to keep it that way until this was done. "I don't know what you're talking about, but you need to get some rest and possibly some fillers before tomorrow afternoon. Everyone will know if I touch up your photos when event members will have their posts out there, too."

There was no hiding the cruel insult, and the way her mother looked was almost too much for Marlow. She didn't like her mother, but it wasn't in Marlow's nature to hurt her or anyone else. The woman already tortured her body enough, struggling to continue wearing the same size she wore in high school. But this was an end to a means, and Marlow would have to keep reminding herself of that until it was over. Her mother, the senator, would never let her go and had never once held back when it came to hurting Marlow.

Michelle looked at Royce and then stalked off toward her bedroom.

As soon as she was gone, Royce whirled around to have a go at Marlow, too. "Why the hell would you say that to her? She works tirelessly for this family and her constituents. Would it kill you to do the job you are overpaid to do?"

Marlow didn't have to take his abuse and stood to face him. "Do you think I care how you feel about it, Royce? The fact that you thought coming here to lecture me was a good idea shows you're an idiot."

His entire face was red as he clenched his jaw. "I don't trust you, Marlow. Not even a little bit. I'll be keeping my eyes on you."

"You, Royce Chatham III, the biggest liar I've ever known, don't trust me? You should be a comedian," she smirked and began to walk away. He'd played Marlow for two years, and she would never forgive him. But she could feel his eyes on her and turned to look over her shoulder at him. He shouldn't have been looking at her body that way, "Enjoy the view, jerk," she said and then slammed her bedroom door behind her.

Marlow locked the door and lodged a chair underneath it.

She didn't feel safe in her own home anymore, and although Royce had never done anything to hurt her physically, she'd never openly challenged him or her mother's career.

Marlow might have fooled them for now, but liars didn't trust anyone, and she needed to watch her back.

She'd planned the takedown of her mother and Royce after reading all those comments from her online friends. But knowing she had the support in Maisonville gave her the strength to follow through with it.

Mentally, she had a check list, and going through it again in her head gave her peace. Securing all her money into a personal account away from Michelle's reach was done. Learning how the online business paid her and when helped her budget accordingly. Plus her new photography sales gave her extra income, and she wouldn't have to depend on anyone else for money again.

Marlow smiled as she thought about firing her mother's attorneys and accounting firm because it had been her most decisive move. They had managed everything to her mother's benefit from the beginning, and Marlow should have realized that sooner. But she'd been young and scared before, and they all took advantage of her.

No one was going to exploit her again.

Her mother would figure out soon enough that she had no power over Marlow. But afterward, Michelle would hold nothing back as she went after her daughter. Marlow had been an easy target for years.

Money was one thing, but getting away from Michelle's subjugation was another, and it would take everything Marlow had in her to make it happen.

Chapter Thirty-Two

Marlow woke up wishing she was in Maisonville with Zachary. It was his day off. She had to remind herself this was temporary so they could be together in the future.

Did she have a future with Zachary Bowman?

They had shared a lot, but she still needed to tell him her biggest secret, the one that bound her to her mother. But that was something she couldn't share over the phone. She texted him Sunday morning letting him know she was okay and had to work.

Instead of sending a message, he called her. "Marlow, you don't have to work for her," Zachary said. And she couldn't explain her plan to him just yet.

"Why do you think you have to protect me? From what? Her? She doesn't have any power over me. Come home."

Marlow felt confident and knew what she had to do, but when he told her to come home, it hurt her heart. "It's fine. I'm fine. I will be with Michelle at a women's event most of the day. Try and get some rest, Officer Bowman. I'll message you when I get home tonight."

When they said their goodbyes and hung up, Marlow held her phone next to her heart. She couldn't wait to explore her feelings with Zachary, but work had to come first.

He was a wonderful person inside and out, but she'd made some mistakes in her life. Mistakes that he might not be okay with. Whether they were together or not, she wouldn't let her mother interfere with his life or livelihood. And what she was doing here with her mother would ensure he and all her friends were safe from the wrath of Senator Ripley.

Quickly showering so she could spend extra time on her hair and makeup, Marlow meticulously dressed for the event. Part of her plan was to undermine her mother's confidence. Michelle had always treated Marlow like she was inferior by criticizing her appearance. It was time for Marlow to prove she could command a room when she walked into it, too.

As she flat ironed her long hair smooth, she accepted that this was all such a shallow world. She didn't want to make anyone feel inferior to her. Looks and beauty were in the eye of the beholder, and Marlow found beauty in so many things.

Still, this was the way of her mother's world. And Royce would be watching so she couldn't falter.

Pulling together her equipment, Marlow was prepared a few minutes early. Holding her head high, she walked into the outer room, ready to go.

Royce was waiting and didn't hide that he was checking out her body. His eyes slowly roamed down to her hips and back up, making her shiver. The pink floral dress wrapped around her curves and accentuated her tiny waist. It was an inch too short, but she had great legs, and he stared at them too.

Last night, when she'd antagonized him for looking at her,

she hadn't considered it sexual. After all, he hadn't ever seemed into her that way. But the way he leered now was carnal and made her skin crawl.

When her mother came out of her room wearing a pantsuit, she saw how Royce stared at Marlow and scowled. Without saying a word, she went back inside, slamming the door behind her.

It was another half hour before Michelle returned wearing a form-fitting little black and white dress. It was clear the competition was on as usual.

Who competed with their own daughter? It was sick. One of Marlow's high school friends had told her that years ago, and it was the first time Marlow had accepted it was true.

Until then, Marlow had been proud to look so much like her mother, who she'd always thought was a beautiful woman. The fact that she wanted to best Marlow at every turn confused her from the time she'd turned fifteen and understood what was happening.

Putting on a happy face, she pretended not to notice the open jealously. Royce walked over and complimented Michelle for several minutes, pumping her up for the event.

When Michelle believed him, her game face was on, and they were ready to go. Royce had ordered a car service to pick them up and rode over to the event center with them.

When the driver exited and opened Marlow's door, Royce pushed past her and told him to get back into the car. He then held the door for Marlow and then Michelle.

It was an odd moment. Marlow couldn't believe she'd ever wanted anything to do with him. And when he insisted on helping carry in her equipment, she decided he was taking the act a bit too far. She snatched her camera out of his hands.

"This is for women, Royce. Leave now," Marlow said, locking eyes with him. Michelle nodded, and the sad look on his face, like he'd been rejected, made her smirk.

She and Michelle headed into the large conference room with all eyes on them. Michelle stepped forward and smiled at the large group, and every woman in the room stood up and clapped for her.

It was still impressive how many people believed in and supported her mother. Michelle Ripley had made that career for herself without any help. If she would just let Marlow live her own life and stop trying to hurt her, then Marlow would walk away and leave things as they were. But as her mother snapped for her to get her attention, Marlow was reminded again that things would not change on their own.

She set up her cameras and lighting as her mother spoke to the event coordinator who wanted to conduct a Q&A segment at the end. One of her assistants had set this up, and Michelle wasn't so sure about answering questions that she hadn't looked over yet. The woman running the event was persuasive, and finally, Michelle agreed.

Her speech was about women in politics and the difference they could make by using their voices for change. It was a moving talk that Marlow had heard before, but it still brought the crowd to their feet multiple times in approval.

But when the Q & A part of the day began, the first audience member asked about Michelle's stance on the Second Amendment.

Michelle did that side-step dance she'd perfected, but the woman pushed back harder. "Those recent videos showed you dining with known gun control lobbyists, and it looks like you are pandering to both sides for votes," she said.

Suddenly, the event was no longer the Sunday Luncheon

atmosphere it had been originally. Half the women were for and the other half against gun control, and the arguing began to take over.

It was everything Michelle worried would happen and exactly what Marlow hoped for.

They left the event quickly, and Michelle let Marlow have it in the car. She threw her purse down and the program from the event. "I told you that there would be hell to pay. That wasn't a women's luncheon. It was an ambush, and mark my words, it was only the beginning."

Michelle was on her phone the rest of the drive home, and when they pulled up, Royce met them at the car. Inside the house, Michelle ranted more about the event and how single-minded most voters were. "Who do they think they are yelling at me? It's always what have you done for me lately, Michelle. They never remember all the good I've done representing the state. Look at my record. I'm a fantastic Senator," she yelled and paced the room.

"Give me everything you took from today," Royce demanded Marlow.

She'd considered keeping some of the video cards back like she did at the birthday party. But this event was more to show her mother that she didn't have the omnipotent power she thought.

Marlow dipped her hand inside her bag and handed the video to Royce. The daggers in Michelle's eyes got her attention, though. "Don't even think about posting anything from that event. You should understand by now that if I go down, then so do you. We are a team, and as far as the rest of the world knows, you have supported me all along. You make me look bad, and your audience will drop you overnight."

Shoving past Marlow, Michelle went into her bedroom.

When Royce started to say something, Marlow held up her hand. "Don't," she said and then turned toward her room.

She needed to hear Zachary's voice and try to reclaim some of who she was without her senator mother.

He picked up immediately. "Hello, Marlow?"

She took a deep breath the moment she heard his voice. "Hey," was all she said.

"I was thinking of driving into the city. Want to come have a cup of coffee with me?"

More than he could possibly know. "Yes."

"I'm walking out the door now and will be there in forty minutes," he said, but he didn't like how she sounded on the other end. "Are you okay?"

"Yes. Just need a friendly face and a few minutes with someone who isn't in politics."

He wanted to tell her that he needed more than a few minutes of her time, but Marlow hurried off the phone, saying she needed to get dressed.

The feeling in the pit of his stomach made him drive faster than usual. He'd been unsettled all day, and the tone of her voice told him he had good reason. As soon as he walked into the Starbucks on Magazine Street and saw her blue eyes locked onto him, the crowd disappeared.

She usually drew his attention, but the way she made him forget anyone else was around was a gift. He wrapped her in his arms and inhaled the coconut and vanilla scent he associated with her. "Everything okay?" he asked, not sure if she would tell him.

"It is now," she said on an exhale.

He bought them coffee and a pastry to split, and they found a spot in the furthest back corner where they could talk privately.

Their chairs touched as well as their legs, and Marlow couldn't understand how another person could give her so much calm. "How was your day?" she asked as if they weren't going to discuss what was wrong.

"Slow and easy like most of my Sundays off. I took the boat out for a few hours and then looked at two houses."

"Did you decide on one?"

Decisions weren't usually tricky for Zachary, but he couldn't decide on a house. "I think I want your opinion."

"You would trust me to help you pick out a home? That's some friendship." She sipped her coffee and looked out toward the street.

He gently turned her chin toward him so he could look into her eyes. "You know this is more than friendship, right, Marlow?"

The almost imperceptible nod was enough for him. There was no reason to label what they were building between them. He just needed her to know how he felt.

He braided his fingers with hers, and she smiled. A lot was going on in that beautiful head of hers, and he hoped she was ready to share it with him. "Are you going to tell me what's going on with your job and your mother?"

She looked past him out the window again. "Is someone coming to meet us, or did something happen today that upset you?"

Marlow shrugged. "We had a women's luncheon that didn't go as well as expected. Michelle blamed me and made some of her usual threats."

"She threatened you?"

Marlow smiled, but it didn't reach her eyes. She'd already said too much. "Don't worry, I can handle it. She's a perfectionist, and if every single event doesn't go perfectly, then she freaks out a little. Royce is probably catching the worst of it right now."

"Royce Chatham is at your house?"

She forgot that he didn't know Royce was there. "He's the one that makes her schedule. It isn't a big deal."

The look on his face told her that it was a big deal. "How can you say that? Your own mother is threatening you, Marlow. And after you broke up with that man, she brings him to your house?"

Avoiding his face, Marlow ran her finger through some spilled sugar on the table. "He's her handler. And I can handle him." It had been a tough day, and she worried that maybe she couldn't handle either of them.

Her mother held what happened to Marlow in college over her. However, this was the first time Marlow had anyone that Michelle could use against her. She felt vulnerable and quite scared for Zachary.

She couldn't talk about this now and needed to change the subject. "So, what do you think Leonie Ford will do when you finally buy a house, and she no longer has a reason to call or see you?"

The way his cheeks turned pink made her smile. Zachary Bowman was a manly man, but he still could get embarrassed. That was rare.

"I don't know what you mean. She's just my real estate agent." He finished his coffee and went to throw away his disposable cup.

She'd successfully distracted him and was ready for the banter he would surely bring. But as he walked back over toward her and she admired his swagger, a lean, attractive woman stepped in front of him.

"Zachary?"

The surprised look on his face made Marlow look at the woman harder.

"Chloe."

Chapter Thirty-Three

Marlow stood there staring at the attractive woman. She had her hand possessively on Zachary's shoulder and gave him the best pouty look Marlow had ever seen. *That was his ex?*

Just when she thought her life couldn't get any more complicated, the universe proved to her that there was always more.

Zachary stepped away from the woman's grasp, and Marlow stood up, giving him a considerate smile. This wasn't his fault, but he had something he needed to take care of, and it had nothing to do with her.

She smiled at Chloe. "Hi, I'm Marlow Ripley. You must be Chloe Patterson?"

Chloe instantly flashed her over-whitened teeth and what she considered her superstar smile. "Why, yes. You know me from television?"

The incredulous look on Marlow's face hadn't given Chloe a clue. "Um, no. Zachary has told me all about you. You know, the way you used him when your college meal ticket didn't pan out and then when you slept with half your coworkers to get the anchor position. How you humiliated yourself and him on the evening news."

"I beg your pardon?" Chloe held her hand to her chest and gave an award-winning appearance of being insulted. Her eyes watered, and she'd acted as if none of that were true.

Zachary grabbed Marlow's arm and pulled her out the side door of the coffee shop as she yelled, "Nice to meet you, Chloe."

He didn't stop until they were beside Marlow's Bronco. "What was that?" he asked, surprised over Marlow's behavior.

"What? Too much?"

Zachary laughed as he cornered her against the side of her vehicle. His body pressed up against hers. "I guess you no longer have a problem saying what you mean."

Marlow tried to catch her breath as his scent surrounded her. "Apparently, when it's to protect someone else, I'm unstoppable."

The warm kiss he gave her jumbled her thoughts for a moment. When he pulled back, she looked up at him, confused. "Wait. I thought you were mad."

"Not mad. At a loss for words, maybe." Zachary gave Marlow that boyish grin that made mortal women follow him all over the place, and she bit her bottom lip.

"You need to go in there and talk to her. Don't you?"

Zachary shook his head no and then looked back through the windows where Chloe stood watching them. He didn't like it. "This doesn't feel right."

Marlow searched his eyes. She wasn't sure what he meant by that comment, and her breath hitched as she asked, "Kissing me out here when she's in there?"

Without a word, he pulled Marlow in for another kiss while his hands threaded through her hair to hold her in place against him. He didn't stop until she was completely breathless. When she searched his eyes again, they were full of mischief. She liked that side of him. "Being with you is never wrong. You understand me?"

Marlow couldn't find a response for that, so she leaned up and kissed him sweetly on the chin. It was the sweetest thing he could have said.

When her eyes watered, he kissed her forehead before opening her car door.

Chloe walked outside. "So that's it, Zachary Bowman? You aren't going to talk to me?"

"Not tonight," he said and leaned down to kiss Marlow again. "I'll follow you home."

No one had ever put her first in her entire life. Marlow didn't even know how to feel about it because her body vibrated and her hands trembled over his behavior.

She gave him the gate code to her house and thought about their impending conversation. She needed to tell him the truth about everything that had happened in her past. This time, she could trust someone, and didn't want any of those secrets to come out later and mess this up.

Trying not to think about whether the truth would make him feel differently, Marlow slowly drove toward her house. She didn't want to play this power struggle game with Michelle anymore. Marlow had to find a way to make the senator leave her and her friends alone. But how could she convince her to let Marlow out of this unbreakable contract?

Pulling into the driveway, she waited for the gate to open and watched Zachary pull in behind her. It was a warm, humid night, which was usual for August in New Orleans.

But she needed to talk to him in private, and the only place she could think of was her backyard. He exited his car and was at her car door as she opened it. "Can we talk?"

He nodded as she pulled his hand so he would follow her. The house looked dark, but the motion lights on the side of her house went off as they slipped by.

There was a rectangular pool back there surrounded by brick and ivy growing up and over the stone walls. In the back corner was a stone and metal gazebo in the middle of a rose garden that hadn't been tended in a while.

They carefully navigated around the thorny stems and into the darkened cave-like structure. It was what you might expect in an old New Orleans courtyard with a little mystery and an eerie feel to it.

"Nice place," he said, watching her.

It was the spot she would run to as a kid. After her grandmother passed away, Michelle became cruel and would take out her frustration on her only daughter.

Marlow had slept out there countless times and cried endless tears in there. It was her very own fortress that held every one of her childhood and adult secrets. She'd never invited anyone to see it.

The quarter moon gave enough light so they could see each other but left most everything around them in the shadows. Lifting a bench seat, Marlow pulled out cushions and a blanket to help when the humidity chilled her skin. They sat next to one another like at the coffee shop, but when she turned to face Zachary, he pulled her legs across his lap.

"This has always been my hideaway. Not that it's a tree house or clubhouse like most kids have, but I'm the only one that ever used it."

Zachary admitted, "My dad built me a tree house in the backyard. It wasn't fancy but had things like a bucket on a rope. My mom would send up bologna and cheese sandwiches."

He did have a traditional family and life. It was what she'd always wanted. "My mother never wanted children. She met my father while she was in law school, and according to her, he was a playboy. He had family money and a carefree attitude. She found out she was pregnant after she passed the bar exam."

"His family owns Ripley Shipping?"

"Yes. But I don't know much and have never felt the need to look him up. The last time I saw him, I was five. Michelle said he didn't want to be a father and one day went out to get cigarettes," Marlow rolled her eyes at the cliche.

Zachary's scrunched up his eyebrows, and Marlow leaned forward to ask, "What?"

He shrugged, hoping to avoid telling her what instantly popped into his mind.

"Tell me."

Rubbing his hands over her calves, Zachary reluctantly said, "If he didn't want to be a father, why did he marry your mom? Seems to me that he would have just refused to be a part of any of it."

The childhood hurt of being abandoned by him kept Marlow from considering anything different than what she'd been told. "Well, he never bothered to reach out or come back."

Nodding, Zachary still had questions about her father, but she had another story to tell, and he would wait.

"I don't have any other family. My mother was an only child, and my grandmother passed away. My grandmother was an only child, too. All the women in my family have girls. Correction, they have one girl. It would have been fine if my grandmother hadn't gotten sick. But she came down with advanced Parkinson's disease. Michelle put her in a nursing home close by, but it was difficult having her leave my daily life overnight."

"Your mother was too busy as a lawyer to care for her at home?"

"She'd already started her political career and was on the city council. I didn't understand why we couldn't get help for her so she could stay at home. But Michelle is unconventional."

He'd always thought that about the state senator but wanted to hear what Marlow meant by the comment. "Unconventional, how?"

"When I was younger, I didn't realize how different my life was. I played with other kids my age, and I wasn't the only one whose father wasn't around. I didn't know anyone who only had a mother and a grandmother, especially a mother who rarely came home for dinner or never attended school programs. Thankfully, Gran was here for all of that and kept things normal. But when she went into the nursing home, my mother had to hire babysitters, housekeepers, or nannies because she was too busy to be a mom. She never liked any of them for very long, and I eventually learned not to get attached.

"Gran died when I was twelve, and it was the only time I ever saw my mother cry. She said she didn't know how to raise a child alone and that was the night she told me I ruined her life."

"When you were twelve?"

Marlow looked past him into the dark. "Actually, on my thirteenth birthday." She still felt that in her soul.

"Michelle won the election that year for Senator and took off to Washington, DC. It was the reason Nanny Lena lasted longer than the others."

"Because she wasn't around?"

Marlow nodded. "When she realized I loved Miss Lena and

her family, who took me along on their summer vacation in Maisonville, she fired her."

"I knew you looked comfortable sitting at the lakefront, but I didn't know why."

Her face warmed, thinking about that sweet family. "They took me out on the water and taught me to ski. I'd never been on a boat before. It was the best summer I've ever had."

Pulling her hand up to his lips, he kissed the back of it as he stared into her eyes. He would take her out on his boat anytime she wanted.

"Instead of hiring another nanny, she dragged me to DC with her. I had a tutor for school and barely saw the light of day. She hated me being there almost as much as I hated it. The spring semester, I was allowed to go back to my private school in the city."

Was she saying what he thought she was saying? "You stayed here? In this big house?" He pointed to her house and yard. "Alone?"

"She would come to town every month or so."

"That's a lot of responsibility for a kid."

"It was scary at first. But Michelle told me that I would have to move to DC permanently, if I told anyone. I could fake an email from her and sign her name on school documents where no one ever suspected a thing. People act like having groceries delivered is a new thing, but it isn't. We had an account with a local market uptown, who delivered it to our house. Michelle would call me every couple of days, and it felt normal."

"You know that's not normal, right?"

Marlow laughed. "Of course. Nothing about Senator Michelle Ripley is normal. She'd be offended if you called her that. She says normal is accepting mediocrity. The Ripley women are not common. Misbehaved women rarely make history, and she wanted to be famous."

Zachary bumped his shoulder into hers gently. "She is a high-profile politician."

Marlow needed him to know about Michelle. "And powerful. You don't want to ever underestimate her."

She sounded afraid of her mother, and he didn't like it. "Sounds like there's more to that story?"

They heard rustling in the dark, and then Michelle Ripley stepped into view. The pure indignation on her face was chilling. "Oh, there is plenty more to that story. Right, Marlow?"

Chapter Thirty-Four

Marlow's hand tightened around Zachary's, and he could tell she was nervous or scared of what her mother would say or do.

"Go ahead, Marlow. Tell the austere police officer about those wild nights in high school. Or how about the drugs and alcohol you were arrested for during one of your epic Mardi Gras parties." Michelle's condescending voice sent chills through Marlow.

She stood up in front of Zachary as if to protect him from the news of her bad behavior. "Stop, Mother."

"Oh, now I'm a mother and not Michelle? You don't get to pick and choose what information you share with the good man in my home, Marlow. You want to make me out to be the villain in your poor little rich girl story, but the truth is that you made your own choices."

Zachary didn't know what to say or do in this situation as the two women squared off. He'd always believed family matters were private unless someone got out of hand, but he cared about Marlow. It didn't matter if he knew all of these things about her past. She was still a minor in high school—one without supervision or guidance.

He stood up and put a warm hand on Marlow's back for reassurance. But it wasn't going to help this situation.

"I never said I didn't make mistakes," Marlow's voice quivered as she defended herself. She'd wanted to be the one to tell Zachary about her bad behavior.

"Mistakes? Really? Having to bail you out of jail has become a regular occurrence, young lady. And that isn't counting all the boys I've had to kick out of here or pay off in college, so your reputation didn't ruin your future."

Marlow's voice shook. "Don't," she said.

And the gleam in Michelle Ripley's eyes shone through the darkness. She gave Marlow the meanest smirk, and that was all the warning she needed. Whipping around without hesitation, she stared into Zachary's eyes. "Please leave."

"What?" He couldn't believe what she was saying.

"Please, Zachary. I don't-,"

Michelle laughed, and it almost didn't sound natural. "She doesn't want you to stay because she knows I'm going to tell you how in college things got so much worse. Right, Marlow?"

"Please, don't. I'm begging you, Michelle, please stop."

Zachary tried to calm Marlow down. "It's okay. I'll go." He stepped past the senator and the thorny roses, but Michelle Ripley wasn't done humiliating her daughter.

Marlow walked behind him, attempting to hurry him along as her mother cackled. "She's a pretty young thing, isn't she, Officer Bowman? All the boys in college thought so, too."

As Marlow shoved him past the house toward his car, her mother followed. "Do you watch pornography, Officer Bowman?"

"Pornography?" he asked, turning to look at Marlow. "It's

not what you think," she cried, pushing him into his car so she could shut his door behind him.

"Marlow Ripley was famous online for more than just her social media posts."

Zachary couldn't believe what Michelle was saying, but the look on Marlow's face told him it was true.

He opened his mouth to say something, and Marlow shook her head, "Just go," she cried, and as much as he wanted to stay, he also wanted to go.

Marlow screamed at him to leave now, and he regretfully did what she asked. As he drove toward Maisonville, the entire night felt like something out of his nightmares. Seeing Chloe had moved to the city and closer to him was not good news. Then, watching Michelle tear down Marlow so effortlessly broke his heart. But he didn't know Marlow. All summer Zachary believed she was tough on the outside but a sweetheart at her core. Growing up in the public eye, she had to accept a lot of criticism, but he was sure she was a good person deep down. Could he have been that wrong about her? He could accept a lot of things but was it too much to ask for a little honesty? And now, after hearing the highlights of her misconduct, would Marlow have ever admitted those things to him?

MARLOW WENT to her knees when Zachary's car pulled past the iron gates in her driveway. She'd wanted to be the one to explain everything to him. If she'd just had a few more minutes, then she could have presented it in her own way.

Michelle walked past her to change the gate code manually. When she turned around, Marlow was still on the ground crying.

"The code is now my birthday. Don't give it out again."

Marlow tried to catch her breath. She was devastated by the look in Zachary's eyes when he drove off. He'd never talk to her again.

Michelle had ruined Marlow's chance with the one thing she truly wanted. She hadn't even believed it was true but being with Zachary showed her that love existed. He'd seen it between his parents and experienced it by how they loved him.

Chasing love was a fruitless game, and she didn't want to play anymore. She couldn't go back to Maisonville. And she wouldn't work for Michelle any longer. She was a heartless monster.

"Get up, drama queen. I warned you. I am not one to be trifled with, and you have pushed me for the last time. Do not forget that I hold all your secrets."

Marlow watched as her mother walked up the front steps to go inside the house with her head held high. She was proud of what she'd done. Proud to have brought Marlow to her knees.

There was absolutely zero love between them, and Marlow was done caring about it. It was an impossible endeavor, and she was giving up on ever having a relationship with that awful woman.

Marlow's wedding should have been the final act of betrayal, but this was it. Michelle had proven the only thing that mattered was coming out on top, and it didn't matter who you stood on to get there.

It would take time to find a new place to start over, but Marlow was leaving this place and never looking back. She stood and wiped the dirt off her knees the best she could.

When she walked into the house, Marlow walked straight

to the bar and poured herself a shot of tequila. She was still shaking and needed to calm her nerves.

The alcohol burned as it went down, and she wiped her nose with the back of her hand. As she poured another shot glass full, Royce cleared his throat. He'd been sitting there in the dark watching her.

"You'll be okay," he said and stood to walk toward her.

Marlow turned away from him as she downed the second glass. Royce stepped closer to brush her hair out of her face.

"She has an uncompromising way about her, but it's a tough world in politics. It's the only way to succeed in DC."

"We aren't in DC," Marlow said, and her voice was hoarse from crying so hard.

"Shhhh, she's gone to bed. Things will look better in the morning." He then pulled Marlow close and tried to kiss her.

She shoved him off her and kicked at him as she yelled for him to stop.

"You don't have to be such a bitch, Marlow. I was trying to make you feel better."

She threw her shot glass at him and hit his shoulder. "You think trying to sleep with me would make me feel better? You're disgusting."

Royce bared his teeth at her, and for the first time, she was a little afraid of him. "I told her not to hire the guys to break into the house and scare you. She could have just wired the money for the car."

Marlow hadn't suspected they would go so far as to hire someone to frighten her. "Well, you guys really blew it because the thugs you hired tried to throw me into a trunk and kidnap me. They weren't going to just scare me."

She drank another shot and felt it when it hit her stomach. It was too much alcohol, but she needed it to numb the pain.

"The Maisonville Police have them in custody and I hope they rat you out."

The anger on Royce's face let her know he was worried about it. "We were doing fine without you and your stupid posts. But no one listens to me. And I am not disgusting. I'm the only one trying to make this family work."

Did he think they were going to be a threesome? He would sleep with her mother and then Marlow too. "We are not a family," she said, throwing her arms up in the air, "Don't come near me again." Marlow knew what she had to do. It couldn't wait any longer. She went to her bedroom and packed all her belongings.

The Bronco held so much more than she'd realized was possible. It was three in the morning when she finished filling her last suitcase and crawled into bed.

She just needed a few hours of sleep, and then she could go. Tears slipped down her cheeks as she thought about Zachary and the hurt look on his face. That square jaw was tight, and his eyes looked solid black because his pupils were so big. He was too good for her, and she'd known it all along. Strait-laced or buttoned-down, both descriptions fit that man, and she wished things could be different.

They had gotten close, and she would remember him for the rest of her life. But after she packed her car and posted her last video online, she would go and never look back.

Rolling over in bed, she put a pillow over her head so she couldn't hear Michelle giggling down the hallway. Royce found the comfort he craved, and Marlow had counted on that.

Three hours of sleep was all she needed, and then she would throw the last of her things into her vehicle and set up her cameras.

As she drifted off to sleep, she thought about Mrs. Bowers

and how she made coffee for her every morning. She sure would love another cup of that coffee along with her sweet company. Of course, she wouldn't mind another piece of pie from Miss Lynn's diner either.

She could almost taste it as she drifted off to sleep, dreaming of speeding through Maisonville one last time.

※

Zachary didn't sleep all night. He walked into the boarding house, furious over what had happened. Just as he'd suspected the first night after he'd arrested Marlow, Senator Michelle Ripley wasn't what she appeared to be.

Always campaigning for the little guy and rooting for the underdog was as big a lie as she could have told. The senator didn't even look after her own daughter. He couldn't get Marlow's pleading voice out of his head as she begged her mother to stop.

He wished the senator had just shut her mouth, but he couldn't unhear what she said about Marlow. If he were a different person, then maybe it wouldn't matter. But he'd lived his life by a specific code, and the truth was a lot for him to accept.

There had been some wild times in his youth, especially his senior year in high school. Most teenagers were curious about sex and didn't every teenager go to parties? It was a natural rite of passage.

Marlow's teenage years didn't sound like the usual rebellious behavior. When her mother said Marlow was arrested for drugs, it took him by surprise. He'd wondered why Marlow would work for the senator in the first place, but it all started to make sense. If her mother bailed her out of trouble as a teenager, then she must have done the same for her in college. *But pornography?* That would have been as damaging to the senator as it would, Marlow. Would Marlow have gone that far to hurt her mother's career?

Against his better judgment, he pulled out his computer and searched every place he could think of to find evidence of what Marlow had done. By dawn, he'd been through every website he could think of and some on the dark web he hoped never to see again.

Most sex on the internet was degrading toward women, and the thought of Marlow being a part of that world was difficult. He would have doubted the validity of any of it if Marlow had told him, it wasn't true. But he saw how she broke down and then how she pushed him to leave.

The worst part about being exploited on the internet was that once it was out there, it never went away.

So why couldn't he find it?

Chapter Thirty-Five

The following morning, Olivia opened the diner for Miss Lynn, who wasn't feeling well. Alexavier would have breakfast with her son, Lucas, before dropping him off at a friend's house. But she didn't enjoy the early shift.

Some regular customers came in right at opening, and they were pleasant enough. Most ate the same thing every morning and drank coffee quietly.

When Zachary walked in and sat at the lunch counter, she eyed him suspiciously. "What are you doing here this early?" she asked, pouring him coffee.

He grunted at her, and she lowered her eyes before walking away to take food to another table. When Olivia returned, she grabbed Zachary's order before busying herself with other customers.

She refilled his coffee twice while he ate, and then she cleared his dishes. The diner remained quiet except for a low hum as the early morning light shone through the windows.

Zachary handed her cash for his bill, and when she brought him the change, she hesitated before putting it in his hand.

"What's going on with you? And don't growl at me again, Zachary Bowman."

He shook his head. Zachary wasn't sure he could tell Olivia. It was more than because of his code not to overshare. He just couldn't bear to think about what had happened last night.

Olivia stared at him expectantly and tapped her hand on the counter. Perhaps it was his lack of sleep or because he needed advice and his old friend would give it to him straight, but he broke down and told Olivia the whole story.

She had to make him wait while she rang up two different customers and refilled coffee for others who were still eating. But mostly, Olivia needed to pull herself together after hearing what had happened.

When she walked by him to sit back down, she whacked the back of his head. "You mean to tell me she was sobbing over her mother telling you her secrets, and you left her there?"

"Olivia. She pushed me into the car and insisted that I leave."

The muscle in Olivia's jaw tightened. "Well, you certainly failed that test, Officer Bowman."

"She's been arrested for drugs, Olivia. And famous on the internet for doing pornography."

"You forget that I knew you in high school, Zachary Bowman. You smoked pot with all the football players after homecoming your junior year. And the only reason you didn't get into trouble was because your dad was the chief of police."

Zachary took a deep, cleansing breath. Olivia Dufrene was infuriating. His eyes felt like they had sand in them, and he regretted not sleeping at all. "You don't know that it was marijuana."

"You don't know that it wasn't."

"Olivia, you weren't there, and you can't understand how this all went down. She went from telling me about her mother leaving her to live alone at thirteen to her mother saying she was famous for doing pornography on the internet."

"If you're going to sit there and profess to be puritanical and to have never watched porn, then I'm going to call you a big fat liar, Zachary Bowman."

"I was in college at a party, and someone put it on the television."

"Well, Marlow was in college, too. Maybe she needed the money or wanted to exercise her freedom from an oppressive mother. What she doesn't need is to be judged the rest of her life for a mistake she made when she was barely in her twenties."

Olivia pointed her finger at his chest and locked onto his stare, "I know I wouldn't like to spend the rest of my life being judged for the mistakes in my past."

Zachary nodded as he thought about how Olivia was treated in their hometown. He wished he'd stood up for her back then. If this was a test, Olivia had been right in saying he'd failed.

Zachary hugged Olivia and then, without another word, headed for the door. He was hard to read but looked upset.

She followed him out. "You, okay?"

He shook his head. It didn't matter if Marlow did any or all the things her mother said. She shouldn't have to spend the rest of her life paying for those decisions.

"Not until I know she is," he said, and Olivia ran to him and gave him a tight hug. It had taken Zachary a moment to get there, but she was proud of him.

"Go get our girl back," she said and waved to him as he

pulled out of the diner parking lot. This time, Zachary did not correct her because Marlow was their girl.

MARLOW WOKE up before her alarm went off at six and tried not to think about Zachary being disappointed in her. It was no use wishing things were different. It didn't change what happened or how Zachary was a staunch rule follower and enforcer. It was difficult to explain how she'd taken a crooked path to end up in the same place as others. And she did regret a lot of those things. Hearing her mother say them with such vitriol hurt even worse. But the truth was that Marlow couldn't take anything back. She wasn't a bad person. She'd just put her trust in the wrong people.

Besides, all those wrong turns taught her to work harder, and this morning, she would take her life back. She showered and blew her hair dry, not fussing with her appearance much. Fresh and clean, which was how she felt today as she used a little lip balm and folded her grandmother's quilt so she could take it along with her.

It only took her ten minutes to finish loading her car. She pulled it out of the driveway to park it on the street and left the gate open in case she needed a quick getaway. Then Marlow sat at the kitchen island with her camera on a small tripod and made the live video she'd planned last night.

Twenty-five thousand people were watching her when she began. "Since many of you have been with me since college, you know I've had as many missteps as anyone. I was often an example of what not to do, like cutting classes or the fashion blunders of wearing super-short denim cutoffs. But I've kept some secrets over the years, and while I thought they weren't hurting anyone but me, I might have been wrong."

Marlow stared into the camera, hoping her sincerity showed. "Like the wedding-palooza that went on for an endless year, I never wanted a big wedding and would have never gone through so many details if Michelle hadn't put me up to it.

"Then, you guys seemed to love it, and I didn't want to disappoint you. But the truth was that I had doubts about marrying RC as soon as the dust settled on that surprise Paris engagement. But again, Michelle wouldn't hear of it. See a pattern here?"

Marlow glanced at her mother's bedroom, there wasn't a sound in the house, and she had time to explain. "You guys have always seen me support my mother, but honestly, she's never stood behind me. It's time I tell you that since college, it has been my job to post her speeches and commend her for helping women. Truthfully, she only does anything if it suits her.

"If you support her because you think she's against guns, then know that she has dinner with lobbyists who support the Second Amendment. On the other hand, if you follow her because she's for the Second Amendment, then know she has drinks with lobbyists who want it repealed.

"You see, if you think Senator Michelle Ripley is for you and your cause, the answer is yes until you turn your back and aren't looking in her direction.

Telling that one truth gave Marlow the confidence she needed to keep going. "The reason I'm telling this today isn't to hurt her career. Don't get me wrong, she doesn't deserve your vote, but that's between you and her and maybe your conscience.

"It's just time for me to live my life without her interference, and the only way for me to be free is to tell you guys that she's been blackmailing me to make me stay.

"When I was in college, I dated the wrong guy. It wasn't serious, and I wanted it that way. But what I didn't know was that he was secretly filming us when we were alone. He posted that video online everywhere, and I was devastated. I tried going to the police, but it was my word against his, and cyberbullying wasn't yet a thing. No matter what I said or did, he would not take it down because he was making money off it. I had no choice but to call Michelle. And let me tell you that it took her less than forty-eight hours to get it wiped from the internet and have him kicked out of school.

"While I applaud her swift action because, let's face it, very few people have that kind of power-nothing in life is free.

"Her lawyers took over my social media contracts and negotiated everything, and her accountants handled the money. I just had to keep doing what I was doing until I graduated, and then she owned me.

"What does this have to do with RC? Well, he works for Michelle. First, he was an intern and then became her right-hand man. I couldn't figure out why she was so happy we were together. Until the day of the wedding."

When she checked again, there were more than a hundred thousand people logged in to hear Marlow Ripley tell the truth about what happened.

She took a sip of her bottled water and a deep breath. "You guys remember I had a professional photographer filming wedding-palooza? I'd had my makeup and hair done before the big dress reveal moment. I teased you guys by showing you the tips of my shoes and then the dress's fabric. The only thing I'd asked for in this event was to do the dress reveal alone with RC, and the crazy thing was that he was the only one who knew about it.

"I guess he'd forgotten because when I walked into the room at the church where he was supposed to be waiting for me, his pants were down around his ankles and——"

Marlow suddenly heard her mother's bedroom door burst open, and a half-dressed Royce and Michelle almost fell to the floor as they mauled each other. Marlow would later refer to it as worse than an animal's gone wild video. But at that moment, she had the wherewithal to turn her camera around to catch them in the act.

"What are you doing?" Michelle asked and then looked at Royce. "What is she doing?" Then back at Marlow. "Have you been listening to us?" And back again to Royce, "Is she filming us?"

Royce scrambled to his feet, "Is that thing on?" He tripped over his pants leg and grabbed a chair to keep from face-planting.

Marlow hopped off the barstool and turned her camera around to speak to her audience. "Sorry for the interruption, but I couldn't have explained the situation better than you guys seeing what I saw that day. I hope you'll enjoy the photographs I have for sale on my site and understand that I won't continue posting as often."

She blew a kiss to the screen just as Royce was about to reach her. As soon as he got his hands around the camera, Marlow let it go. He thought he would have to wrench it from her hands and dramatically swung it around, almost hitting her mother in the face.

When Marlow began to walk toward them, Michelle screamed at Royce not to let her have the camera back. Marlow smiled as she stared down her mother. "Oh, I don't want or need the camera anymore."

Michelle pulled her sleeping shirt into place and glared back at Marlow. "Royce, double-check that the video card is still intact. I don't want her posting any of that."

"Michelle," he said, attempting to explain what just happened. "She doesn't need the card to post it."

"What?" Senator Ripley waved her hands around to talk like Marlow when she was excited. "I know she can't post a video without that video card."

Marlow picked up her purse and headed for the door as she heard Royce explain that it was a live video, and everyone had already seen it.

From outside, Marlow could hear her mother scream, "Go get her."

Before Marlow passed the gate, Royce grabbed her by the arm, making her drop her bag and quilt. "Let me go, Royce."

"Or what?" he rolled his eyes as he began to drag her back toward the house. Michelle could make her post another video retracting her earlier statement. Perhaps, make her say she set them up somehow. He shook his head. By far, this was the worst thing Marlow had done to them, and he knew things were about to change.

He shook her arm roughly and yelled. "Or what, you'll throw a vase at me?"

"No, she'll have her boyfriend beat the crap out of you."

Royce turned just as Zachary's fist collided with his jaw. He practically bounced when he hit the ground.

"I told you to keep your hands off her, and I don't like to repeat myself," Zachary said, stepping aggressively toward Royce again.

Scrambling across the asphalt, Royce was desperate to get

away from Zachary. He managed to get his feet under him and ran back into the house.

When Zachary turned around, Marlow folded her arms in front of her. "I'm sorry. Did you say you were my boyfriend?"

"Too presumptuous?"

"A little."

Zachary pulled her into his arms. "I'm willing to beg for your forgiveness, Marlow. I don't care about any of that stuff from your past. We all make mistakes."

She shook her head. "You've made mistakes?"

"I made a mistake last night when I left you here. I was wrong, and I promise to make it up to you. I'll try to do better."

Marlow tried not to cry over his apology.

His eyes watered, too. "Why don't we go home and talk about it?"

"Home?"

"The boarding house. Yes, home."

Marlow squealed when he scooped her up into his arms and carried her down the driveway to her loaded-down Bronco.

"No speeding, Miss Ripley," he said and then winked at her.

He was such a rule follower.

Chapter Thirty-Six

When Marlow pulled into the driveway of the boarding house, Mrs. Bowers was there waiting on the front steps. It was the sweetest greeting Marlow could have asked for, and she couldn't get to the lovely older woman fast enough.

"It's so good to have you home, child," Mrs. Bowers said with happy tears. After giving Marlow a warm hug, they walked into the house, where she had fresh coffee waiting.

Marlow promised never to leave again without telling her, but Mrs. Bowers said, "Darling girl, you can come and go as you please, just as long as you understand there will always be a place here for you."

It was that generosity but also Mrs. Bowers' sincerity that got to Marlow the most. At that moment, Marlow realized the entire summer she'd been there, Mrs. Bowers had never referred to the boarding house as her own but instead called it their home.

After enjoying coffee together, Marlow and Zachary unloaded her Bronco. It took her a while to unpack things, and Zachary stayed with her for the entire thing.

As she emptied each suitcase or bag, he stowed them in the top of her closet out of the way. Marlow had more clothes than anyone he'd ever known, and he teased her that she was now Wardrobe Barbie.

His latest nickname for her was accurate because she loved clothes. But he would flip when he saw how many shoes she had, too. But she didn't unpack those because he cornered her near the closet and kissed her breathlessly.

Zachary Bowman was showering her with affection, and it was everything she'd hoped for, yet didn't know if she'd ever get. Before things got out of control, he pulled back and smiled at her.

"I'm wasting away, woman. Can we go get something to eat?" It made her laugh because Zachary ate more food than anyone she knew.

Mrs. Bowers was with her garden club friends for the afternoon, and Marlow and Zachary decided to go to Miss Lynn's Diner to get something to eat. Before Marlow got inside the door, Miss Lynn and Olivia were there to hug her. "So glad you're back home, my baby," Miss Lynn said.

Olivia winked at Marlow, but when she leaned forward, she smirked. "This guy treating you well?" she asked, gesturing at Zachary but talking to Marlow.

"I'm standing right here, Livvie," he said, and Olivia shrugged. Marlow laughed because Olivia would always be there to set Zachary straight if he needed it.

They enjoyed lunch and had just finished sharing a piece of chocolate icebox pie when Leonie Ford interrupted them. "Good afternoon," she said to Zachary and Marlow. "I'm sorry to admit that I've tried everything to find you the right house, Zachary," Leonie said, looking forlorn. "I just don't think this will work out between us. You're going to need to find another real estate agent."

Marlow elbowed Zachary to say something to Leonie. While she didn't want the woman flirting with her man, Marlow did admire Leonie's ability to step aside gracefully.

"I understand. Thanks for trying, Leonie," he said, maintaining a straight face.

Marlow elbowed him again because he looked like he was about to laugh. She decided to step in. "Leonie, I might need to find a small house to turn into an office for my new marketing company. It won't be until the end of the year or the beginning of next year, but still, I'd appreciate your help when I'm ready."

Leonie's face perked up. "Absolutely," she said and immediately fished a business card out of her purse. "Here you go. Call me anytime."

They watched her leave the diner and flirt with several local firemen walking toward the door. "She doesn't stay down long, does she?" Olivia said as she walked over to refill Zachary's tea glass. They all laughed, but Marlow knew Olivia still hadn't forgiven the poor girl for flirting with her boyfriend.

Miss Lynn had overheard Olivia's comment and shook her head. She walked over to remind Olivia and Marlow that Leonie was on their team, and they had to admit the girl had great taste.

It had been a long summer season, and the last crowds were waning in Maisonville. Marlow hadn't helped at the diner since she'd broken her hand and owed Miss Lynn and Olivia. "I haven't been available, but if you ever need me to help, anytime, just call me," Marlow said, and then explained that she was staying on at the boarding house and helping Mrs. Bowers run things.

They all agreed Tenille was too busy to do it as she focused on her properties with her husband in New Orleans.

Miss Lynn and Olivia looked at each other and then at the lunch counter. Frances Heaton, a local girl in her late twenties, was alone, drowning her sorrows in a strawberry pie. They weren't sure if she needed a job or just a shoulder to cry on. But they were confident they would find another waitress to fill that spot again very soon.

Olivia smiled at Marlow slyly. "I heard the marketing business is hot right now. Hot like those new doctors at the clinic, am I right?"

She watched Zachary cut his eyes her way but didn't break under the scrutiny.

Marlow laughed and leaned into her jealous boyfriend. "I think it's going to be great."

Marlow received an email from Evie Mae and Felicity saying they loved her logo idea and were ready to have coffee sleeves made along with new signs for their business. But when Marlow called to talk to her about it, Evie Mae was discussing something with her brother, which sounded heated. It wasn't easy to get her to finalize any plans, and Marlow made a note to reach out to Felicity in the next few days.

As usual, plenty was happening at Renaissance Lake, but Marlow Ripley was relieved to finally not be the one everyone was watching.

The couple said their goodbyes to everyone at the diner. It had been a long day, and they both needed rest. When they returned to the boarding house, Mrs. Bowers was sitting at the kitchen counter and happy they brought her some dessert.

She told them about her garden club meeting and their secret plans to start putting flamingoes out in the middle of the night for random people around town. There wasn't a single member of the garden club under the age of seventy, and it tickled Marlow to imagine them dressed in black running around town at midnight to surprise others with a random act of flamingoes.

It would be the perfect Instagram post if she were going to do that anymore. But, at the moment, she wasn't.

Zachary went upstairs to shower, and when Marlow heard him finish, she bid the sweet older woman goodnight and went upstairs for her turn. Sharing a bathroom with him now felt normal, but the idea of sleeping with him anytime she wanted made her nervous.

It was silly, but she took an extra-long time with her bedtime routine and changed pajamas three times. When she walked out of the bathroom, Zachary was standing there on the landing, smiling at her.

All her nervousness was instantly replaced with a desire she hadn't felt in a long time, maybe ever. Her face felt warm as her eyes took in Zachary's beautiful, hard body. He was the type of person who constantly was busy, whether it was mowing Mrs. Bowers' grass, taking a run around the neighborhood, or working on his new boat. His toned abs showed the natural effect of his hard work.

When her eyes perused down his body and back to his face, the look of approval was all Marlow needed. He stepped into her space, and she dropped her bathroom towel and toiletries onto the floor to wrap her arms around him.

His hands were everywhere, and his lips covered hers as they explored each other's bodies. It felt like Marlow had never been with another, and waiting as long as they did made this moment special.

When Zachary picked her up, Marlow wrapped her legs

around his body, and they never broke the kiss. He laid her across his bed and pulled the covers up over them.

Marlow wasn't sure she'd ever get enough of his affection and loved every minute of him loving her. An hour later, she was in his arms, still trying to catch her breath.

He'd slipped his white tee shirt that he'd worn as an undershirt over her body, and she felt surrounded by him again. It was a small gesture, but to her, it wasn't small at all.

Zachary's fingers roamed over her back as she nestled beside him with her head on his chest. Her hands rested on his taut stomach. There was comfort in being wrapped in Zachary Bowman's arms, and Marlow had never felt this loved or this free.

She sat up in the bed to face him, and he looked a little confused. "Hey beautiful, what's going on in that head of yours?" he said, and it instantly made her think of the first time they'd had coffee at Espresso to Geaux.

The truth was that Zachary had paid close attention to her back then, and she hadn't known what to do with all that attentiveness. This time, she did. "I want to set the record straight over what my mother told you."

Zachary sat up in bed and leaned against the headboard to face her. "Marlow. You don't owe me an explanation. None of it matters anymore."

"I wanted to be the one to tell you everything, and if she hadn't walked out there when she did, I would have," she said. And more than the details she would give him, the fact that his girl wanted to tell him the truth about everything meant something. But he'd already decided she was his, and nothing would ever change that.

Zachary tugged her hand to pull her into his arms. He was

perceptive, and it would take time for Marlow to get used to being connected to someone like that.

She straddled his lap and pulled the covers around her body as she faced him. "When I was in high school, I did throw huge parties. I drank underage and smoked cigarettes, but I didn't do drugs. Some of the guys that came to my parties smoked weed, and during a particularly wild Mardi Gras night, the police were called to my house because of the noise. When they discovered the marijuana, no one would claim it, and so they arrested all of us."

Zachary immediately thought about all the times he'd been called out for noise violations. It was up to the officer whether to take it further, and he understood how that moment could have gotten out of hand with a high-profile politician's daughter.

"I did try marijuana when I was in college. Everyone there had a prescription for it before it was legal. And so I tried it, and after eating half a pizza, I threw up all night. It was not for me."

Zachary smirked. He'd wanted to eat an entire refrigerator when he was a teenager and had tried it. He would tell her the truth later about how his father was the one who caught him and his friends.

Marlow looked nervous to tell him the next thing, but his girl took a deep breath and powered through. "I know you're the most troubled over the internet sex video."

Zachary shook his head. "You're wrong, babe. I'm not concerned about anything that happened before we met. Unless you need me to be."

Marlow leaned up to kiss him. He was such a great boyfriend. "First, I did not set out to make a sex video like

Michelle tried to say. I had zero knowledge of it until a friend told me he saw it."

That got Zachary's attention because Marlow hadn't consented, which was completely different and illegal.

"I dated this guy casually in college and thought he was cool. It was never serious. After the attraction ran its course, he posted a video he'd covertly taken of us. It was on some site where he made money off it, and I couldn't get it taken down on my own. I tried everything before calling Michelle.

"He'd named it *Sex with the Senator's Daughter* or something ridiculous. My mother is a jerk, but she can be effective when necessary. I truly don't know how, but the internet was scrubbed clean, and there isn't a trace of the video anywhere. Somehow, he gave up his copy and was kicked out of school. Last I heard, he'd moved across the country."

Zachary looked angry, but she was learning that was on her behalf and not aimed at her. She reached forward and laid her hand across his heart. "Thankfully, I did not become famous online because of a porn video. I was mortified because some of my professors and classmates saw it. I was ashamed over the whole thing and didn't go out with anyone again until Royce."

Marlow shrugged. "I haven't dated much at all. Guys never really asked me out. I think they were scared of my mother."

How could this woman not know that she was the most beautiful person in every single room she walked into? Zachary would make sure she knew it without a doubt.

He pulled her in close, and she leaned into the warmth of his hard body. "Guys weren't scared of your mother, Beauty Queen Barbie. They just knew they weren't good enough for you."

Marlow laughed, and Zachary loved to hear that sound. He

turned off the bedside lamp and showed her again what he thought of her beautiful body.

※

OFFICIALLY RELOCATING to Maisonville had been the best move of Marlow's life.

In two weeks' time, her permanent address was Mrs. Bowers' Boarding House. Every morning, that sweet woman would make her coffee if Marlow didn't set an alarm and get to the kitchen first.

She'd learned that when Mrs. Bowers was a young bride, she spent a summer in Paris training as a saucier, which is a sauté chef. She loved to cook and had already given Marlow three cooking lessons.

Zachary was the beneficiary of all that great food, and he only had to sit in the formal dining room with them, wearing a jacket to enjoy it.

Mrs. Bowers pretended it was a fancy dinner party and told them it was how she and her husband had done it when they were first introduced into society.

There was a lot they still needed to learn about this fascinating woman, and she slowly shared bits and pieces of her early life over food, of course.

Today was Sunday, Fun-day, as Marlow liked to call it, and one of her favorites because she and Zachary got to spend it together. They went to church with Mrs. Bowers, and then had lunch together.

Zachary had big plans for them that afternoon but wouldn't tell Marlow a thing. Mrs. Bowers was in on it because she couldn't stop smiling as she made an excuse and left them alone.

When he drove them to the marina, she figured he'd wanted to take her fishing and held his hand as they walked to his boat. As soon as she stepped on board, Zachary led her to the interior cabin. There, she saw brown craft paper everywhere with rudimentary drawings.

"What's all this?" she asked as she spied a huge bouquet of wildflowers where the kitchen would go.

"I've been meaning to discuss something with you."

She grinned, "Are you going to admit that you've been picking me flowers from the wildflower patch in front of the police station? Because the garden club will come after you, Officer Bowman, when they catch you."

"I've already been caught. I promised to look the other way when they vandalize, I mean decorate, people's homes and businesses with those flamingoes. And they agreed not to say anything when I pick flowers."

Marlow laughed until she couldn't catch her breath. Was Zachary Bowman breaking the rules for her? She was a bad influence on him, but she kind of liked his naughty side.

Looking around the room more closely, she realized he'd drawn cabinets and furniture on all that craft paper. She smiled because he'd gone to a lot of effort. "What is all of this?" she asked, her blue eyes shimmering with curiosity.

"I figured out that the reason I couldn't decide on any of the houses Leonie showed me was because I already have a place that feels like home."

Marlow leaned up to kiss him. "The boat," she said, knowing this was his dream boat, and perhaps it made sense for him.

He shook his head. "No, babe. The boarding house with you and Mrs. Bowers."

He guided her around the cabin so she could get a closer

look at the drawings he'd made. "But I think we might need a little more privacy sometimes, and that's what all this is about. We could set this place up like a vacation home, and maybe on the weekends or when the boarding house is busy, we could stay here."

Marlow watched him excitedly share his plan.

"I'm not an artist like you, but I thought if I laid out where everything should go, you would have a place to start. I'm good with whatever you want."

Marlow wrapped her arms around him and hugged him for the longest time without speaking. She usually had a lot to say, and their roles had reversed.

When he realized he'd done all the talking, he stopped, too, and tried to regroup. He was moving too fast, but he knew what he wanted. He just needed to make sure Marlow was on board. "What do you think? Does that sound like something you'd be interested in?"

Marlow couldn't find her voice. Tears filled her eyes, and she tried to speak, but then she took another deep breath. He held her close but couldn't find the words either. He didn't want to rush her, and he was worried he'd overstepped.

Marlow put both hands on his face because looking into his eyes focused her like nothing else. "I'm still stuck on the fact that you said being at the boarding house with me feels like home."

Zachary kissed her with more passion than she'd ever known. That woman shouldn't be so easy to please. He'd give her the world if she wanted it, and one day, he would make her understand.

"Come on, Marlow, I have more to show you," he said, and they went upstairs so he could teach her how to maneuver the boat out of the slip. They headed past large, beautiful homes built on the waterfront. The largest one was white and looked like a mansion set amongst the old oak trees.

Finally, they found a quiet spot, and he pulled her next to him so they could watch the sunset. No words were needed as the sky turned a burnt orange with streaks of purple, red, and gold.

Marlow had believed her entire life that love wasn't worth the chase. But right there at that moment, next to Zachary Bowman, she knew that getting caught by love was worth it.

Before dark, he took her past the old lighthouse and watched her take at least twenty photographs. When he let her drive the boat back to the marina, she didn't stop smiling.

It would never get old, making her happy, and he would tell her that the day he married her.

Read the next book in the Renaissance Lake Series
Coffee and Twinkle Lights

Get a Copy of Dixieland absolutely free

When love is not enough.

This Southern Gothic Tale is set in Dixon Springs. A spot so far off the map that the highway and train tracks both end here. Home to Meg and her big sister, Sophia, all they want is a chance in life and to get out of this dying place. With only each other to depend on, can they find a way to escape or is there no way out of this nowhere town?

Just click the link below to sign up for the author's New Releases mailing list and download your free copy of Dixieland now.

http://www.lisaherrington.com/Dixieland

About the Author

LISA HERRINGTON is a Women's fiction and YA novelist, and blogger. A former medical sales rep, she currently manages the largest Meet-Up writing group in the New Orleans area, The Bayou Writer's Club. She was born and raised in Louisiana, attended college at Ole Miss in Oxford, Mississippi and accepts that in New Orleans we never hide our crazy but instead parade it around on the front porch and give it a cocktail. It's certainly why she has so many stories to tell today. When she's not writing, and spending time with her husband and three children, she spends time reading, watching old movies or planning something new and exciting with her writers' group.

Connect with Lisa, find out about new releases, and get free books at lisaherrington.com

Made in the USA
Middletown, DE
25 September 2023

39357290R00170